MOONLIGHT DESIRE

# Moonlight Desire

## The Witch and the Wolf Pack
### Book One

## K.R. Alexander

Six Wolves Press

Copyright © 2018, by K.R. Alexander

ISBN-13: 978-1-7177457-7-4

All rights reserved.
No part of this book may be reproduced in
whole or in part without written permission
from the publisher, except for brief quotations
in critical reviews or articles.

Run with the Moonlight Pack at
kralexander.com

And hunt up *The Witch and the Wolf Pack*
series on amazon.com

K.R. ALEXANDER

## ○ C̲H̲A̲P̲T̲E̲R̲ ̲1̲ ○

I'VE BEEN DIFFERENT all my life: always something to hide. Keeping magic secret is as easy and comfortable as wrestling bears. Still, it's only magic. I've never had a secret this big before.

It started with the kidnapping.

No, it started with the flight to London, stepping off the plane at Heathrow for a last summer vacation before launching my career. A final trip to see my sister and the dreamy Englishman she'd run away from Kansas City to Brighton to marry.

She was determined to set me up with a British guy as well. We'd tried before. Turned out, they weren't all as swoon-worthy as her Henry—accents aside. Now I'd have a wide pool. Melanie had proudly informed me via Skype that she had four men lined up for me to meet. Plus, this trip was about beach- and pub-hopping and living the last summer between college kid and hardcore adulting to the fullest. There would be more than four meetings by the time we were done.

But there was another reason for my trip. The one Melanie didn't know. My secret.

I'd already visited Melanie and Henry twice in the three years since she'd moved to England. That was how I'd met members of Broomantle, a society of local witches and magi in the South of England who based annual meetings out of Brighton in plain sight. Their weekend conference was my first priority.

Attending lectures on animal familiars, maintaining mundane/magic relations—i.e. hiding—herb lore, spell lore, plus discussion panels and meals together, would take most of my weekend.

They'd also asked me for a presentation. Saturday evening and Sunday morning I would do some of the teaching. Then dinner with members on Sunday night, hand-shaking, home to Melanie, bikini on Monday, and let the vacation—and matchmaking—begin.

Of course, that's not what happened.

I collected my small suitcase at Heathrow and met Melanie at arrivals.

After hugs, shouting, and, "Oh, my God, I love-love-love your new bag, Cassia! Purple! Love it!"—sisters, natural blondes, it happens—I got a hug from Henry as well and he led us to the airport's "car park."

He opened the passenger door for me on his scarlet Lexus while I was already heading for the driver's door. England. Wrong side of the road. All coming back.

Hour and a half drive from the airport to their bright terrace house with beach view and seagulls screaming outside. I was so crashed after two flights and twenty-four hours of travel from Portland, Oregon, I did nothing but ask questions.

What was Henry's marketing firm working on? Did Melanie really have four guys for me to meet who she thought were so wonderful?

So the two of them did all the talking. Perfect.

I could have fallen asleep on the foyer rug but managed to remain upright for dinner prepared by both. Oh, yes, Henry also cooks. Chicken and vegetable curry followed by sweet Victoria sponge cake piled with strawberries and crème fraîche.

By the time we'd finished, Melanie was trying to paint my nails. It would have to wait.

I hardly remember dropping on the soft, white guest bed with windows open to sounds of the English Channel, sun just set, and I was gone.

It wasn't until morning that I was kicking myself for having flown in on Friday. That ticket had been so cheap—perfect idea. Get Broomantle and my teaching assignment out of the way as soon as I arrived, then nothing but fun and sun and sexy accents for the next two weeks with Mel.

So jet-lagged my head spun, I dragged myself to the shower on Saturday morning—no time for fresh nails—dressed, hair, five-minute face, coffee, too tired for the breakfast Melanie offered, and out the door.

"Who comes all the way to Brighton for *history* lectures in the middle of summer?" she shouted after me on my way down the front steps.

"It's only two days, Mel. Then I'm all yours. Can't wait!"

Everyone in my family who didn't know about my magic—meaning everyone besides my late mother and grandmother—thought I was a history buff. Easy to pretend. I did know something about history after all the study I'd done for my own career path in teaching. Even as a teen all I'd had to say was something like, "Oh, that reminds me of the Russian Revolution—so tragic." And everyone nodded like they understood and never asked questions.

So it was another history conference for oddball Cassia and her scholarly brain below all that flaxen hair. If I'd really walked into a history conference, those balding old historians would probably have swallowed their fountain pens.

These conferences, though, groups like Broomantle, were diverse. Magic can happen to anyone as long as you know how to spot it and have a little guidance. I'd had my mother and grandmother, Nana. These days I was on my own besides a few friends and contacts. Nor did I want more since I was committed to living a normal life. A mundane life. Trying.

I'd seen how hard it was for my mother. And how hard it was for me just keeping secrets from Melanie and everyone around me—forget a husband and kids. Time to break the cycle.

One magical stop on the trip, since I'd agreed to do it last year. Then this witch was putting out the fire under the caldron and hanging up her pointed hat.

I needed a bumper sticker for my VW at home: *Mundane Forever!* But hadn't been able to find it yet.

From Melanie and Henry's house, I walked to the Seastar Hotel, a sweeping Victorian, expertly restored, overlooking the red pebble beach and Brighton Pier.

Tourists already clogged the sidewalk. Sun well up, beach hot and inviting, people in flip-flops, snapping pictures on their phones. Me running late.

Why had I agreed to this? When I could be having breakfast with Melanie, giggling over descriptions of those four guys, in sandals instead of flats, sunscreen instead of eyeliner?

Was I just a sucker?

No, I'd said I'd teach Scrying 101 this evening and Advanced Scrying on Sunday morning because we were a small community. That was how I'd been raised.

Nana—who'd been the famous scry, not me—in particular had been adamant about this.

*We do not merely carry the magic; we are the magic. We are a collective of remaining humans and magical beings and we must be our own allies, our own family, or this community will continue to fade.*

Just what I was doing, willing myself to fade: turn my back on my own magic. Mundane forever.

Unless asked, very nicely, to lecture on scrying, to be a valued member of that community. One more history conference.

So, yes, maybe a sucker.

A doorman—or bellboy?—opened the massive wood panel door of the Seastar Hotel for me and stepped back, sweeping his arm out to take in the lobby as if I were a duchess and he an 18th-century courtier.

"Thank you. I'm here for the conference, if you could show me…?" I may have grown up small town USA, but, after a big city wakeup call for so many years of college, I didn't get tongue-tied just because a cute guy opened a door.

Even so, if this did not happen to be one of the local men my sister intended for me to meet, I may have to come back here and find him myself.

Had they hired him to stand at the door purely on his looks? Chiseled face, sleek appearance, and dramatic manner to lure tourists?

He gave me a bow when I said what I was here for. I wouldn't have been surprised if he'd produced a red rose as well.

"Right this way." With a smile like we shared some intimate secret.

I felt flushed at the voice, and look in his eyes, as if he'd said something entirely different—inappropriate.

Settled in the conference room, still warm, I caught glimpses of him escorting others to the open double doors. Not like it had been anything personal about me.

Fueled on espresso, the day passed quickly. The crowd rounded out to perhaps one hundred individuals from all over Great Britain. Easy environment to meet people, but also to get lost.

A few years ago, I'd have hoped to meet. Now, plotting my own escape, knowing this wasn't a life I wanted, I avoided eye contact. I made notes or doodled, going over material I had to deliver later on, and sat alone for lunch when I'd usually have found a group to chat.

My resolve not to interact was tested late in the day, myself about to go up, when I heard snatches of conversation about, "How many dead now?" And, "Of course they keep to themselves—"

Disjointed, cut off, I looked around for the speakers yet couldn't tell in the group.

Casters dead? Mundane gossip?

Too late to ask even if I'd wanted to.

An hour talking about scrying, journeys, aids to the seer, spells, meditations, inducing trance, and how to get started as a scry—small, with a clear mind and clear intentions. Then half an hour of Q&A. And, finally, freedom.

I'd meant to take Melanie and Henry out for a drink, Saturday night, visit their favorite pub. Instead, jet lag clobbered me, the long day caught up, and I was asleep by 8:00 p.m.

Sunday morning. Same hottie at the door. In fact, some noticeably good-looking people in this crowd who I didn't remember from yesterday.

Like that tall guy with the ponytail and eyes like gold flakes. A willowy woman with hair the color of burnt honey, long enough to tuck into her waistband. And that broad-shouldered one with the torn jeans, high cheekbones and a carved jaw, young as myself, staring at me while I did the advanced talk on scrying into distant places, unknowns, even across time. All you have to do is understand that time makes the same difference to scrying as distance—which is none at all.

While I talked, those eyes fixed on me.

Everyone else occasionally glanced around, took notes, nodded, checked their phones, or frowned as they pondered a question. These newcomers only stared, sitting at the back of the room. Three or four that I knew hadn't been there yesterday. I'd at least have remembered the muscles in this room of intellectual spellcasters. But, with faces like those, I should have remembered more.

By Q&A I felt creeped out, yet intrigued. What did they want? Who were they?

They must have questions. Maybe I could ask some myself. At least approach one once I was clear of the podium.

Questions for me about seeing out of time. That one tended to be a hang-up. I was having to clarify and follow with another answer along the same lines when I noticed the willowy young woman slip out of her seat. By the time she reached the doors, ripped jeans, ponytail, and another dark, handsome guy with noticeable biceps, had also left their seats.

No one seemed aware of them drifting out. Except me—hardly able to finish Q&A.

They remained on my mind by the end of the conference and dinner with Broomantle members. I almost asked someone about them. But what would I say? *Who were those beautiful, fit people who only showed up for my talk this morning?* It didn't make sense and, even if I did want to know, it could only be getting more involved to ask questions. Not less.

I bit my tongue, thanked Broomantle representatives who'd invited me, praised the lovely venue—thinking again of the doorman—and bowed out.

Tonight, late or no, I had to take Melanie to a pub and force myself to stay awake. I'd never adjust to the time change otherwise. With the worst of the trip already behind me, I was once more glad I'd booked that cheap flight to land on Friday.

I started back, winding along side streets, leaving the tourist Brighton behind and walking down rows of pastel houses in residential parts of town.

I knew the way from previous visits and felt myself decompress as I went, again worn out from the day, yet looking ahead to the next ones so much more. Until I rounded a corner, saw a blur of motion, a man moving fast, and everything went black.

## ○ C̲H̲A̲P̲T̲E̲R̲ ̲2̲ ○

IT TOOK ME ABOUT one second to understand a bag had been dropped over my head. I had enough of a glimpse before the lights went out to know where he was, even if I couldn't see anymore. In that instant the self-defense class my grandmother had paid for me to take at nineteen when I'd left home flashed back to me. Had I been asked a moment before, I'd have said much of that full-contact course had faded from memory. Not true.

I was knocked forward by the force of impact from the bag smashing into my head and shoulders, propelled by two powerful hands. I used momentum to throw an elbow, making contact yet feeling a solid impact. No flab here. It was like hitting a refrigerator.

Along with fast movements, I started shouting, "No!" Stomping down hard, catching his foot and met by swearing.

"No!" Throwing my head into him as he grappled with me. I hoped to break his nose but caught his jaw, the force of the blow making me see stars. The guy was tall as well as strong.

"No!" A knee slammed up and in with all my body and fear and anger behind it. This, at least, made good contact.

Violent cursing, the man knocked back, me ripping at the nylon bag around my head, and *wham*: another set of arms shoved me into a solid wall.

"No!" I stomped again, trying to twist, shouting, jabbing out to catch a nose or eyes, then felt my face smothered by a large hand over the bag.

Fighting to breathe—forget yelling—I felt a horrible sensation of weightlessness, leaving my stomach behind while I was yanked into the air. Multiple hands: two or three men crushing my mouth and throwing me around like a sack of flour.

I wasn't heavy. But I wasn't a shrimp either. The way these guys moved I might as well have been a doll. Their strength further terrified, but also shocked me.

When I heard a car door and felt the sensation of being thrown forward, suffocating, still lashing out, I thought for the first time of doing more: using all my resources.

Then *crash*—sick pain in my shoulder as I landed in some sort of vehicle. My hands were wrenched around to my back, tape at my wrists, cord or drawstring pulled tight on my neck, keeping the bag in place. All in the time it took me to cough and suck in a breath with the hand gone from my mouth and the bag still stifling me.

I thrashed like an eel against tape, kicked out, and *thwack*. Foot hitting something relatively yielding.

A different man shouted in pain, possibly more swearing. I couldn't understand the language he used. Not German, not French, maybe something Scandinavian.

Slamming noise from the back of an SUV or station wagon and I realized that was what I'd been thrown into. The vehicle shook. Another door slammed. A deafening engine started.

I'd been walking past rows of parked cars on the street. I saw it in an instant—this one at the end of the row where I'd turned. There had been … was it a Jeep? Yes, a silver Jeep, not like the little sedans and compact cars. They had been waiting for me with this vehicle.

I was being kidnapped. The absurdity, impossibility of it, left me as reeling as the blows and blindness. Two or three men had lain in wait for me on a street corner in a foreign country, grabbed me, and thrown me in a Jeep.

It was just … didn't even … couldn't be…

Impossible.

Had anyone heard me yell? Called the cops? England was covered by CCTV nose to tail. Someone would know. Yet, this particular street and corner, even if it had been recorded, who would see it? When? How soon and how would it help if they didn't know where the Jeep was going or who I was or who the men involved were?

Impossible. But not impossible to fight back.

Engine roaring, dashing off through the streets of Brighton.

In those first moments the idea to fight with magic had not entered my head. Beyond instinctive defense. Even if I'd thought it, I would never have been able to call it up.

Magic is an effort, draining to the user, an act of will: focus and resolve. Yes, a skilled witch can summon magic she needs in a relative flash, but only relative. Much like a gun can be loaded and fired rapidly. If the gun is not loaded in the first place, however, no amount of pulling the trigger will make a bullet fly.

With my heart hammering, struggling for each breath through that nylon sack, smelling wet dog and sawdust, with pain beating through my bruised shoulder and knees wadded up toward my chest, I tried to think.

Kidnapped, being driven away, fight back. I was still a witch—like it or not.

Two problems. First, the magic mindset. If I didn't clear my head enough to focus on it, I couldn't get anything to happen. Suffocating and panicking were not going to make magic. Second, mundanes involved. I couldn't use magic in front of mundanes unless they were unaware of it. Not to stop a crime. Not to save my own life. Not to prevent a war. Never. Ever.

Which left the dilemma of calling magic, harnessing it to work in a time of stress, while also channeling it in such a way as to not appear to the mundanes that I was using it.

Example: blow out a tire, break the tape, pull the sack off my head, get out, and run. Coincidence, a shock about the tape, but still believable events.

And if they caught me? This time we'd be face-to-face. I could fight back, channel greater strength, be seen by other drivers.

I focused on breathing.

One tire. I could gather the force to blow out one tire.

Focus.

I'd hardly heard mumbled voices of the men, not registering as my mind raced. So I hadn't noticed the movements until something touched my ear through the bag and I realized one of them was leaning over a back seat above me.

"No tricks," he said, breathless. It was the one who'd been speaking another language. Yet his accent was nothing but English. "We know what you're thinking and you can't get away with anything. Right? *Nothing* at all."

Two fresh horrors. First, they knew what I was. Second, that cold, round metal pressure through the nylon was the nose of a gun.

I waited, motionless while my thoughts sped and didn't get anywhere.

I needed a list. I needed to balance alternatives, weigh options. I needed points A and B, choices One or Two. Instead, my mind replied with white noise of panic.

Minutes passed, the vehicle making turns, then rapidly gaining speed, leaving the city.

Focus. Gather force.

My magic couldn't stop a bullet. It might help—twist the gun from his hand—but it could also get me killed if I made a mistake in timing. And they knew. Which meant that if something weird happened, such as a tire blowing, they would assume it was me even if I'd done nothing.

*Goddess, grant us a smooth journey.*

Then what? Once we arrived ... somewhere?

What did they want? Should I try to talk?

I feared my voice shaking—betraying myself, losing my own strength.

I kept silent. Only struggling for that energy, ready to harness once the gun was off my head.

The gun did not stay, however. The pressure soon vanished. I sensed the man looming above me, keeping an eye on me. They said no more as we drove.

Ten minutes, twenty, thirty? I wasn't sure how long, how far.

Then slowing, turns, a smooth road becoming rough, more turns, worse road, bumped and jarred.

At last, we stopped.

Doors opening, shutting. Still, I lay motionless, arms aching, heart pounding, but ready to act, to fight if at all possible.

How long before Melanie missed me? Was the sun setting? Even if it had, she would think I'd gone for a drink with my historical society friends.

Heavy steps on gravel. The back opened. Quick hands, strong and impatient, yanked me up by an arm. I stumbled and pitched forward as I was dragged from the back, caught and steadied on my feet by those same hands.

I didn't fight or speak. I focused on the magic. Ready. Ready for what?

Tape was cut and ripped off my wrists with a sudden pain that almost made me cry out. I sucked in a breath and bit my tongue instead. Breathing even faster, rigid with the effort to stand and keep my magic ready.

Two guys pulled me forward, one to each side, a hand on each upper arm, and we crunched over gravel. Only two of them all along?

Next thing I knew, I was tripping and stumbling through grass or weeds, a rough lawn. No, a field, maybe a hay field. Across tall grass and jagged earth and cool evening air.

Several voices ahead, low, male and female, growing louder as we seemed to be coming up to them.

Then, abrupt silence.

# ○ Chapter 3 ○

"What—?" A woman's voice.

"Told you we could get her, *cataja*." Voice of the man immediately to my right. The one with the bag. The one I was sure I'd kneed in the groin. Now, though, his tone was cheerful, even smug.

Unseen hands shoved me forward. I tripped and dropped to my knees as voices murmured ahead and around us. They sounded alarmed, not threatening, but I wasn't sure beyond that. English mixed in with that strange language.

My focus had to stay inward while my pulse raced, skin damp with sweat. Prepared to fight.

Fight who? What?

Hands free, I snatched at the hood over my face, loosening the drawstring.

"What have you done?" Same female voice.

"Just what I said we would." The bag was yanked away by the owner of the voice above my painful right shoulder.

I sat back on my heels, breathing hard, envisioning inner power, the fire in my chest ready to be guided by my will. Even with the murmurs, however, I was not prepared for how many there were when I finally saw.

It was twilight, the sun below a little wood to my left, while I was indeed on my knees in an unkempt field. I faced dozens of individuals arranged in camp chairs, on logs, on the ground, or standing up in rows behind them for a look at me.

As I blinked and regained my sight, an older woman before me was getting to her feet. Face drawn, she approached. Her blazing eyes were directed above me.

"If you cannot complete a simple task, Kenaniah, seek guidance from your *orataj*." The same one who'd already been speaking.

"We did complete—" he started.

"You said you could retrieve the scry!"

"We—"

"Not maul and torment her!"

"What were—?"

Still holding the magic, prepared to escape any way I could, I stole a glance around. To my right was the protesting Kenaniah. I knew him at once. The carved jaw and high cheekbones, ripped jeans and intense eyes from advanced scrying this morning. He'd also been the blur that dropped the drawstring bag over my head.

"I thought ambitions for core meant more to you than this," she snarled and Kenaniah flinched. "And you, Jedediah, will wear the cuff if you ever treat another human this way."

I didn't recognize the one to my left, Jedediah, though he was cut from the same mold. Young, powerfully built, jeans and T-shirt—all black in his case. While the other tried to argue, Jedediah only stood there, scowling, shoulders hunched. His biceps made three of mine in circumference. Above the square jaw and black stubble, I was pleased to see flecks of blood that he hadn't mopped up from his nose.

Must have been his face I'd kicked in the back of the vehicle.

An older man and a young woman moved forward.

The two flanking me took a step back from the one reprimanding them. She managed a deep breath, her gaze dropping to me. A relatively small woman, though still as tall as myself, with silvering hair twisted up on her head, wearing a black summer dress with a gray half cape across her shoulders.

Not only her expression but whole body changed when she looked at me. Her eyes softened and grew sad. Her back eased, her chin lowered, and she opened her palms toward me.

"The council welcomes you to the South Coast Cooperative," she murmured in a voice like someone else—a shout become a whisper, a warning become an endearment. "You have been treated unfairly. We must beg your forgiveness."

I blinked, staring stupidly up at her in the gloom, still on my knees. "I…"

"What would you have us do, *cataja?*" Kenaniah was having another go to argue his case. "When the council asked them before, no worm would speak to us."

"So you have explained nothing to her?" The old woman snapped, back to the sharp tone and glare to face him.

"Plenty of time for that. She's here, isn't she? That's sorted. You said 'bring her' for Moon's sake! Not chat her up."

"Watch your tongue!"

But the two others had come up to us. The woman from this morning, burnt honey hair, very young, stepped past me to take Kenaniah's arm, shushing him. The older man offered me his hand, also apologizing.

"Are you all right, miss?" He had a graying beard and eyes crinkled with laugh lines, though the eyes looked concerned now.

I didn't want to take his hand, afraid to break my own focus, but, slowly, I did and allowed him to help me to my feet.

"She'd never have come willingly—" Debate still on.

"If you had no intention of explaining the situation, you should have said so. Peter and Isaac could have talked to her."

"Like we've 'talked' with worms before? She'd have told us to boil our heads. Like any other worm would!"

The long-haired young woman was tugging his arm. "Kage, that's enough." She must have been stronger than she looked because he stumbled, breathing hard, and checking his words.

"Your pardon, *cataja*," Kenaniah—Kage—mumbled, finally averting his eyes.

"It's not too late," the young woman hurried on, glancing between them and me. "Maybe she'll still help. It's not the council's fault this happened, *cataja*." She cast me a mute appeal, her eyes desperate. For what? For me to say, *Sure, no harm done*, and laugh the whole thing off?

Then, somehow, they were looking at me. Every one.

After the yelling, I'd just about vanished. Or so I'd hoped.

The older woman inclined her head as she faced me, about to speak. I didn't want her groveling. I just needed to know what the hell was going on.

I spoke first. "What is it you want? Who are you? Council of what?"

She looked up, startled, though she knew they'd told me nothing. "Why ... council of wolves."

## ○ Chapter 4 ○

The three of them, Kage, Jedediah, and the honey-haired young woman, stood sideways to the old woman, all eyes downcast. This shift in their postures also changed tension in the air. No more arguing, no more fighting back.

Everyone who was looking at anything was looking at me.

"Please." After a breath, the old woman offered her hand. "Will you allow us a moment of your time? We will not harm you. More," she added with a hint of a growl, eyes darting to Kage and Jedediah—who had remained silent.

I took her hand briefly, unable to resist stepping back even so. No one moved to stop me.

"I am Diana, silver of the Sable Pack and member of the South Coast Cooperative, humbly requesting your forgiveness. This is Elijah, silver of the Aspen Pack."

The one who'd helped me up nodded.

Still easing back, I said, "Cassia Allyn. So you're … shifters?"

It didn't make sense. There were supposed to be werewolves in Montana and Canada, maybe elsewhere in North or South America. Some remaining in Europe and Russia. But a whole gathering here in the South of England? How?

I didn't know much about them. Not many humans, even in the magical community, did. Elusive, shunning human company, keeping to themselves. So what was this?

If there *were* werewolves running around densely populated England, why were they kidnapping humans and demanding ... what?

Diana nodded in answer.

"Why have you brought me here?"

"To ask your assistance." Soft voice.

"Right," I said, facing her and not backing away anymore. "And sending a couple of thugs to drag me here with a gun to my head was a good start?"

"Gun?"

Many of them looked around to each other, or Kage and Jedediah, who smirked. Kage chuckled.

"We don't have a gun," he said, startling me with a lopsided grin. "That was the nose of an old hammer. Just couldn't have you thinking you'd use your ... magic ... duff..." He faltered and looked away again in the heat of Diana's glare.

"Kage, really?" The young woman started.

"Jed's idea," Kage muttered. "I thought it was pretty canny, actually." He seemed surprised. Maybe Jedediah didn't have many good ideas. Or Kage simply didn't like him.

"Jed—" But she stopped and looked to me. "I'm sorry. I should have stayed in Brighton and talked to you myself. They're proper daft sometimes; dead from the neck up."

I hated it when people apologized for other people. Obviously, Kage could speak for himself—although I was beginning to wonder about Jed. And "sorry" didn't look like it was cracking the top ten of how he was feeling. Jed had gone back to scowling at the grass while Kage gazed off into the distance as if hoping to catch a view of the sunset.

It was beyond true twilight. The western sky faded to indigo. Getting tough to see. Not a comfortable feeling in the silent crowd. No one made a move to light a campfire or even an electric lantern. They just watched in gloom.

Diana seemed to have been ready to follow up about the gun charade. Instead, she took a long, careful breath, dragged her gaze away from Kage, and focused on me.

"Our pack, and, perhaps, the whole South Coast Cooperative, is in jeopardy." Her tone was gentle as she ignored the two delinquents. "As to you, however, you were brought here unfairly, and are free to go." She opened her arms. "Rebecca can give you a lift back to Brighton whenever you wish."

The young woman with Kage nodded.

I hesitated.

"Or I can explain the trouble here and you decide for yourself." Diana gestured with her arm to take in the group. "If you will allow us a moment of your time we would be in your debt. It will not take long. Perhaps you would care to sit?" Maybe one was still smirking because the soft tone sharpened. "Kenaniah, Jedediah, find places in the circle."

Dismissed, Kage and Jed slipped away, skirting behind her. Other dark figures enfolded them into the group.

Rebecca waited, presumably to see if I wanted her chauffeur services.

I swallowed. There were the obvious issues about even agreeing to listen—all that had just happened, the situation, the dark, the "wolves." But there was an even worse issue coming to mind: no more magic.

A witch giving up the craft.

*Mundane forever.*

Inviting in magical creatures, leading to greater entanglement into my life, could only be bad news. For me.

What about for them?

Did they really need help? If so, why me? In all of Broomantle—a human group they knew of—they could have asked anyone. Why have their eyes on me today?

Did they have something for, or against, American witches? I'd stood out in that regard. Otherwise I was nothing special. Just a normal witch. There had been dozens of spellcasters there with greater power and skill than myself.

And what was the trouble? Were they really in danger?

Nana used to say we were fading: human casters, shifters, undead such as vampires, and the faie. We were all that was left, few and far between. With the possible exception of the faie—elementals and the very essence of magical spirits.

*Collective of remaining humans and magical beings. Be our own allies. Or this community will continue to fade.*

I took a breath and spoke slowly. "No promises, but I'll listen." So I really was a sucker. "*If* you'll start a fire or bring lanterns, or there's somewhere we can go inside."

This caused a stir. I couldn't hear what all was whispered, but got the gist. *What did she say? She wants what?*

"Do you always have council meetings in fields in the dark?" I asked, catching my tone and hoping I sounded more confused than as if I were accusing them of anything unintelligent.

"Moon rises. There is no room for us to gather indoors here," Diana said, also careful in her tone, diplomatic. "We do have a fire pit beside the barn. We can group there and build a fire?" Like a question. *If that would suit you, madam?*

She made me feel like a prima donna. Lifting her eyebrows after I'd chipped a nail and burst into tears over it. But this was crazy enough as it was. They could humor me with a light.

"Thank you," I said again. "Then maybe you can tell me what's going on."

She nodded to her fellows and several jumped up—presumably for firewood.

Diana led me to a new meeting site, others straggling after, some with objects they'd been sitting on. The mood was subdued, tension, even fear, thick in the air. Fear for what was happening to them? Fear I wouldn't help?

My own heart still beat too fast, palms sweaty in the cooling night. Maybe it was my own fear getting the better of me, making me sense it in them.

It took only minutes to have a fire going and our gathering repositioned near a crumbled stone barn. Then I accepted a seat from Elijah to face Diana by the growing blaze, and she began.

## Chapter 5

"The South Coast Cooperative comprises the packs of southern England. The Aspens in Devon, Greys in Somerset, Beeches in Hampshire, and the Sables, my own family, here in West Sussex."

At mention of the Beeches in Hampshire I heard muttering in the crowd.

Diana added, "The Beech Pack opted to forgo these gatherings, and much interaction of any sort between themselves and others, a generation ago. Which is their prerogative." A firm note at the end.

There had seemed like a lot of them when I first got a look. Now it struck me how few there were if these represented members of three different groups and, presumably, much of this Sable Pack who lived here. Forty or fifty at most.

"What about the rest of the country? Europe also? I hadn't known there were werewolves in England at all."

"I'm glad to hear that," Diana said quietly. "There is a pack in Wales and a few who keep their own council in the North of England and Scotland, as well as some on the Continent. France, Germany, though mostly Eastern Europe. As far as I am aware, their numbers are low as our own. I have a correspondent, distant relations, in Bavaria in a pack made of only two families.

The same in France, though more in Romania. Beyond this, I could not say."

"Sounds like casters, now that you mention it. But you do still have four packs in this part of the world? That's no small feat."

"Life here can be challenging. Rewarding as well, while we seek a balance between our shared lives with humans and honoring our ancestors and ourselves. Now, though…" She looked away into the fire.

"What is it that's happening to your pack?"

The field was so quiet, deathly still besides the crack of the blaze, I heard an owl hoot at the top of the wood.

Slowly, Diana shifted her gaze to meet my eyes. "Wolves are dying. Since last winter, one Grey, two Aspens, and four members of the Sable Pack have been murdered."

I sat still, not only hearing the word *murdered* beating in my brain, but floored by the numbers. Seven of them? They had a serial killer in their midst who'd taken down *seven* werewolves since winter and they just now thought they'd ask a witch for help?

"I'm sorry," I said after a breath. "But if you're trying to solve a crime you've come to the wrong witch. Can't you track the killers yourselves? And what about mundane police?"

It seemed there was a shudder, a ripple of breath and murmuring not unlike the one following the name of the Beech Pack.

"Our affairs are not human affairs," Diana said. "To involve human police would be to explain, justify, and open our lives. Which could be a greater risk than what we already face."

This seemed improbable, given what they faced right now, but I held my tongue.

"As to finding them, we have been attempting to since January. The killer, or killers, as we believe this is more than one person, knows what we are. They dowse the bodies and trails in petrol, citronella sprays, solvents, or other masking agents. We've never even come close."

"So it's the same? You do know it's the same person? Or same people?"

"All seven have had their throats cut, bled out like game. Their eyes were removed, hearts staked, clothing gone, and skin and area splashed, generally with petrol as if they were to be burnt."

"But they're not?" I swallowed. "Burning would seem like a safeguard against tracking."

"We suspect the killers don't want a fire to draw attention."

"Draw attention? How are you finding them? How could the human community not know about a scene like that?"

"They're always near home, or left where we will be. They mean for us to find them. Of course, we do, and tend to our own dead."

"When you say staked … like vampires?"

"Yes. Since there are no vampires here it doesn't seem possible someone could mistake such identities. You must go to London or Birmingham to find vampires in this country."

There were *vampires* in London? How had I not known any of this?

Thinking it made me remember. "Some humans know. I heard them mention deaths at the conference. So the magical community knows? Why haven't you asked them before now?"

"I couldn't say as to the community. But a few individuals know because we told them. We have exceedingly few contacts in the world of casters. After a number of deaths, however, when it became clear we were making no progress, we did ask for help."

More unease than ever in the crowd. I felt tension like a shadow cast across the fire.

That argument; Kage insisting they'd had to drag me here because talking wouldn't have worked—that if I'd known what they wanted and who they were, I wouldn't have come.

Nana's teaching; werewolves and humans didn't mix. She'd said if I ever met a werewolf it was best to think of it as I'd think of meeting a wild wolf. Keep my distance, mind my own business. Because one thing I did know about them, or thought I'd known, was that they really didn't like humans. One of the reasons, besides privacy, they were said to only live in places like Canada these days. Not the most populated parts of overpopulated England.

Plus my own inklings about them there in the dark: they didn't *want* help from me or any other human, witch or mundane. They wanted to be left alone and solve their own problems.

Probably a few—Diana, Elijah, likely some others in authority—must have decided that, in desperate times, they would go to humans. Not the cops, heaven forbid. But at least a caster.

"So what happened?" I asked, feeling an oppressive sense of an uphill battle that I didn't even want to be fighting.

For the first time, Diana hesitated. "Last spring, I spoke with a mage in Brighton. He could not, or would not, help us. Yet he presented the idea of needing…"

"A scry," I finished quietly. "There are other scries in the magical world. You didn't have to wait to prey on a tourist."

"It was not our intention to prey on anyone. I regret the way you were treated. As to your powers, however, you were invited from America to teach the art of scrying to other spellcasters, were you not? You are clearly the best."

"That's why you sent some of your family to crash my talk? To make your selection? You've been watching Broomantle to find one? I'm sorry if you got the impression that I'm some elite seer. My grandmother was the renowned scry. Yes, I can do it, and teach it, but I'm no great shakes. There were better ones than myself there this weekend."

Hush. Many eyes glinted eerily in the firelight.

I thought about telling them I was ready for that lift back to Brighton. Melanie probably wouldn't be worried yet, thinking I was out with my peers. Most likely delighted to imagine I'd met a cute guy. Well … there were very attractive guys around. I could tell her that later in all honesty.

Instead of her, I was the one worried. Whether they actually wanted me here or not, some of them had been smart enough to see they needed help. And to ask.

I took a careful breath under the watchful eyes of dozens of predators who'd found themselves turned into prey. It might have helped if they moved about, or had drinks in their hands, or started their own conversations. No. They watched.

"So you're wanting me to scry for these killers? Then what? What if I see them? First of all, seeing someone doesn't mean I will have any idea of the context. Looking for something like this by scrying … it's such a long shot. Secondly, what will you do if I do find them?"

More silence. And stares.

"If you're not involving the human legal system, I can't see how this could end up any better than a bloodbath—even if I could tell you right now what's going on. I sympathize for what's happening to you. But I'm not comfortable pointing a finger and more people dying either."

"I can't tell you what would become of the killers if we catch them," Diana said. "Justice is not what concerns our packs at the moment. It is fear for the lives of our parents and siblings—our young, friends, and neighbors—that robs our sleep. Knowing the face of this killer represents life, at least a chance, be that defensive or offensive. While continuing in ignorance as we are now means another mother, or mate, or brother could be dead by morning.

"We are not asking you to be our council, Cassia Allyn—judge, jury, police, or jailer. We ask only for a witness, a clue, a path to follow. Though we have no right to ask you favors, you may be our one hope. If there is anything at all … anything you think might shed light…" She trailed away with her eyes briefly shut before meeting mine again.

I looked into the fire, turned my face from the heat, and nodded.

## o Chapter 6 o

THEY SEEMED TO EXPECT me to need my witchy wares—perhaps to perform the scry in my designated magic room with my magic wand and crystal ball. All I actually need to scry is my mind. Outside induction of a trance state is, however, a huge help.

I asked Diana if any of them drummed, or did they know a chant they could use?

"We shall sing Moon's blessing," she said. "A prayer and lullaby. Repeated, it should sound like a chant."

It turned out to be a perfect melody not only because of the repetitive nature, but because there were no words in the song I could understand. That language again, round and lyrical, too many consonants and as strange to my ear as Russian. Still, it was beautiful.

They chanted this moon prayer in rhythmic tones, no louder than wind whipping through autumn leaves. The fire cracked and flashed.

I sat on the ground with my legs crossed, still uneasy about closing my eyes in front of them—not to mention worrying about spiders lurking in the long grass. Like shamanic journeys, though, I would never be far gone, always aware of this space. If anyone tried to, say, throw a bag over my head, I'd know.

I interlaced my fingers, chin down, eyes shut, and let the song carry me to a place of meditation. The waterfall I always retreated to for personal energy, to call my magic, settle my mind, escape, or gain insight. In this landscape, I gathered my intentions and goal.

*These people are being attacked. Shifters of the South Coast Cooperative have been murdered.*

*Help. Reveal: the killer, the way, the next step.*
*See truth without distance or time as barriers.*
*Open doors.*
*Answers.*

The grove was not my own. Space in standing stones. An emerald green pastureland. Rolling slopes, cliffs to the sea. Figures in dust-brown robes.

A great calm settled over me. The first peace I'd felt since falling asleep in Melanie's guest room last night. Wind whistled over standing stones. Dark symbols on them vanished into shadows cast by the setting sun.

*Reveal.*
*Answers.*

I saw no more, only this quiet place of meditation, a small group with hands folded. They also seemed to be praying or chanting.

I felt no fear, no malice. Rather, a kinship. A sense of connection. Often, if the way is unclear, a feeling can be as significant as a sight in scrying. I listened to the feelings.

*Answers.* The word came back on the wind, in the chant, as if I could see it painted in the stone circle.

Nothing else.

I stood beside my waterfall with my spirit animal, the red-eyed tree frog. I looked into her blood-red eyes. My frog looked back from river rock at the edge of the pool.

*Are these answers? Or only the questions?* I asked.

She gazed for a long moment at me, then jumped into spraying white water and vanished.

When I returned from the trance I sat for a long time, looking at flames, still thinking of the feelings as much as the sight.

The chanting voices faded and gradually fell silent when they saw I was awake.

Diana sat in a camp chair before me, fire to her right and to my left.

I shook my head. "I'm not sure if this is much help, but ... do you know any druids?"

Many glances were exchanged behind her.

"What is it?" I asked.

"The druids have lost someone as well," Diana said.

I felt a chill.

*The right answers begin with the right questions.*

"You didn't mention that."

She looked around.

Elijah was already moving his chair more into the light beside her. "We heard in the Aspens that a druid was murdered some months ago. I don't know if the pattern was the same. There's one my daughter and others have seen on occasion on the Teign, or we wouldn't know at all."

"Druids and werewolves?" I said. "What's the connection? Why would someone target both?"

They shook their heads.

"You'll have to speak to them." I made my tone more brisk. "Start with this one you see at the ... is it a river?"

Elijah nodded, yet he looked uncomfortable. "I've never met this person. Even those who have go months between a glimpse, much less a conversation. Like us, druids keep to themselves. I couldn't tell you where they live."

"Cornwall."

Elijah and Diana turned in their seats. I looked past them.

The speaker sat at the edge of firelight, a young man with black hair down to his shoulders. Or a young male? I supposed it was wrong of me to identify them as "men" and "women."

"Come forward, Eleazar," Diana said. "You think so? It is said these days there are no proper druidic orders closer than the border country."

He stepped up to her, but sank to his knees to join us on the grass, between Diana and myself so the three of us formed a semicircle facing the fire. He kissed her hand, then rocked back on his heels.

"We don't need a proper order, *cataja*," he said. "We need only one druid to ask what's happened to them. The old texts say there have always been druids in Cornwall—one of their sacred lands."

"You refer to history books, Eleazar." Diana looked tired, face deeply lined in the skipping light.

"Do we not study the past in order to understand the present, *cataja*?" He smiled from her to me, meeting my eyes. A real smile, gentle and warm as the glow to my left. The first sincere, pure smile I'd seen since arriving here.

I returned it without meaning to, surprised how the sensation relaxed my own shoulders.

College-age, maybe younger than myself, that long, wavy hair, black T-shirt, boots, and the leather bracelets he wore all would have fit perfectly with a guitar in his hands. And he could have been on his own album cover. His smile was beautiful. Not a very manly word, but it was: faint dimples in his cheeks, perfect teeth—not all together common in the UK—and sparkling eyes reflecting dancing firelight.

Diana had already answered him and looked to me before I'd noticed.

"Well," I said, dragging my attention back to her, past Eleazar. "I ... suggest you find some. Cornwall or anywhere else. The connection is critical or I wouldn't have seen druids. Since you already know they've experienced a loss, it's the obvious place to start."

Murmurs and stirring in the crowd, at last not so fixed on me.

"For all we know," I added, "they're on the trail of the same killer. Or already have answers. Even if both your groups are solitary, surely you could work together on something this important."

Diana nodded thoughtfully. Elijah said something to her that I couldn't catch and she frowned, tapping her fingers on the fabric arm of her chair.

Eleazar still smiled at me while everyone else grew restless. He offered his hand, then switched from left to right in a flash.

"Sorry," he said. "I forget most humans are *dextel*. I mean ... uh..."

"Right-handed?" I asked.

"Yes." Beaming even more. "I'm Zar. Only elders call me Eleazar. It's a gift and a privilege to meet you."

"It is?"

We still had some audience but others were finally talking among themselves.

"Of course it is. You honor us by being here."

I wanted to push hair back from his face. See those eyes better since I couldn't tell the color, only orange reflections. I wasn't usually crazy about long hair on guys. On him, though…

"Zar, nice to meet you. I'm Cassia." I shook with him, surprised to find his grip mild.

I could have held on, thinking of all the men I was supposed to meet with Melanie. Why bother? Not that werewolves were an appropriate substitute. Still, nice to see that some of the younger ones didn't hate humans.

Other things I was supposed to be concerned over just now.

Even so, I had to ask. "Are most werewolves left-handed?"

"Left, or even ambidextrous, are more common than right-handed. Right-handed wolves are what we call a *dextel*."

"In your own language? What are you speaking?"

"Lucannis, the wolf tongue." Talking fast. I wasn't sure if he was nervous or only eager to share with me. "You must think us frightfully rude. We don't often have people around who can't understand it."

"No, it's … gorgeous."

Zar lowered his voice as he went on. "Kage, your inviter—" Grinning. "He's a dextel and he's always been touchy about it since it makes him look human. I wouldn't be fussed. Not with humans like you around." He inched nearer, very much in my personal space, yet I couldn't say I minded. "Your eyes are moonlight ripples in woodland pools. If I had your eyes, I'd never be able to pull myself away from a mirror."

"How can you see my eyes in firelight?"

Zar leaned even closer. "I'm sorry Diana didn't ask me to bring you back. Things would have been different. You could have come to the whole council meeting if you'd wanted to. If you didn't want to…" A little shrug.

"I know all the hidden coves and inlets up and down the beach from Kent to Devon. We could have found other places to be."

"Is that so? Why didn't you go with Kage and Jed then?"

"Oh … you know." He finally dropped his gaze, twisting a stalk of golden grass around a finger of his left hand. Somehow, he was still holding my right. "We should give them a chance, like the elders have been trying to. Let them fail on their own if they must."

"I see. You're very noble."

A shy smile, his focus back on my eyes. "Jed's my brother and Kage is my first cousin. Who am I to look after them all their lives? If they're going to maintain shambolic reputations around here it's best if the poor sods do it on their own."

"You're the brother and cousin of those two? I'm surprised you're willing to admit that. Especially to me."

"Love makes fools of wise wolves and pups of silvers. I would admit anything to you." He kissed my hand on those words while I suddenly wished he wouldn't: Diana was again addressing me.

Not that I knew what to say. Or had heard the first bit of what she was saying.

"And we will protect you, of course," Diana said. "It's possible you could be in danger if this killer finds out you seek them."

What?

I had to wrench my gaze from Zar. He still smiled at me, head a bit tipped, eyes tossing back firelight, dimples showing.

"I … uh," I said to Diana, thinking of hidden coves by moonlight. "I don't see why anyone would know. If you find druids and start asking awkward questions, I suppose it would be nice if you didn't drop my name. Otherwise…"

"What about your search?"

"Search?" Had I zoned out that much?

*Dammit*—he was still smiling. Didn't he have anything else to look at?

"To find the murderers. We recommend you start in Cornwall." As Diana spoke, Elijah nodded. "Eleazar knows lore and ways of our magical kin."

"I'll go," Zar said at once. "Thank you, *cataja*. It will be my honor to protect Cassia and track our foe."

"You have your pack's gratitude, Eleazar. Others…" She looked back as hands went up—which startled me.

Wait. First of all, what was going on?

I wasn't running off to Cornwall with or without a couple of werewolf bodyguards. I'd never even hinted that I would be willing to do such a thing—had I?

Plus, I was done. I'd scried for them. Now I was ready to start my Brighton vacation after that lift home to my sister.

Besides, even if they were thinking I'd tear off to Cornwall, why were there volunteers? Other than those speaking to me—Diana, Elijah, Rebecca, and Zar—I'd not noticed one whisper to imply that they were happy I was here. I didn't belong. Yet now they all wanted to join in?

Diana paid no heed to silent requests to be chosen. "Kenaniah, Jedediah, you will accompany Eleazar and protect the witch."

"I'm not sure what—" I started.

Standing up, she waved them forward, still speaking. "She is our hope. Will you watch over her? See to her safety and each other's? And help in any way possible?"

"I will," Zar said, scrambling to his feet before the others could answer.

"Wait a minute," I said, following him, brushing grass from my pants. "What is it you're expecting?"

"Only that you help us find them," Diana said. "Starting in Cornwall. If you can locate druids and ask after their own situation, perhaps that will lead you to enough information to scry again for this killer. With you, the druids, and the wolves working together, I'm sure we can save our pack."

I mouthed while she talked.

Everyone else also stood, or those I could see, by firelight.

Kage and Jed answered her, giving an affirmative that, yes, they would aid and protect me, Kage getting in some bit about making this up to his "elders and core." Jed hanging back, grudging at best, looking like he'd rather be anywhere else.

As if I wanted them along either. As if there had been any point where I'd agreed to any of the stuff she was talking about.

Diana turned, taking stock of them. Rebecca stepped forward. As did another female in a sweeping dark skirt, a wiry young male with rumpled black hair, the guy with the ponytail from this morning, and more.

I was reeling, trying to get a better look at faces in twisting shadows, when Diana waved them back and made her selection.

"Isaac? Will you join them?"

"Honored, *cataja*." A big male even taller, also much paler than the others, stepped forward. As powerful in appearance as Kage and Jed, yet older, past thirty—though that may have been the short trimmed beard.

Slower and more deliberate in his movements, his light hair was combed back. He wore a blue button-down and looked all together tidier and more pulled together then most of those assembled.

The pale one stepped to Zar, Kage, and Jed around Diana. I noticed Kage ease away, uncomfortable. Both he and Jed avoided looking at Isaac. This made me take an instant liking to him. I wished Diana would send Kage and Jed back. Let Zar and Isaac come with me.

Then I kicked myself. Wait, so I *was* doing this? I was dashing off to look for druids with a bunch of werewolves? Had they slipped something into my drink? But they hadn't even given me one. Forget tea or roasting marshmallows, no one had so much as a mint or bottle of water.

Diana removed a silver pendant from her neck and held it out.

Zar, Kage, Jed, and Isaac reached to hold the chain, their hands touching, linked back to her as she held the silver orb.

Diana looked up. As one, everyone else did as well. So did I—pack mentality.

There was the moon, three quarters, above the little wood beyond the stone barn.

"Moon grant light in darkness, good hunting, our families safe from harm," Diana said. "Grant your light to Cassia, this witch, our hope. Grant strength and wisdom to these four wolves who will keep her safe on her journey to unmask our enemies." She looked to the four before her, each with his left hand extended to hold the chain. "Will you swear to honor your pack and Moon by protecting this woman from whatever dangers may appear in her search? To help in this fight against forces that would hunt us?"

"I so swear," they answered in unison.

Diana held up the pendant as they dropped the chain and, one by one, each bent to kiss the orb in her palm. Then each made a gesture I'd never seen. At first, I thought they were crossing themselves. Instead, they touched their temples, then chests with two fingers, at the end of the movement tipping their faces back to the moon as if to give it a nod.

Diana hung the silver orb back around her neck and faced me. The group of four parted for her to do so, Zar and Jed to her right, Kage and Isaac to her left, all looking at me.

A shiver flickered down my spine: new awareness of cool silver moonlight cutting into the orange heat of the bonfire, facing the silent packs who were placing their lives in my hands—even while many did not look pleased by the idea. Well ... they weren't the only ones.

But I nodded. I don't know why.

Looking to Zar, Kage, Jed, Isaac, then into Diana's eyes—strong, yet afraid—it was as if I had no choice. As if I'd already made the choice the moment I'd heard people were dying and it may be within my power to do something to stop it.

I nodded again, meaning it this time, taking a breath. "When do we leave?"

## ○ CHAPTER 7 ○

I THOUGHT THEY weren't going to let me leave them. The whole lot seemed to think I would set out for Cornwall tonight with four werewolves I didn't know from Adam.

Maybe the fact that I'd said I would go at all had given them the wrong impression as to how crazy I really was—i.e. totally, as opposed to only borderline crazy.

When I explained to Diana that I wasn't going anywhere until I'd talked with my sister and had a good night's sleep, she sent Rebecca to drive me home. She also insisted one of them would return in the morning to pick me up. As if I wouldn't be safe going out alone. I wanted to tell her that was absurd, I was capable of taking care of myself. But I'd just been kidnapped by two of her clansmen so I didn't have a leg to stand on with that argument.

Perhaps she was only afraid I wouldn't come back if she didn't send someone to get me.

I was too tired to engage Rebecca as much as I wanted to on the drive. She had a little green sedan that may have been a sweet ride about thirty years ago. Now I was startled it ran at all. It smelled doggy, musty, and sweet like candy.

It was so dark out there, I couldn't get any sense of where we were, only that it took ten minutes to the suburban edge of Brighton and another ten to get home, myself struggling to navigate, looking up Melanie's address on my phone.

She asked if I was all right, clearly worried. But worried for me or about something happening to me or only about her family or becoming involved with a human like this, I couldn't say.

Then she apologized for what had happened with Kage and Jed. I wished she'd stop doing that.

"Are you two involved?" I asked as we reached the city. "You and Kage?"

"No," she laughed. "I'm his sister."

"I'm sorry."

More laughing. "I guess he takes getting used to. We grew up with Jed and his brothers also."

"How many?"

"Just Kage and me in our family. For Jed, two brothers. But Gabriel is gone so it's only Jed and Zar now."

I didn't ask what she meant by "gone." One of the victims?

"I wish I could come with you," she added. "Or do anything to help. The killers have mostly targeted females. I bet that's why Diana was scared to let any of us go."

Another thing they hadn't mentioned. What else did they know about the case that they hadn't told me? It probably didn't matter, though. I would soon have plenty of time to ask.

I sighed, brain foggy, waiting for my phone to load a map. "Any advice for having to spend ... what? A couple days to go to Cornwall and back with those two for company?"

"Don't let them get under your skin. Between Kage and Jed there's hardly been a day they haven't been in trouble with someone in the pack since they were pups. But Kage will look out for you like he says he will. Just be prepared for a lot of showing off and ego along with it. Most of the males that age think they're silver. And Jed ... I stay away from Jed myself. Most wolves do. Zar's a good sort. A lovely storyteller—but don't tell him I said that."

"Secret's safe with me. Do you know Isaac?"

"Not much. Isaac isn't close kin. He joined us from the Mountain Pack in the border country a few years ago and I've never had much to do with him. He works among humans. Many of us do, of course," she added hastily, as if she didn't want me thinking she meant this as a slur on Isaac. "My father does, and Kage some of the time. Isaac is just ... more involved. Some wolves are better at blending in than others. He's one of them."

"Anytime you can get off this road and turn right would be good. Then I think I can give directions. So that's why Isaac sounded like he had a different accent? The farthest north I've ever been in England is the Cotswolds."

"You should go sometime. The North of England is beautiful. The Lake District, Yorkshire Dales. Our coast is lovely too, but..." Rebecca sighed. "I'm not sure why Isaac wanted to be down here when he'd had mountains and lakes like that to explore." She put on the turn signal. "Where are you from? American accents make me think of human telly and California, but you have such a huge country."

"Close, north of California. I'm here from Portland, but from Kansas City originally." This was a white lie I told routinely because the single main street town forty-five minutes outside of Kansas City where I'd actually grown up was hardly a speck on any map. Anyway, after my teen years in the high desert of New Mexico with Nana, I didn't think of myself as from Cattahoo, Missouri, regardless.

I went on. "I've been in Portland for years—college, interning, working. About to start my first real teaching job at an elementary school in a great district at the end of August. I was lucky to get the job."

"So you really are a teacher? Your presentation today was smashing. You seemed so comfortable."

I gave a little shrug. "I've had a lot of practice. Spiders, no. Swimming in open water where I can't see the bottom, no. But I can do public speaking." I didn't want to keep talking about myself, head aching, still jet-lagged and stupid and needing to come up with a story to tell Melanie.

Instead, after more directions, I thanked her for doing this and asked, "Are you okay, coming out on your own?"

"I'll go straight home. No worries. They haven't been grabbing wolves off the road. It's right around home and out on foot that has us concerned."

"I'm sorry. I can't imagine how hard this has been on all of you." They must all have lost loved ones, if not close family.

As we pulled up before Melanie and Henry's house, beside cars parked on the street, Rebecca said someone would call at dawn to pick me up. I'd been in England enough before to know this meant "come by." Not call on the phone, in which case she'd have been more likely to say they'd ring me. But I stopped her mid-sentence anyway.

"Sorry but I'm not going anywhere, with anyone, at dawn. I'm going to talk with my sister, get a good night's sleep, have breakfast with her in the morning, and pack an overnight bag. I will be out to meet whoever is calling at ... nine in the morning. Not a minute before."

Rebecca nodded. "Nine it is." Offering a tentative smile.

I thanked her again and let myself in with my key from Melanie before Rebecca drove away.

All spellcasters are liars. Unless you live so remotely that you never come into contact with mundanes and cut yourself off, you're going to have to lie.

The story came easily while Mel and I sat up with herbal tea in our pajamas on the couch. For me, night attire meant a thick white cotton tank and blue pajama pants that matched my eyes. She actually wears a nightgown. She got into them after moving into this Victorian house. I'd smother in such a thing. I needed my freedom, waking or sleeping.

I told her about the great group of people I'd met at the conference, how we'd lingered over dinner and I'd lost track of time. About a conference in Cornwall going on through the week, visiting historians lecturing from all over the world, how these friends had booked a vacation rental and there was plenty of room for one more.

I said there was still space so I'd registered for the conference. Not that I planned to stay for the whole thing, of course. I wanted to get back to her so we could spend this time together—plus meeting all those guys.

Melanie isn't stupid. "People your age at this stuff? And women? Gee, Cass, I thought you were the only one. Next thing I know you'll be telling me they're all blondes." We make jokes about our blondness. We can. Other people can't.

I didn't address these questions. More like one big, "I know, right?" And telling her I was sorry, but I'd be back soon so we could hang out.

"No, don't worry about it. This is your jam. You should totally go." She sounded confused. "Last big adventure before 'settling down' to a full-time working adult, right?"

Having a great, supportive sister only makes it harder to lie.

I wanted to cry by the time I went to bed. Call the whole thing off. But I lay there in the dark, bruised right shoulder still aching, listening to waves, and thought of seven bodies—throats cut, eyes carved out, hearts staked—and knew I would do no such thing.

More doubts over breakfast and coffee with Melanie. Henry was there for part of it: eggs, tomatoes, fried bread, bacon—not to be confused with toast or with American smoked bacon—then he kissed her goodbye and waved to me.

I left my rolling bag, only taking my newly reloaded backpack for overnight. Strictly essentials and a change of clothes that I hoped I wouldn't need. One night out should mean toothbrush, hairbrush, underwear. But I'm one of those people who always has things like Band-Aids and ibuprofen, hand sanitizer, tweezers, a keychain flashlight, and tissues in my purse. Better to be prepared.

Easy to pack light, in jeans and a summer top, though it looked so cold and foggy out there this morning I zipped on my favorite purple and pink cotton hoodie as well.

Approaching 9:00 a.m., I flexed my shoulder, feeling all right now, grabbed my bag, brushed my teeth, touched up lip gloss, and stared at my own eyes for a minute in the mirror, remembering Zar.

Was it too late to bring Zar, Isaac, and Rebecca instead of Zar, Isaac, Kage, and Jed? And what was up with their names? Were they all biblical? Odd connection for people who apparently worship Moon.

*Watch your tongue.*

What had he said? Something about the moon. For Moon's sake?

Good to know. Don't take the name of the moon in vain around werewolves.

Who would they send to fetch me this time?

One more hint of manhandling me and they could find their own murderers.

Worse than my personal pride and safety concerns, though, what would Melanie think if those guys showed up in their Jeep?

Pulse quickening, I said goodbye, hoping she wouldn't come out front with me. Of course, she did, wishing me a fun trip, telling me to keep in touch and be careful. An odd thing for her to say. The product of us both growing up? No. She knew I wasn't telling everything.

I hugged her on the threshold. Just as Rebecca's old car came up the street.

*Thank you, Goddess.*

I shouted back love to Mel, hopped in, waved, and we were off.

This time, I could see where we were going, out into the countryside beyond Hove, north of Portslade, past a sprawling golf course, and west on a motorway called A27. Then it was north, leaving the coast behind for open green farm country with few homes.

On high ground of fenced fields and roads needing mending, away from suburban sprawl, we took a final potholed road, past a small apple orchard, out to a mobile home park. I was pretty sure they called them caravan parks in England—unless that was only for vacation type trailer parks and not long-term living.

That was it. A mobile home park with dozens of homes: lawn chairs, a dusty drive, only a few old cars and SUVs, a long field with a partly broken rail fence, a little woodland on the far side, and, in the center of the homes, a two-story timber building that must be on a permanent foundation. I wouldn't have known the place in daylight except for the stone barn with the caved-in roof out in the field.

Not that I'd had any reason to think of werewolves as glamorous. But there was something about the bleak setting and signs of poverty, with the untended road and old cars, that was not only sad but, somehow, intensely disappointing.

Several of them stood outside—arguing, to go by dramatic gestures and shaking heads—when we pulled up. They stopped when I climbed from the car with Rebecca.

Chill wind whipped up from the south, making the place seem even bleaker and less welcoming.

Diana, with the silvery half cape around her shoulders in the cool morning, approached to welcome and thank me.

I struggled to return her smile. Indeed, it was all I could do not to say, "Let's get this over with."

## ○ C͟H͟A͟P͟T͟E͟R͟ ͟8͟ ○

THEY HAD A LITTLE camper trailer—which they called a caravan—hooked up to tow behind the dusty silver Jeep for my living quarters. I'd assumed we'd stay in a hotel in Cornwall overnight. Apparently such things were too expensive, and too detestable, to consider. They intended to sleep out under the stars and I could have the caravan. I could manage for a night. Anyway, I didn't have a whole lot of cash to blow through on this trip either.

Kage actually mumbled an apology about the previous evening as he opened the passenger side door for me. I was impressed. Jed, with two-day stubble and a scowl on his face, didn't bother.

Zar, who'd been trying to get my door before Kage, retreated to the back with his brother after wishing me good morning. The pair of them looked even less alike in the daylight than they had last night, complexions aside. Both Zar and Jed had black hair, mottled brown eyes, and warm skin tones that were almost caramel—making me feel as bleached and dull as glue.

Otherwise, Jed was taller, broader, square-jawed, mouth set as if having received terrible news, just rolled out of bed grooming, a general air of looking like he'd eaten a bucket of nails for breakfast and followed it up with a workout that included breaking crowbars across his knee. At least he'd cleaned blood off his face from my kicking him. While Zar, although still pushing six feet and with the kinds of muscles I wasn't used to seeing on Portland hipsters—or any other humans in daily life—was slighter, more elegant, clean-shaven, obviously the younger brother, and smiling the whole time he looked at me like he'd been waiting for me all his life. His long hair was wavy. Jed's was short and on the verge of curly.

They did share a few other traits. Both dressed in nothing but black and gray, both in leather motorcycle boots—so was Kage, though he had on faded blue jeans and a dark red graphic tee—and both disconcertingly handsome in their own ways.

Disconcerting because they all were—male and female. I saw only a small group, and only briefly, in the light of day, but this was something else that struck me about them. Something else I'd never heard about werewolves. Were they like this everywhere? Their gene pool, limited as it was, must be made of stout stuff.

Before I climbed into the Jeep—no running board and a weirdly monstrous, American feeling vehicle—Isaac stepped up to properly introduce himself.

He didn't offer a hand, instead giving a little bow and asking me to let him know if there was anything I needed, or that he could do for me on the trip. All very old-fashioned, not a term I'd ever applied to myself. Yet ... I liked it.

I had no more than a chance to thank him before we were all clambering in, Diana having a last serious word with Kage, myself settling my backpack between my feet in the front passenger seat, then we were off.

There were many things I hadn't known about a Jeep Wrangler, having never been in one. I'll summarize here with the caution that they may vary from US to UK. Plus, there was this particular vehicle with a charm all its own. I'm not sure how old it was; at least ten years. And there was certainly a "special charm" to the driver in this one.

1. The seats are as comfortable as park benches.
2. The 2.8-liter diesel engine is very, very loud.
3. Manual transmission and small roads with a driver on your right leaves the unpleasant impression that he is constantly reaching toward your leg when he's really reaching for the gear shift.
4. The suspension is ... strange. Built for rough terrain, I felt as if we would roll and sway right over on every turn. An alarming experience when taking turns at three times the speed intended.
5. Dashboard is minimalist: cheap plastic, climate control, radio, not much going on. It's certainly not going to navigate for you.
6. The pervasive odors of male college dorm mixed with a gamy reek of wet dog, and fur and greasy fast food wrappers fluttering around—due to opening the window for fresh air—are almost overpowering enough to distract from those terrifying turns. Almost.
7. No worries about driving on the wrong side of the road. Why choose a lane when the whole road is your kingdom?
8. Noise from the wind, two brothers snapping at each other about their cramped space, and creaking and bouncing of the caravan only compete with the diesel engine. While none, sadly, drown out the others.

Five minutes into the drive my breakfast was flooding my throat while I clenched my teeth. Five hours to Cornwall. We hadn't even reached the motorway to really start the trip.

Any more and my stomach was going to turn inside out and I would murder my driver. Where would we be then?

On top of it all, the bickering. I couldn't hear all the voices in the back distinctly with my window open, wasn't even sure who was talking. But there was some kind of argument going on. Besides this, I could hear Kage right beside me quite clearly.

"Moon and stars, Jed! If you don't stop kicking my bloody seat I'm going to rip your fucking legs off and shove them down your fucking throat!"

Oh, how I wished they did have a gun in here. I didn't know if I wanted to turn it on Kage or myself more but one of us had to go.

Heading for the motorway, Kage picking up speed on a straightaway, trailer banging behind, engine roaring like a bear.

"You wanker, Jed!"

I gulped back bile and shouted, "Pull over!"

"What?" Kage glanced at me.

"Pull the damn car over! *Now!*"

He hit the brakes. It took a minute, but he got the thing slowed and pulled onto the left shoulder before a traffic circle.

"What's wrong?"

I was already out, fist against my mouth. I'd never thought of myself as susceptible to motion sickness. Now, I'd never be able to think of my stomach the same way again.

But I didn't toss Melanie's lovingly prepared breakfast on the side of the road. I walked into long grass by a hedge, caught my breath, feeling the cool morning air already warming as the clouds burnt off and July sun rose higher, and turned back to the Wrangler.

Isaac had stepped out, maybe concerned.

Others watched from inside.

"Everyone get out!" I shouted.

Slightly to my surprise, they did.

Kage frowned. "What's going on?"

Jed looked resentful, keeping silent.

Zar was wide-eyed, glancing around. Like he thought I'd spotted a murder clue out here.

Isaac appeared calm.

I was the one wide-eyed when a fifth young male scrambled over the backs of the seats where their rucksacks were stowed and joined the four on the shoulder.

"What—?" I gasped. "Who the hell are you?"

No one else seemed surprised to see him. In fact, surprised by my reaction, they glanced between us.

He stepped back, though I was well away from them in grass. "Um ... I'm Jason. Sorry. I waved. I thought you saw me when you were getting in."

"Thought I...? What are you doing here?"

Jason shrugged. "Wanted to come along with Kage. I told him I was coming. Diana said four was plenty but ... I just ... wanted to come." He bit his lip and looked away over the hedge to the crop beyond.

All the arguing and voices. Isaac, who'd been sitting right behind me, hadn't been saying anything in the car. It was the other three in the back. That's why I hadn't been able to catch anything.

If he wanted to ride in the cargo space all the way to Cornwall, that was his problem. And maybe the driver's if cops spotted him and pulled us over. But not mine.

I took a breath, also looked across the field, then faced them with my hands on my hips.

"We're going to change drivers," I said clearly as traffic zipped by.

"Whoa." Kage stepped forward. "That's my four-wheel."

"You should have thought of that and taken better care of it."

"I'm not letting anyone else drive my Jeep."

"Fine." I walked past them, back the way we'd come.

"Where are you going?" Kage turned with me.

"I'm going to get a ride into Brighton."

"You can't do that."

"Watch me."

"Hey! Bloody hell, what are—?" Kage jogged after me.

I drew up my magic. A tight ball ready to burst. If he so much as laid one finger on me...

But he didn't. He walked backward in front of me.

"What's going on?" he asked. "Why are we stopped?"

"I'm not riding with you all the way to Cornwall."

His eyebrows jumped. "That's it? That's what you're upset about? My driving?" Kage shook his head, incredulous. "I've been driving for years. Moon and stars, I learned to steer when I was just a pup on Mum's lap. My family always had a four-wheel."

"Well, maybe she should have taught you how to use the peddles."

"What?"

"Just because you *do* drive doesn't mean you're competent." I stopped and so did he. "How many people spend years doing things like cooking or writing poetry or raising kids who suck at it?"

Kage stood there with his mouth open. Hostile and clueless as he was, he remained irritatingly stunning in the fresh morning sun. Carved face and body, medium brown hair and hazel eyes that I could see clearly for the first time, variegated with greens, browns, and grays.

"Now, if we're all five—six—going to Cornwall," I said calmly, "someone other than you is going to drive. If you don't want them driving your Jeep, why don't we go back to your pack and see if anyone will lend us another car?"

Shaking his head. "Have to tow the caravan. We only have a few four-wheels that can do that. I've got the best one."

"Then let's return to the car." I jerked my head over my shoulder. "And I'll assign a new driver."

Kage mouthed at me for a second.

I held out my hand. "Do you want to give me the keys, or go home and discuss the situation with Diana?"

Blink, lips moving. "Hunt Moon." Under his breath.

"I'd drive myself, but I've never driven a stick, or on the left side of the road, so let's try to be a tiny bit sensible."

At last, he passed over his car keys. "Jed can't drive."

"He wouldn't have been my first choice. Don't worry." I took the keys, which needed another moment as Kage didn't let go even once my hand was on them. I finally had to use both hands to pry loose a couple of his fingers.

"Thank you." I walked back to the four waiting at the Wrangler.

Jason must be another relative. Black-haired and dark like Jed and Zar, with eyes that looked black as well. I thought I'd seen him the night before. Wiry, sharp nose and chin, lighter in his build than Kage and Jed. Yet he still looked like he spent a lot of time in a gym. Although I doubted this was true.

It crossed my mind, seeing how toned this lot were in their short sleeves, that canines in human guise might look this ripped.

Dogs are disproportionately strong compared to humans. My dad used to keep sporting dogs, pointers or setters that he trained to work in the field. They were amazingly strong. For lean, light animals, they could give a lunge on a leash and nearly send me spinning, even as a teen. So I knew a bit about dogs from my dad, even if I'd never been an animal person.

It didn't take long to choose a driver.

Irritable Jed was a nonstarter. His beaming, adorable brother I did consider. Zar, though, no matter certain other appeals, concerned me by how young he looked. He'd probably never driven anything like this combo before. Jason was out because he'd elected to ride in the back in order to come along. No one else should be forced to take that fall for the fifth wheel to drive.

Isaac was the obvious choice. Older than them, quiet, only watching me as I returned. I could see him properly now as well. As broad-shouldered as Kage and Jed, he had a couple inches even on Kage, well past six feet. The short beard lent maturity to a still young face without looking scruffy. His light brown or dirty blond hair was also neat. He wore dark khakis and a white polo shirt instead of black or blue jeans—or frayed cargo pants in Jason's case.

For all his differences from the rest, pale, tall Isaac's common ground was looking like he would have no trouble finding paid work to stand in front of a camera should he ever wish it.

I glanced around to Kage on the side of the road: arms crossed, glaring at the ground. Torn jeans, boots, graphic T-shirt from some death metal band in red and black. The kind of tousled hair he'd probably gelled but wanted it to look careless. I was surprised his arms weren't tattooed. Noticing this, though, I realized I hadn't seen a single tattoo or piercing on any of the werewolves, including those hanging about in the light this morning.

Was I being shallow about Isaac? The kind of sap who'd trust a guy with neat hair and a clean shirt over a punk in scuffed up motorcycle boots? Just because?

Maybe. But I had last night, and this morning, to back me up on this one. I'd give my own judgements, unfair or otherwise, a try.

I handed the keys to Isaac. "Would you be so kind?"

"My pleasure." He inclined his head. At close range, I saw how devastatingly green his eyes were. Not hazel like Kage's. Isaac's were as green as my eyes were blue. Again, I remembered Zar's mirror eyes comment as I wished I could look into Isaac's for a while.

When I passed over the keys Zar grimaced and looked away as if Isaac had insulted him but he was determined to let it slide.

Jason faced Kage, who still stood like a stump, glaring at gravel while traffic flashed past him.

Of the four, only Jed, weirdly, seemed pleased. He didn't exactly laugh. Yet I thought I saw one corner of his mouth lift as he turned away.

No love lost between him and his cousin. Was he only enjoying Kage's suffering? It made me uneasy along with what Rebecca had said about staying away from Jed.

My passenger door was already open but Isaac stepped to it, waiting for me to climb in and close it.

He watched the road for a break to get in on the driver's side.

The motley crew took their time about getting in the back. Jed slid in, then Zar. Jason trotted down the shoulder to fetch Kage and talk him around to the Jeep.

While they got this sorted out, Isaac looked at me. Slight smile, eyes like emeralds. "Are you all right?"

His voice was softer than the others, yet clear. It wasn't just his accent that didn't match the locals. He didn't seem to think he needed to project and prove a point. Not fighting for his place. Secure in his place.

"I'm fine. Thank you. And I'm sorry, I didn't mean to cause a scene. I just couldn't ride with that for five hours. And a wreck to cut it short and kill us all didn't sound much better."

"Some better, though?" A touch more smile, mostly in his eyes. Like sharing a secret.

By the time I got back to Melanie would I still want to meet men she had lined up?

I had to remind myself these were werewolves. I'd never heard of such a pairing.

Then again, there were many things about werewolves I'd not known. Like that they existed in the British Isles. And the whole faith thing. And the gorgeous thing. Those emerald eyes…

"Is your necklace a religious symbol?" I asked while Jed and Zar settled behind us, Zar trying to get his brother to move over in the narrow space.

Isaac lifted the gold chain from under his shirt to show me the moon pendant. Not a full orb like Diana's silver one, but still somewhat three-dimensional. A gold circle with relief of a crescent moon within the full one. I was sure it was real gold along with the chain. There was nothing masculine about it.

"That's beautiful. And a unique design." For how simple it was, the piece was arresting, something Nana might have kept, and I could also appreciate.

"Come on, Kage!" Zar shouted outside as Jason reached the door.

Jason scrambled again into the cargo space.

Isaac reached to the back of his own neck to unclasp the chain. "For you." He offered the necklace.

"You can't give me that." I laughed a little, breathless.

"Why not?"

"Why…?" I met his eyes again.

He still smiled gently. He might have been offering a drink or change for a five.

"No, Isaac, that's yours. It's valuable." I shook my head.

"If it makes you uncomfortable, perhaps you could borrow it? If you wear this sign our kin will recognize you as a friend if you happen to cross paths."

Since werewolf and caster relations were not great I hoped we weren't meeting more in Cornwall, but there was something to what he said.

Still hesitating, I offered my hand. "Okay … I'll wear it as long as we're on the road together."

"I'm glad." He let the chain coil into my palm and folded my fingers over it. His hand was warm and strong and I longed to keep that contact when he touched me.

I looked from our fingers to his eyes, then broke the gaze quickly with the slam of Kage's door and sat back, heart beating fast.

"Thank you." Giving Isaac another fleeting smile, hoping it was casual, easy: how the contact should have felt. It should have felt like two people who'd hardly exchanged a word and essentially been acquainted for half an hour. It should not felt anywhere near as intimate as it had.

I'd have been glad to visit a quiet cove with Zar last night. Now I wished it were Isaac.

*Werewolves. These are not human beings.*

Their culture and society were not my culture and society. When I'd planned on meeting British men on this trip I should have been more specific. This felt like Goddess having a joke.

*You wanted English guys? Here's a whole pack.*
*No, I wanted normal, decent, gainfully employed human men.*
*Should have said so.*

I fastened the chain around my neck while Isaac put on sunglasses and started the rumbling diesel.

Kage didn't say a word. Jed did not kick Isaac's seat. Zar kept his voice down in some kind of argument with Jason.

We set off again for the motorway. This time, I was pretty sure we'd keep going.

○ C̲h̲a̲p̲t̲e̲r̲ ̲9̲ ○

Everything went well until we stopped for lunch. We were outside the historic and charming city of Dorchester. We didn't get to take in the good parts.

When Isaac stopped at a "petrol station" for diesel all heads turned in the back.

"Burgers," Jason said as Isaac opened his door.

"That's a Saucy," Zar said, sniffing toward the open window on Kage's side.

I had mine down as well. It really felt like July now, somewhere between hot and flaming. I'd folded away my light hoodie in my backpack.

"It's just McDonald's," Kage said.

Jason shook his head. "Pretty sure it is a Saucy."

"Like corpse-nose can tell the difference." Jed snorted.

"You can do better, knob-head?" Kage leaned over Zar to get at Jed, a growl in his voice.

"You think that's challenging?" Jed asked, sneering. "A dead eel could catch a scent twice as far off as you can."

Zar pushed Kage back with limited success.

"Moon-cursed *verus* arsehole—" Kage was apparently going to climb over Zar to reach Jed, but Jason joined in holding Kage back, looping his arm around Kage's neck to pull him into the headrest.

"I can't smell anything," I said.

They looked around, startled.

Jason appeared embarrassed for me and Zar worried.

"What do you mean?" Zar asked. "You can't smell at all?"

"Sure I can. This Jeep and gasoline. But not food."

"You can't smell the burgers?" Jason asked. By his tone and expression, you'd have thought he was saying, "You lost your whole family in the flood?"

I shook my head. "Not a hint. You all have better noses than me, including Kage."

"Worm nose." Jed curled his lip and looked away out the window to the station lot where Isaac was filling the tank. "Doesn't count."

"What did you say?" I asked.

Kage also frowned. "That's right. Can't smell popcorn at the cinema until they're already inside, can they?"

"It's not your fault," Jason said quickly. "We just forget. When you said you couldn't smell anything..." Still that worried, tragic look.

"What did he call me?" I addressed Jason.

"She means worm," Kage said. "Get off me, Jay."

Jason let go of Kage's neck.

"We don't mean anything by it," Zar said.

"It sounded like he did," I said.

"'Worms' are just humans," Kage said. "Some of the elders think it's rude."

Zar lifted his eyebrows. It seemed he'd never heard that "worm" might be considered derogative.

"It's just slang," Jason said, still looking anxious as he leaned over the back between Kage's head and Zar's. "Like toff or wobbler or ... yearling or..."

"Kage?" Isaac reappeared at the open driver's door. "Did Diana send you with cash?"

"Yeah." Kage shifted, starting to try for his wallet from a pocket.

Isaac shook his head. "That's fine. I've got it this time, but I'm not filling it again." He returned to the pump.

Kage mouthed and muttered about who was driving and paying and Isaac's "whinging", speaking of slang. Half of this stuff I wasn't sure if it was British or wolf.

By the time we left the station there had been no bloodshed, and it turned out they were right. Only a few blocks away was a red and white building that looked like a fast food chain.

It was indeed Saucy. I'd never heard of the place, dubious of any junk food but even less impressed with the slipshod appearance of this joint.

I might also just mention that, by my standards growing up in small town middle America, parking in England is *tight*. I've spent several years now in Portland and it's still nothing to the apparent prevailing feeling in England that all cars are about three feet by two feet.

Isaac couldn't actually park in the lot. He couldn't have parked the Wrangler in Saucy's lot without taking up two spaces regardless. With the trailer, he could hardly even get in and out. He didn't seem troubled.

With a quick scan of the lot, he drove over the curb, up onto the sidewalk, and turned the Jeep back into two spaces. It was a good thing Saucy did not appear to be popular. Already an hour past the lunch rush.

We ended with the trailer across the sidewalk at a corner, Jeep in two spaces. No one hurt. Grateful we wouldn't be here long, apprehensive about the legality of the situation, I was nevertheless impressed with the driving.

Jason scrambled from the back, almost falling on his face in the paved lot as everyone exploded from the Jeep.

Zar ran to open the greasy red door for me before Isaac could get there. Breathless, sweaty from being crammed in the back seats with his brother and cousin for hours, he beamed at me.

I wanted to tell him to quit it—no matter how cute he was. My arms weren't broken. But, like the parking, this whole thing wasn't going to last long.

Jed brushed past. Kage started to follow, then saw what Zar was doing and stopped so abruptly Jason walked into his back.

Kage held out both hands in an exaggerated *ladies first* gesture, accompanied by a grimace that he may have meant to be a smile and it fell flat. Or maybe, like Jed, he really did just mean to be a bastard. A sarcastic bastard in his case.

I ignored him, thanked Zar, and went in, also ignoring the snarled oaths behind me. Zar had probably dropped the door on Kage. Or deliberately hit him with it. Isaac and Jason brought up the rear.

Jed was already ordering and, judging by expressions on the faces of the mundane couple behind him, I wondered if he'd cut in line to do it. I'd have been more surprised if he hadn't than if he had.

Kage stormed over, walking past the older man and woman and apparently ready to jump in with his own demands of the pimply guy at the register.

Really?

"*Kage*," I snapped.

To my surprise, he spun around to look at me, halting mid-step.

"Come back here," I said, voice firm and quiet.

"What?"

"*Come here.*"

He walked over, frowning around at Jed as if already having to watch his cousin eat while he had nothing. Every affront was so personal around here.

Zar, Isaac, and Jason also gathered by me, though distracted, glancing toward the counter and fryers and grills beyond. I hadn't smelled it down at the petrol station, but the aromas of burgers and fries in here were powerful as waves breaking on the beach.

"Do you not see those people waiting to order?" I asked Kage.

"Not a queue. Jed's already up there." Kage didn't meet my eyes.

I was startled he'd even bothered to come back to me. Now I could tell he actually did care that I was upset, turning sideways to me, as he had when he'd capitulated to Diana the night before.

Why? Was it grudging respect? A respect he didn't want to be caught in? Was it only because of his agreement to protect me? Remembering what his sister had told me, was he upset because I was getting in the way of his showing off with all my demands and criticisms?

I was no stranger to men hitting on me. I knew that different personalities showed their interest in different ways. If he did want to impress me maybe that was why he would do as I asked, grudging or not.

"Yes, actually, that is a 'queue.' Just because Jed is an ass doesn't mean you have to be. You can wait."

Kage's expression went rather blank. He looked over at Jed, out the window, then frowned more.

"Did that not make sense to you?" I asked.

"Not really." Addressing the distant door.

"Which bit?"

"None of it."

I sighed.

Jed moved on.

The older couple stepped up to place their orders.

"Okay," I said. "Thank you for waiting. You four go up after them. I have to look at the menu."

"Your lunch is on me, Cassia," Zar said, moving over to my shoulder to indicate his commitment.

"They're all supposed to be on me," Kage said irritably. "Diana sent cash for us."

Oh, yes. That's what Isaac had asked him about. Now that I thought of it, though...

"She trusted you with that?" I asked.

Kage shrugged, watching the couple at the counter, ready to swoop in. "She's my grandmother. Wants to think the best of us, doesn't she?"

"How foolish of her."

"Anyway, lunch is on me." Muttering, clearly not wanting to include the others but doing his duty.

"All right," I said. "Thank you anyway, Zar. That was nice to offer."

Zar smiled at the menu board mounted on the wall behind the counter. Kage's glare sharpened.

I told them to go ahead when they could, making a choice while they ordered. A grilled chicken sandwich with mustard, lettuce, tomato—not breaded, not deep fried—and a big ice water to bring along. That part sounded the best.

I grabbed paper napkins and a straw and made my way to tables to await our trays.

Jed sat at a red booth and Zar slid in opposite him, smiling as he invited me to join them. Of course, I did, assuming the others would follow and pull over chairs.

No; Jason and Kage took another booth and Isaac a third. They didn't seem to want to be anywhere near each other.

A number was called and Jed, who'd only sat frowning out the window at kids licking ice cream off their fingers that ran down their cones in the heat, went to fetch a tray.

I was surprised they'd fixed all the orders so quickly, but Jed returned with about eight burgers. I was ready to tell him mine was the chicken when I noticed they all looked the same. Brown and red sheet of paper around each, split into a couple of red plastic baskets.

Jed whipped the paper off one and stuffed it into his mouth, chewing as it went, swallowing, and ripped the paper off a second.

I swear, it was that fast. These were not sliders, but normal fast food burgers with bacon and soft sesame seed buns. He did about two swallows, maybe three, per burger, each one taking a max of five seconds to vanish.

Two, six, eight, and they were gone. Eight burgers. Gone. I couldn't eat a chocolate chip that fast. It would still be dissolving in my mouth.

Ever had one of those moments when you're not quite sure what's happening? Like watching an accident that you can do nothing about, can't even believe it, and it's all over in a blink?

I sat there, mouth open, brain dead. No... That wasn't even...

Jed gulped and licked out grease from one of the papers. Zar was also interested in their aromatic wrappings and leaned in. No food still in sight. All the same, Jed growled at him. *Growled*. It did *not* sound like a human imitating the growl of a dog. It sounded like a wild animal National Geographic growl.

Zar sat back, leaving Jed's papers untouched. Expression still amicable, he went on talking to me about the delightful smoky flavor in this particular burger joint's burgers. He'd been on the same subject before. I think. I could hardly hear him.

"How did you—?"

"Fifty-five and fifty-six?" Calling from the counter.

The old couple had already taken their tray.

These were mine and Isaac's. Three more followed for Zar, Jason, and Kage as we started back to our tables. I didn't rejoin mine, however. I sat at a little table in the middle with my chicken sandwich and ice water.

Zar had six cheeseburgers. Isaac had bacon burgers, seven or eight. Jason had a mix of chicken strips and burgers. Kage had a pile of double burgers and cast aside some of the bun tops. That was all. No fries. No greens or tomatoes. Only mayonnaise or ketchup for some. No drinks.

By the time I'd eaten a quarter of my sandwich, they were done. No conversation, no looking up from their trays. Like they had vacuum hoses attached to their faces.

I ate and tried not to stare.

Jed got up for the restroom. Isaac delicately wiped his short beard with a paper napkin—he was the only one who'd bothered to pick one up. Kage licked house sauce off one of his buns and dropped it into the heap of bread he'd discarded on the table. He shoved it at Jason, across from him. Jason sniffed, licked off sauce from another bun, but didn't seem much interested.

Kage went to order a couple more burgers.

Holy hell. How much cash had she sent?

Isaac and Zar tidied up their tables and went to dump papers in the trash and drop their trays on the waiting platform there. All four of them glanced toward me and my chicken sandwich.

While he waited, Kage also cleared away his mess, not fussy about crumbs and sauce he left behind. Zar lifted one of the sesame tops clear and Kage whipped around. For a second, I thought he was going to punch Zar, who only retreated with the bun. Kage dropped the matter, though, and threw away remaining bread.

Zar gulped and smiled at me. "That all right?"

"What?"

"Your chicken? Is it off color? It smells right enough."

"No, it's good. Thank you."

Zar nodded but he looked confused. As if to cover, he added, "You have brilliant hands. The delicacy of fine glasswork, strength of a swan."

I looked down at my own fingers on the sandwich.

Isaac jerked his head at Zar and the two moved on, leaving me to finish. Maybe Isaac knew that it took most humans more than forty seconds to eat lunch.

I did soon finish, went in the bathroom myself, and by the time I came out, Jed and Zar were arguing in the corridor about Zar having been in the middle seat all morning and wanting to relocate.

Isaac was nowhere in sight. Kage and Jason were stepping outside into blazing sun, each with another double burger in hand that they seemed to be eating as a leisurely dessert. Like an after-dinner mint.

I followed them out to hear Jason say, "Should those be open? It creates drag."

Kage frowned at the trailer windows. "Thought they were closed this morning. He pushed sunglasses onto his nose and took a bite—the burger already half gone—as he walked over to the caravan.

Kage tried the door, then glared around at me and Jason, following.

"Oh, right," Kage said coldly. "I don't have keys to go in and check."

"You shouldn't have the keys anyway," I said. "Isn't that my room for the night?"

"Did you fill the water tank?" Jason asked Kage. "We might not have camp hookups." He gulped the rest of his dessert and wadded up the paper.

I was surprised, feeling my estimation of Jason rise. I couldn't imagine the likes of Kage being concerned if I had such luxuries as running water or not.

Kage waved him off. "It's got water." He stuffed the next quarter of burger in his mouth and tried the door handle anyway.

It flew open.

"Bleeding Moon—" Kage started back as a man hopped out.

## ○ Chapter 10 ○

"Smashing to see you, Kage. I was beginning to think you didn't care about us back here."

I knew that guy jumping from the trailer. But where?

"What the fuck, Andrew?" Kage did not appear impressed.

"For me? You're a proper pal. Famishing in there." He snatched the rest of the burger out of the shocked Kage's hand.

Kage leapt at him, a snarl coming from his throat, obviously ready to pound the thief into the side of the trailer.

Instead, he dodged, fast and nimble as a cricket.

"Just kidding." He shoved the paper and burger bundle back at Kage. "Pull yourself together, mate. But you should watch where you put that thing. A parched traveler couldn't get his own around here, could he?" His gaze fell on me.

"Andrew—" Jason had rushed forward, perhaps to stop Kage from killing him, but paused as Kage swallowed his treasure to keep it safe. "What are you doing here?"

"A quest in the company of a beautiful lady? Who could resist?" Andrew's eyes were fixed on mine, smiling.

"The Seastar Hotel," I breathed. "You opened the door."

"Yes, I know. How could I forget your ravishing countenance? How could you forget mine? Truly a charming match, wouldn't you say? Moon's luck, even." He took my hand and kissed it. "Andrew, m'lady. At your service day or night." Drawing out the last word with a touch of emphasis.

Jason still looked worried, and Kage annoyed.

"You're ... with them? One of them?"

"Of course I am." He straightened with a flourish and chuckle. "Does this face look human to you?"

In a meeting on a street context? No.

He looked like a fashion plate. Not as muscular or as tall as the others. Lean and sharp, all high definition, elfin. Reddish brown hair. Eyes like amber jewels. It was weird but his hair and eyes were an awfully similar color.

Yes, the whole pack was striking. These young males all worth much more than a second glance. But this one, Andrew, I couldn't take my eyes off him. I hated that. Hard-to-get had been my whole adult life. Watching and waiting to be as lucky as my sister had been in meeting Henry.

The perfect man was out there. Finding him didn't involve going all gaga over a pretty face and letting a guy like Andrew know what you were thinking.

I was spared by voices behind me as Jed and Zar came out to the lot after us.

"What in Moon's name is shit-head doing here?" Jed's alluring tones.

"Thank you, Jed." Andrew grinned even more. "That's the nicest thing you've ever said to me."

"Stowed away in the caravan," Kage said.

"Weren't you roasting?" Jason appeared concerned. "It's got to be an oven in there."

"Why do you think I opened the windows? But, yeah, it's not been a picnic. A burger and shake would set a wolf right." He smiled sweetly at Kage. "I seem to have heard Diana say you were core provider for this adventure?"

"Members only," Kage snarled. "Get yourself something if you want it."

"Andrew?" Isaac also out with us. "Does Diana know you're here?"

Andrew chuckled. "Diana doesn't care where I am as long as I'm not near her."

"Makes two of us." Kage's tone grew even angrier. "After your lunch, get a train home." He walked to the Jeep, started for the driver's door, paused, balled the burger paper into a lump in his fist, then stood waiting at a back door for it to be unlocked.

"You can't just kick him out," Jason said. "If he wants to come—"

"Like you?" Kage cut him off. "What do you lot think this is? We're not on holiday."

"I agree," Isaac said quietly.

Everyone looked around. Even I, who didn't know them, was startled by such a sentiment coming from Isaac and directed at Kage. Kage looked slightly mollified.

"Having so many wolves here will not make Cassia safer," Isaac continued. "Or help with the job. It's only going to draw attention. We have too many involved already, Andrew."

That may have been the most logical thing I'd heard in days. All the same, I don't know why, other than to look at him, I wanted Andrew along. Anyway, I didn't like the idea of throwing a wolf out of the group and sending him to fend for himself. What if the killers really did know about us being out together? What if a lone wolf traveling back to Brighton by train was exactly the kind of thing they were watching for?

I wouldn't say all this. No jumping at shadows or provoking more arguments.

Instead, I said, "He's here now. It's fine. But we can't all ride in the Jeep. Is it legal for you to ride in one of those things at all? Does it have any sort of seating with a belt?"

"No need to worry, fair maiden," Andrew said. "Even the suffocation bit isn't so bad with windows wide."

Just to Cornwall and back.

"Okay?" I looked to Isaac. "Not ideal, but ... let's move on and find the people we need. That's the priority and the faster the better."

I noticed tension, bristling in the others from the corner of my eye and edges of my senses. But who else was I supposed to look to for a reasonable opinion? If they didn't want me favoring Isaac maybe they could come up with logical points themselves.

Isaac nodded, though I couldn't say he seemed pleased about it. "As you wish." Still speaking softly. "Andrew, Jason, you were uninvited. Perhaps you could both ride in the caravan and give the rest more space?"

"Sure," Jason said while Andrew gave a bow as if being offered the Queen's carriage.

Jason checked the water tank just to make sure. I was really starting to like him.

Zar climbed in the far back so he didn't have to sit between Kage and Jed, both of whom seemed even more put out with Andrew along than they had been anyway.

Andrew ran in for burgers and a milkshake.

I settled in the passenger seat and started to fish my phone from my purse. I needed to see how much longer we had on the road. But the phone wasn't there. Through the bag, all around the seat, under, in the door, in my backpack, everywhere.

I hurried inside to check tables I'd been at, ask at the counter if someone had turned it in, check the bathroom. Starting to panic as I went out.

*Think.*

When had I used it? Recently. Looking at maps of Cornwall as we'd come into Dorset. Not as if I'd left it behind. It had to be here. Unless I had dropped it in the restaurant and someone walked off with it. But there was hardly anyone even here.

Heart pounding, I headed back out, looking across the sidewalk and parking lot.

Andrew walked ahead. He passed Jason a milkshake at the door into the trailer and both stepped up. Weird how they gave Jason food but no one else. Not top of my thinking space right now, though.

"What's wrong, Cassia?" Isaac asked through the open door.

Everyone else was settled. I was the last unaccounted for.

Bubbles of panic made my breath short.

"I'm looking for my phone."

"Does it have a blue case?" Andrew called from the trailer.

I spun to face him.

"Nice new screen protector?" Grinning, he held my phone out from the trailer doorway.

I almost ran to snatch it from him. "Where did you find it?"

Andrew shrugged. "I always find what I'm looking for."

"Thank you."

He winked and shut the door.

It wasn't until we were pulling out of the interesting parking job that it dawned on me: Andrew hadn't "found" my phone. He'd stolen it.

## ○ C̲H̲A̲P̲T̲E̲R̲ ̲1̲1̲ ○

ONCE WE REACHED Cornwall late in the afternoon—after a relatively peaceful drive and having been unable to carry on conversations due to noise—we faced the problem not only of where to stay but the more pressing one of finding druids. The image I'd seen showed open green pastures, then coastal cliffs.

Isaac, calling through the din of engine and open windows, told me that could be any number of places on the Cornish coast, aside from the standing stones. A search for stone circles around here on my phone also yielded no promising results. At least we had water to go on, although even that was a problem. Most of the county was coastal.

Another concern: they wanted a public woodland where they could stash the caravan out of sight, so inland. I wanted a real campground with water and electric hookups. But I would settle for a wood—mostly because I didn't want to see mundane campers. As much lying as I'd done in my life, I just didn't have a story to explain us. Six English hunks and one all-American cheerleader. On a camping trip.

So, before heading to the northwestern coast we made our way to a wood and nature preserve in the center of the county. Here were scenic landmarks Golitha Falls and Cholldon Falls on the River Fowey. The latter waterfall was smaller and less visited, while being surrounded by a lush wood that eventually gave way on all sides to roads or farmland.

We dropped off the caravan in the gravel parking lot at the trailhead for Cholldon Falls. Then, after far too much debate, left Jed, Jason, and Andrew with the caravan to figure out a way we could get it into the wood and make a campsite. Again, I was sure this was illegal. There were legitimate campsites in Cornwall where we should be paying to park overnight.

I said nothing about it. As far as I was concerned, it was a tossup. Sneak and break the rules, or do everything legit but involve mundane outsiders? Anyway, there was no question that the whole lot of them were in agreement on this one: camp illegally and unseen. If they could make this work and we didn't hurt anything or damage any property I didn't mind.

This left Isaac, Kage, Zar, and myself to continue for the north coast and start looking.

Less harebrained than it sounds for two reasons. First, I could scry once I was in the area, likely to pick up more information. Second, Zar seemed to know a good deal about druids and magical creatures. He should have insights into this search as well.

He'd made a shouted effort on the ride over to tell me that many druidic groves were coastal because the druids placed them in best proximity to elemental properties; that a few hundred years ago Cornwall was host to one of the largest wolf packs in the British Isles; and that the kindred—called the faie by the magical human community—still dwelt throughout the British Isles, yet spotting one was as common as spotting an albino badger.

Isaac also seemed to know his way around Cornwall. That left Kage as the dead weight in the company. I'd have rather had Jason along. I suspected Jason could actually talk to mundanes and behave like a normal person in public. But Kage, having already handed over his keys, would not leave his Jeep and, really, he had a point.

By the time we reached Wadebridge, I felt ready to stretch my legs on the beach, druids or no. But there didn't seem to be a beach here. Only the River Camel flowing out to sea.

"Can we get to any cliffs?" I looked out to the estuary through the windshield. "A physical connection to an object or place for scrying is a huge help. I'd love a walk anyway."

On to Padstow, then Trevone and the tiny village of Harlyn.

We walked to Trevose Head Lighthouse above the beach.

It wasn't right. None of it.

Where were the vertical cliffs? The sweeping green?

This place was breathtaking, worth the trip. But all scrub and rolling, miles of beach and more miles of the Irish Sea or Atlantic Ocean. I hadn't expected we'd pick a random spot in Cornwall and march right to the stone circle I'd seen, yet I had expected familiarity.

Wind was so violent here on what felt like the tip of the world, I struggled to find a hairband or ponytail tie in my pockets. No luck. Not far from the white lighthouse, I sat above the sea, hands over my face to keep hair from lashing my eyes. It probably struck a dramatic pose—holding my own face, communing with my magic. My three escorts remained silent on the bluff above the lighthouse tower.

I mentally opened my third eye and drew from my magic and helpers, asking myself and powers of the natural world for the sight. A different question now. Different intention.

*Druids of Cornwall. Show me where they are. Guide me to their door. Take me to a druidic grove in Cornwall.*

A path of water, a circle within rock. Water dropping through the circle. A pool, a river, mounds of stone in the water. Small, graceful. Not standing stones. River rocks stacked in the stream. White waterfall beyond black rocks made a striking picture.

*But where?*

Zar. Standing behind, watching me, frowning slightly. I saw him clearly, the focus of the other two misty, while Zar, with his long hair streaming out as if sticking his head out a car window, remained crisp.

That wind was stunning, magical in itself. I have always loved and respected the wind. Now that image of Zar leaning into it captivated me, drawing me with him. I longed to invite him to share the magic journey with me, to show him what I saw.

I thanked the magic, the wind, the helpers, Goddess, and stood to return to them. I focused on Zar—this time with my eyes open.

I twisted back my hair and held it spiraled around my fingers at the back of my head. Even so, wheat-colored strands stung my eyes as it flapped into my face. I had to raise my voice to call to him in the wind, though we stood only feet apart.

"We're close. There's a waterfall. Maybe near here?" I used my free left hand to gesture, giving a sense of the shape of the thing. "Water flowing down, then a circle in the rock. It's as if you look into the water through a ring out of stone. The pool below is dotted with stacks of river stones."

I thought he would look puzzled. I should have known the magic better than that.

Zar was already calling back when I'd hardly stopped, "That's Saint Nectan's Glen. I'd have to look at a map, but it's in this part of the county. I'm sure it's only a short drive."

The other two looked at him, then me. They had no trouble with their hair, though Isaac's now looked as rugged as Kage's.

"How did you know that?" I shouted.

Zar shrugged. "Anyone who knows anything about the kindred and Cornwall knows that. The Saint Nectan's waterfall has been associated with the kindred for as long as anyone can remember. I didn't know it had a druidic link, but it makes sense. It's a mystical place. Although it's not standing stones, or on a cliff over a beach." He cocked his head.

I shook mine. "Forget about the cliff. One lead at a time. Scrying can be like that—a treasure hunt. This waterfall may be why we're here. Come on."

## o CHAPTER 12 o

WE HIKED TO THE JEEP and I pulled my zip hoodie back on. The only warm garment I'd brought for the whole trip besides a thin rain jacket. I also found a brush and ponytail ties before climbing back in to navigate to Saint Nectan's Glen on my phone.

It was getting late, sun sinking, past dinnertime, my stomach growling, by the time we reached the Saint Nectan's Glen wood.

There was a car park, almost empty as tourists were leaving before twilight, and a walk to reach the falls.

This time I knew the instant I saw the waterfall that it was the place. A great sense of relief, of calm, came over me.

"We've found our druids," I said. "I don't know when or who but I know we can find them here."

Kage looked around as if to catch one while Zar seemed transfixed, as I was, by the glorious sight of the waterfall. There were only a couple of mundanes still out taking pictures, making their way back on the trail.

I walked to the edge and squatted to see the little stone mounds.

"How did you know I would know?" Zar asked behind me.

I smiled at the river rock. "Magic."

"So—" Kage also walked up. "We're supposed to do what? Wait for druids to show?"

"That's a good question. Yes. We should." I stood slowly, feeling jubilation slide away as if into the crystal water. "But I don't think I can. It feels like the middle of the night to me. If druids come here to perform rituals or meditate they must be doing it before dawn or after dusk."

"Yes, too many visitors during the day," Zar said. "So we could wait now."

"We have to go back and shift the caravan," Isaac said.

"We're probably forty-five minutes from them," I said. "Maybe we should bring it closer. Although…" I bit my lip.

"Nowhere near here to put it," Zar said.

"No," I said. "But it's quite a commute."

"I'll stay and watch," Zar said. "You lot go back and make sure camp's sorted."

"No one's doing anything alone on this trip," I said.

"Kage can also stay—"

"That's my Jeep—"

"Or all of us just for a bit," Zar went on.

Ravenous, jet lag once more all over me, wishing we could get the caravan squared away before it was pitch dark, I shook my head and walked along the water's edge, having to think.

When Zar started to speak again, I said, "Give me a minute."

I knelt on the stones where I faced the circle of rock looking through to the white water in purple shadows, then rested my right hand on the surface of the icy water. I felt a tingle of energy in that water, making the hairs on the back of my neck stand up.

Was it only what Zar had told me? Or could I sense the faie here, their gazes upon us?

I let the sound of the waterfall be my chant and took a moment for a light trance, counting backward in my head, hand on the water.

I looked through time of the approaching night. The moon rose, crested the sky, sank. Water flowed, silver and endless through the hours of darkness. No one came forward. No human figure in the glen. Only deer to drink, a fox trotted past like a shadow, and an owl's wing flickered across the moon.

I came back to myself on the bank and stood.

"They won't be here tonight," I said, watching the waterfall. "Just as well. Let's get back to the others and return before dawn. We'll try in the morning."

"If you can tell they won't be here tonight, why not pin down when they will be so we don't have to guess?" Kage asked.

His tone irritated me. Sarcastic. I tried to ignore this. The past twenty-four hours, starting with me kicking him in the balls and his grandmother giving him a public dressing down, hadn't gone that well for him either.

"I could try," I said. "But none of this is certain. Scrying is a window across time and space, neither foolproof nor pinpoint. Either way, we should be here in the morning to watch. At least I'm fairly sure no one will be around tonight, but I can't keep looking. I'm exhausted and hungry and I'm going to have a migraine if I try anymore. I already told you I'm not a very accomplished scry."

"Does it hurt you to use magic?" Zar asked.

As I turned back to them, he and Isaac appeared concerned, watching me. Kage was stalking around the grove, apparently searching for hidden druids behind trees.

"No, it doesn't hurt me. But it is a huge drain. I can only do so much and I'm not exactly starting at my best right now. Why don't we pick up dinner that we can take back to the others and see what we can do about the caravan overnight?"

"Dinner?" Kage stopped patrolling and looked at me. "We already ate."

Zar cocked his head.

Isaac smiled faintly. "We'll stop at a pub. Don't worry about us, though."

"Don't ... what do you mean?"

"Didn't you get enough?" Zar asked.

Isaac was already explaining. "We don't tend to eat as often as humans. One meal, perhaps a snack, generally suffices for the day. Or two meals if they're small."

"How do worms—? I mean, how often do humans eat?" Zar asked.

"In theory, three meals a day. In practice, we can be a bit random. But a single huge meal and nothing else is not generally considered ... healthy. That would be fine, Isaac. Maybe a baked potato, or—?" What did they call them?

"Jacket potato?" he said, still smiling.

"Thanks. I've never understood that one." Picturing russet potatoes in raincoats.

We returned to the Jeep in diminishing light.

Minus the pub stop, it did indeed take nearly forty-five minutes to get back to the caravan, though no one had a better location to suggest for camp.

I ate my potato, topped with mixed sautéed vegetables that were quite good, if over-cooked, in the gloomy Jeep on the way while we discussed how and what we were looking for: best times to be there, questions we hoped druids could answer, and when we could expect sunrise.

We reached the car park at Cholldon Falls after night had settled and found our fellows ready with a route to tow the caravan into the woods behind the falls.

I followed on foot with Zar. Kage was back to driving, off-roading the two vehicles into seclusion. Andrew and Jason walked in the tracks and fluffed up the sparse undergrowth so no one would see where the Jeep had passed. The weather had been dry for some time and the ground was able to take the force without ruts.

Jed seemed to be in an even nastier temper after his time alone with Jason and Andrew. He steered Kage wrong in the dark, then smirked when he ran into a fallen tree. Kage, cursing him through the open windows, was trying to back to get around it when Isaac told him to leave it—he had a good spot anyway. No footpath, road, or human anything within sight.

They made sure the trailer was stabilized before disconnecting the Wrangler.

Deeply uneasy about what we were doing, and still cautious about my company as well, I tried not to think about all of the above while I collected my pack.

Kage gave me the caravan key. Jason lit a battery-operated lantern and showed me around the trailer.

It was ... small. And old. And smelled like mildew and rust and stale grease from someone cooking. A toilet and shower stall, a burner and sink, cabinet, tiny table and booth, a little bed over the trailer hitch and storage space. That was it. The whole thing was about the size of an SUV.

There was water in the tank, even if it wasn't hooked up. Limited toilet and hand/face washing and no shower. I had bottled water to drink and brush my teeth.

At least I wasn't sleeping in the dirt. And room and board were free. So many blessings on this trip.

Lantern in hand, I stepped back outside with Jason, asking if they didn't have a tent or anything else to set up.

He smiled like I'd asked him if he'd brought his parka. "We don't need tents. I wouldn't even know how to set one up. Don't worry about us. I hope you're all right, though. It's not exactly posh in there. If you want an inn I'm sure we could—"

"It's okay, Jason. Thank you. I actually used to camp in New Mexico, believe it or not."

"I thought you were from the States?"

I hesitated. "New Mexico is a state. Mexico is a country."

"Right. Well, if you do need anything, just let us know."

"Sometimes, when English people say 'us' or 'we' they mean 'I', don't they?"

Jason chuckled. "I suppose so. Did you get enough to eat with the potato? Andrew said you'd be expecting dinner."

"How did you know I had a potato?"

"Smell."

"What else was on it?"

"Caramelized onions, summer squash, bell peppers, butter, salt, vinegar. Not sure what else…"

I regarded him in lantern light on the caravan's step while Jason looked up at me from the ground. The rest of them were going through things from their bags at the Jeep, Kage and Zar arguing—something about Zar having brought books along and the waste of space.

"How?" I asked. "You look human. Is your nose really different on the inside when you're like this?"

Jason shrugged. "We can't smell much in skin. A lot better in fur. So ... I don't know. Zar might know. And Andrew and Isaac know humans the best. Sorry."

"It's okay. Thank you for your help."

"I didn't do anything."

"Showing me the trailer. We're going early back to the glen, before sunrise, if you want to come. We can't take everyone."

He nodded. "I'd like to. I don't mind early."

"And I'd appreciate everyone's phone numbers. I have an international plan for the trip."

"Sure. Mine's in my bag."

"We should be able to reach each other in the morning when we're split up again." I stepped out with him while Jason went to get his phone from his rucksack in the Jeep, where Zar and Kage still stood with their own stuff. It seemed Jason did not know his number, having to find the thing.

Zar was brushing his teeth. Kage, with his shirt off, sat in the open back to pull off boots and socks. Andrew sat sideways in an open side door, doing something on his own phone as we walked up. Isaac, around the other side of the Jeep, had just pulled off his shirt and was folding it into his bag. Jed was nowhere in sight.

"Fancy staying out with us instead?" Kage asked me as we approached.

I shifted the lantern into my left hand to pull my phone from my pocket with the right. Must charge it some tomorrow if I could. I had the plug and adaptor. Just no power.

"I should have your numbers in my phone. What's yours?"

"Numbers?" Kage frowned. "I didn't bring a phone. I don't think…" He grabbed his bag to feel inside.

"What do you mean you didn't bring a phone?"

"I can tell you mine," Zar said around his toothbrush. He held up a cell off his own bag.

I stared at it as he spit into the brush, then started to tell me the number.

"Is that … like … twenty years old? Do those phones still work?" I didn't mean to be rude about it, but I was shocked. It had been a long time since I'd seen a phone like the little black thing with the inch-square glass screen and plastic keypad that he held.

"It's not that old. Just a pay-as-you-go SIM. But it works. It even has a good signal out here." Zar added the last with a smile as if to prove how delightful it was.

"Oh," I said. "Could you tell me the number again please?"

I input it with the exit code and country code, then Isaac's as he told me his from across the Jeep. While they talked, I noticed Andrew, who hadn't looked up, was smirking at his own iPhone screen, which lit his face with a gentle glow.

"Nope," Kage said. "Didn't bring mine."

Jason looked sadly down at a phone exactly like Zar's in his palm. "Battery's dead."

"There's a charger in the Jeep," Kage said. "Plug it in tomorrow."

"So neither one of you have phones?" I asked.

"At home," Kage said defensively.

"Like Jason's? Does Jed have the same too?"

Zar shook his head. "He doesn't have a mobile."

"At all?"

"I don't think he's ever used a phone."

"Excuse me?"

"Doubt it," Kage said. "Why would he? He's a stranger. Doesn't want anything to carry, does he?"

Stranger? I didn't ask what he meant.

"It's all right," Zar told me. "You have mine and Isaac's. Andrew will give you his." Like this vast number of people able to communicate was something to be proud of.

I walked over to Andrew, who was still smiling and still hadn't looked up.

"Are you the only one here with a real phone?" I asked him.

"Isaac has a smartphone, if that's what you mean. And you were just about thinking you were on the road with normal people, eh?" Andrew finally looked at me, eyes hooded, smirking.

"Just tell me your number."

"Like to be the active one, do you?"

"What?"

"Most human women seem to like to be chased. Not do the chasing. So you should be giving me your number, leave it on me to ring you. Isn't that right?" Corners of his mouth curved up, yet the hooded eyes were calculating, not smiling.

"Forget it." I turned away. "I have Isaac's and Zar's. I'll assume they can get in touch with you if we're in different places." My face felt hot as I stalked back to the trailer.

Zar dashed after me. "Moon bless, Cassia. All right in there? Can I get you anything?"

"Good night—"

"You step like a moth."

I turned to face him from the door. "I what?"

Zar had that smile on his face again. Adorable, sincere, faint dimples showing in his cheeks. "Your movements are so elegant. How you walked just now, with your lantern, was light and quick as a moth." It hadn't occurred to him that I'd moved quickly because I wanted to be left alone. "Do you know the story of Moon's light and the field mouse?"

"Maybe ... I could hear it another time. Good night, Zar."

"Moon bless—good night."

I eased the door shut, giving him a brief smile to soften the blow. Funny how he made me feel guilty for abandoning him out there. Like shutting a lost puppy out in the snow.

I tried to put Zar, Andrew, phones, and druids out of my mind as I got ready for bed, then faced the prospect of actually going to bed.

This was the part that scared me, but, taking my lantern for a careful inspection, looking for spiders, centipedes, mold, rot, stains, fur, anything else creeping or crawling, I found there was a fresh cotton sheet on the foam mattress and a worn, but also clean, duvet on top with an extra wool blanket at the foot. Diana's work preparing for me?

No ... I remembered Rebecca and smiled.

"Thank you," I whispered as I settled in.

But I needn't have worried about spiders. It turned out the problem wasn't my aromatic bedchamber. The problem was the night.

## ○ CHAPTER 13 ○

PARDON MY IGNORANCE, but I'd thought they liked personal space. Territorial, or whatever. And if they wanted to risk local authorities by parking their caravan away from real campgrounds just for a night, fine.

It took me five minutes after turning out my lantern to understand what was really afoot—why we had to stay away from civilization and human camps. That was how long it took for what sounded like the world's biggest dog fight to break out beside the trailer.

I sat up in bed and *whack*—had to move slower in here. Rubbing my head, I stumbled from bed in pajama bottoms and tank top, slipping into flip-flops.

I felt my way to the open window in the dark and peered into shadows. Woods were touched in moonlight, revealing a tangle of thrashing, snarling, yelping forms.

What I'd been taught about werewolves in my education from Nana could fill a postcard: There weren't many. They didn't like humans. Some remained in a few areas where they lived isolated lives. Not much more.

I'd always assumed that full moon thing was a mundane myth, yet had no idea even that they could change into canine form at will like this, much less that they'd do it at the drop of a hat. If they could shift whenever they wanted, why didn't they have more sense about it? What if some tourist or local farmer happened to hear, or even see, a wolf pack in the nature preserve?

They had to be stopped. Not only the noise—which was appalling at close range, whether it attracted human attention or not—but the damage they may be doing. What if someone was badly hurt? In the screaming and snarling and whirling out there one could even be killed. Would they do that? Listening to this carnage, it was easy to believe.

Then … it stopped.

One huge tangle broke apart into groups, one or two ran off, a few more scuffles, then it seemed everyone was circling away, still growling. A couple of shapes were only black moving on black, yet the rest had pale enough fur to make out hints of the long limbs and large bodies. Only one showed clearly: a single white wolf. This one stood out not only because of his color and great size, but because he seemed to be the center of focus. When the group parted, the white wolf remained at the middle of our clear grove off to the side of the trailer.

They circled him while he growled like a bear.

Another scuffle among some of the darker shadows. Focus on the white one broke. The squabble dispersed.

Again, one or two moved in on the white wolf, snarling and bristling.

A tense standoff, circling. He raised his head, ears pricked, moving toward his opponents. A pause, low growls, then the final two slipped away into the woods like wraiths.

The white wolf stood alone in the moonlit clearing which had a second before been the Colosseum. Ears twitching, he seemed to be waiting for another attack. Had the whole lot of them been going for him?

He looked up, as if hearing something to catch his interest, though he faced the caravan, gazing, perhaps, directly at me. I wasn't sure if he could see me through the little window screen at the side of the trailer in the dark. Even so, I felt a chill, sure he met my eyes.

I reached unconsciously to finger the gold charm from Isaac around my neck. I hadn't taken it off for bed.

The white wolf turned and also walked away. Limping.

I lay back with my heart pounding.

Had they really tried to kill him because I asked him to drive? Showed him favoritism? There must have been something else involved. He was already the outsider, here from another pack. Then again, was I even sure that was Isaac?

Did hair color and complexion have anything to do with fur color? Just because Isaac was paler than the rest might not mean he was a white wolf. Still ... I couldn't really believe it in this case. I was sure that wolf had been Isaac. Just as sure their ganging up on him had something to do with me.

Footfalls outside, sniffing, another scuffle and yelp, frequent growling without escalating. A moment of quiet, then paws galloping past.

Much running and pounding about.

Quiet again. Were they hunting something? Playing? Chasing each other?

Were they dangerous to humans?

Did they think clearly when they were in this form? Did they retain themselves—their personalities?

What if they happened upon livestock? Or some innocent person walking home from a pub? Or me?

It took me an hour more than it should have to drift off as I wrestled with these questions. Strange, how what I'd wanted to ask about on the noisy drive had been more information on this murder case—more clues? Any solid suspects already? When what I should have been trying to ask about was much closer to home.

I jerked awake to sounds of another fight. Short-lived but plenty to jumpstart my pulse and leave me wide-eyed. This one also petered out.

Drifting off.

Yelping.

Awake.

Yaps and low howls. Maybe they had some sense about the noise level because they were short, broken howls, quickly cut off.

More running about.

Drifting off once more.

*Wham.* Something crashed into the side of the trailer and I sprang out of bed.

Paws bounding away.

Silence.

I lay back.

Another fight in the distance.

Did they not need sleep?

Another problem, though: now the trailer was cold. Much colder than I'd thought it would get in July. A summer night near the English coast should not be underestimated for temperature drop.

By the time I finally closed the windows, ready to take the musty stink over the noise and now the Arctic conditions, I was a popsicle.

I pulled on my hoodie and two pairs of socks, spread the wool blanket and my thin raincoat on top of the duvet, and it still wasn't enough. I felt damp, shivering, and jarred by sudden noises even with all the windows shut.

I lay there, fabric of the hood over my nose to combat the smell, thinking of Melanie's guest room and the sound of the waves, then what I'd agreed to—wondering why. And prayed to Goddess for morning.

I had set my alarm for 4:30 a.m. so we could drive back to the falls by 5:30 and watch for any sign of druids. Turned out, I didn't need the alarm. I was awake anyway.

In a stupor, I got up and washed my face with scant cold water and the glow of the lantern. I dressed, including light hiking shoes, then looked back out through the window with the lantern out behind me.

There, in predawn moonlight, was nothing but quiet. A peaceful scene of silver-edged blackness. The whole pack curled on the ground in furry balls, tails over their noses. A couple of them nearest the trailer were even curled up together. How sweet.

I wanted to crash cymbals in their ears, set off fireworks, blast a foghorn—the bastards.

Shaking for a whole other reason, jaw set, I silently unlocked the trailer door on the side, then threw it open as hard and fast as I could to rocket off the outside trailer wall and ricochet into my face, where I caught it. Not fireworks, but the huge *bang* in the silent dark of the night was nevertheless satisfying.

The grove exploded as six piles of fur shot into the air, landed on their paws, and spun about, snarling.

"I want *two* volunteers—not three, not six—for the druids' glen so we can stake it out until tourists start arriving. I want you two to be bipedal and dressed and in the Jeep in ten minutes. And I don't want to hear another fight break out or I'll walk into the village, call a taxi for the train station, and you can figure this out on your own. Do you understand me?"

Silence.

Twelve gleaming eyes watched me in moonlight. *Did* they understand? Were they themselves, only furred? Or were they ... wolves?

"Thank you for your cooperation." I slammed the door and locked it.

I could get by with cold water to splash on my face and wash my hands and a quick makeup ad lib, but, oh, how I longed for hot coffee. The glen first. Then straight to the nearest town for the nearest, hottest expresso.

While I waited, I wanted to study Cornwall maps on my phone, or read about Saint Nectan's Glen. But I had to save battery. I packed up my bag with the phone cord and raincoat—and everything else just in case we got back to find the trailer had been towed.

I gave them nine minutes and—heart pounding in my throat as I again wondered about their mental states—returned to the Jeep.

Morning songbirds chirped, even if the sky was still dark, and it made me feel a bit more awake. Not nearly as much as coffee would have.

They'd already had the Jeep disconnected, facing out, behind the trailer. Now Kage sat in the driver's seat with the inside light on in the vehicle, pulling on his boots.

Zar was just dragging his shirt over his head, motorcycle boots already on. His disheveled hair had bits of woodland in it.

Three wolves still stood around the campsite, watching. One, solid black, sat by the Jeep. He got to his feet when I approached, clearly visible by interior lights from the Jeep.

I stopped by Zar, not going around to my door as the wolf faced me.

They'd obviously understood what I'd said, yet they'd spent half the night trying to kill each other. And there was something else that made me uneasy about facing that black wolf in the now illuminated woods. He was so ... wolf.

He was not monstrously large or saber-toothed or glowing-eyed. He looked exactly like a wolf in a wildlife documentary or a zoo. Just as there was nothing to distinguish them from handsome humans with a gym fixation in that form, there was nothing distinguishing this black animal from a big wolf.

Yet that was enough to pause. Wolves, it turns out, are not howling versions of dogs. Wolves are very large, very intense, long-legged, large-boned, golden-eyed. Facing that wolf was as much like facing a pet dog as facing a domestic cat is like facing a tiger.

The wolf stepped toward me, wagging his tail.

"What does he want?" I asked, stiff beside Zar, working to keep my voice level and firm.

"To come along," Zar said, buckling a leather belt on his black jeans.

"I already told him," Kage said, not looking around at us. I suspected he didn't want to meet my eyes and call attention to the fact that he was driving again. "We thought you'd want Zar along because he knows about the glen."

"You're right," I said, surprised by this consideration, still not taking my eyes from the wolf. "Thank you."

"Sod off, Jay," Kage said and yawned. "She said two. You're making her uncomfortable."

Jason, however, seemed to be aware of this. He sat down on his haunches and held up one massive paw. A paw like a club with talons curving off the end.

I just stared at it.

He dropped the left and lifted his right paw, cocking his head, whining.

I licked my lips, wishing my heart wasn't beating so fast, sure he could hear it, and reached to shake his paw.

Jason's tail swept the mulch of the ground. He licked my hand before I withdrew it from the shake. Jason. Right. I had told him…

"I suppose … if he'll stay in the Jeep?" I said. "We can't have him out there and be seen."

Jason stood, tail swinging, opening his mouth in what seemed to be a panting smile, sending bits of debris dropping from his bushy tail.

The other three wolves—one white, one black, and one smaller and mottled with markings I couldn't make out in the dark—shifted uneasily as they watched us. Of course, I shouldn't have offered. It wasn't my fault if they were all jealous pricks, but, in their defense, I had said two. Not two plus animal companion.

Too late, though. Jason nudged past Zar to jump in the open door. Zar followed him in, also yawning.

"You swot," Kage said, apparently to Jason, and shut his door.

In the passenger seat while Kage started the engine, I looked to Jason and Zar in the back. Jason took up much of the space, standing with his hind paws to Zar's right and forepaws to his left, scratching at the glass. Zar could only see over the top of his back by mashing down the thick fur.

"He wants his window down," Zar said irritably to Kage.

"Anything you need, princess," Kage muttered, rolling down the electric window behind my seat for Jason to stick his head out.

"Are they going to hold this against him?" I asked, glancing at Kage as he let out the clutch.

"Sure they will. Think no one noticed you said two but invited puppy-eyes on the side?" Kage eased the Jeep between two trees, shifted gears, and rubbed the back of his neck. I could see marks there. What looked like newly healed pink flesh, but it was hard to tell in the light. He sighed. "Doesn't matter. The wankers. Moon curse their hides."

"Rough night?" I asked, glaring at him.

Kage didn't say anything.

A long black snout poked up between my headrest and door and the wolf licked my ear. I jumped. His teeth brushing my skin was not a pleasant sensation.

"Sorry," Zar said. "I guess ... we made some noise?"

"*You guess you made some noise?*" I looked around at him.

Jason moved to meet me between the two seats and licked my ear again.

"Jason!"

He lay down across Zar's lap and the full bench seat, pinning back his ears and rolling his eyes up at me.

"He was only saying he was sorry too," Kage said, but he was smiling as we bumped out onto a real road. Enjoying my snapping at someone other than him, no doubt.

I sat forward, letting out a breath. "Will you please roll up the window?" I was freezing.

Kage did so. Behind my seat, Jason heaved a sigh.

Other than my giving directions, Kage sarcastically asking if he was going at a suitable pace and using a suitable technique in his driving for my taste, and Zar swearing at Jason for stepping on him and telling him to get in the back, we made the trip to Saint Nectan's Glen in silence—although the window did go back down for part of it.

I was prepared for a long wait in the dark, dreading reaching the spot, in fact, longing for my coffee. But I forgot all about this as we pulled into the car park to find not only was it already occupied by a little electric car, but there was a faint light glowing from the glen.

## ○ CHAPTER 14 ○

"SHHH, LET ME DO THE TALKING."

"Cassia, wait—"

"Might just be worm tossers lighting a fire in there."

"We're here for your protection."

"Please, Zar, keep your distance. Let me talk to them."

I moved stealthily down the dark wooded trail while Zar and Kage followed only a few paces behind. The only one who did trail from a distance was Jason. Zar had let him out of the Jeep as soon as we'd stopped. So much for staying behind. I didn't say anything about it. I was starting to feel like an uptight nag around this bunch—which I hated. Those weren't words I'd usually use to describe myself.

I also remembered Jason being the only one who thought to ask if I would have enough water in the caravan and his attempt at an apology just now on the ride over—though I'd snapped at him for it. Maybe I owed him one.

Werewolves had been keeping their lives private from humans for thousands of years. Jason could probably manage to stay out of the way.

As I walked carefully toward the falls, not daring to bring a flashlight, though Kage had offered a "torch" from the car and I had my own keychain light, I watched the warm glow in the woods fade like lingering sun spots in my eyes. At first, it looked like someone had started a fire out by the falls, as Kage noted. Then the place seemed to slide away, fading as if flames were being covered until the soft orange light became a very faint blue-white one.

By the time I reached the footbridge and could see the waterfall ahead in predawn gray, the light was gone. Just as the surface of the water had made my skin tingle, awareness of energy left behind sent air shivering around me: magic essence like heat lightning. The tips of my fingers tingled. A chill raced down my spine.

I'd meant to move into the open, show the druidic circle I didn't mean any trouble and introduce myself. No skulking or looking shifty.

Instead, I hesitated. "Zar?" the merest whisper. "Druids aren't casters. So what...?"

"That's not human magic," he whispered back, almost into my ear, and I knew he could feel it as well. "It's the kindred. Has to be."

My heart leapt. Would we see one?

The faie: elementals, magical spirits, fairy folk, guides, and ancient companions of both the middle and lower worlds. Nana had seen them, even had pet names for some. I'd felt them around in her high desert domain where I'd hiked and camped with her but never seen a faie in person and awake.

Yet the energy was fading with the light, the air itself seeming to settle just as if a wind were dying—hiding from us.

I started over the bridge, stepping silently as I could and holding my hand out to tell Zar and Kage to stay back. They ignored the warning, following on my heels until I turned and glared. This made them pause on the bridge while I moved on toward the pool.

Noise of rushing water filled my ears. Subtle smells of earth and moss and river rocks filled my nose. There was something about the ground beneath my shoes that breathed.

For a moment, I thought it hadn't worked. Not only had any faie fled when they sensed our approach, but the druids had abandoned their circle and also slipped away before risking explaining themselves to mundanes.

Then I saw the woman.

As if I'd been looking at her all along. Like I'd known she was part of the stones and water and breeze. Yet, as if she'd just appeared there.

She stood motionless, her back to me, her arms out to the waterfall, palms up, praying or meditating.

With my escorts still at the bridge, I waited at some distance to allow her to finish her ritual. She must know I was here. If for no other reason than the faie's vanishing. But where were the others?

Druids followed a nature-based faith and this sort, the kinds of druids loosely connected to the magical community, were generally members of druidic orders much as Broomantle was to casters. Diana had said the nearest order was around the Scottish border. If Zar was right, however, and my own scrying, there was still one order in Cornwall. And this glen was a gathering spot. Yet ... here she was. One woman facing the waterfall.

For the first time since spotting her, I felt uneasy. Was this right?

I took a gentle step back, waiting, wondering if I should speak or leave her in peace, running through what I knew about druids.

There were people Nana used to reference as "fringe magic." Not mundanes, nor casters in our world. People like Wiccan practitioners, mediums, and shamans.

Then there were druids. A collective joined to the Earth and natural spirits. I hadn't the faintest idea what all they did to practice their faith, or much else about them, though I respected the idea of their connection to nature. Nana had held them in great esteem.

And now ... being attacked? Someone in the South of England murdering shifters and a druid?

My worries of what to do next, of interrupting a ritual, were resolved when the woman—with long, pure white hair and a gently lined, weather-roughened face—turned to me.

In the gloom with the eastern sky growing lavender, the birds calling, the waterfall roaring at her back, she smiled at me.

"Good morning" she said in a soft voice that hardly carried over the water. "I didn't know anyone else came to the glen so early."

"I was looking for you," I said, hoping on second thought that this didn't sound creepy. "I think. My name is Cassia. I'm trying to find the druids in this area. I hope we can help each other."

Her eyes widened as she took me in anew, though she didn't seem alarmed. She offered her hand and I stepped forward.

"Well," she said slowly, "you've found her." A smile crinkled the corners of her eyes as she pressed my hand in both of hers. Her skin was silky, smooth and fine.

I felt calmer with the contact, certain this was right: where we were supposed to be, who we were supposed to find.

"'Her'?" I asked. "You mean … there are no other druids in Cornwall?"

The old woman's expression grew sad and she again squeezed my hand as she said, "We have long been a dying breed."

I glanced around to the two on the bridge. "That's what I was hoping to talk to you about."

She saw them as well.

"Friends of mine. Could we talk to you? They tell me your people may possibly have been attacked as theirs have."

This time, she did look alarmed as her gaze went from Kage and Zar, then up to my face. "This is a sacred place." I could hardly hear her in the rush from the waterfall. "Might I beg your grace and time to meet later? I believe I know what it is you are referring to. Two druids have…" Again, she looked at Kage and Zar.

"Two?"

She nodded.

"Anywhere you like," I said. "Where could we see you?"

"Come for lunch, if it's not too much to ask. No— my granddaughter will be over. Tea, then? Five?"

"Five would be perfect." *Anything would be perfect.* "Thank you so much…?"

"Ellasandra. And thank *you* for coming to find us. May I give you my address? You young people know how to get anywhere without directions these days."

I smiled, fishing my phone from my hoodie pocket. "We're spoiled." I typed in the address to my notes. No idea if it was near or far but it hardly seemed to matter.

I introduced Kage and Zar, both keeping back, nodding, before thanking Ellasandra again and we left her to her glen.

*Thank you, Goddess.*

The magic was right. It was myself I didn't trust. Follow the magic and I would find the answers. Sometimes I just needed reminding.

We made our quiet way back to the Jeep while I looked up the address. Now, though, I couldn't catch a signal.

They'd heard all we'd said, though I couldn't imagine how when I'd hardly picked up the old lady's words a foot away from her.

"So who's going to tea?" Kage asked in an offhand way.

My little bubble of euphoria at this clear path burst.

"How about I go alone?" I said as we reached the Jeep. "Will that keep the peace?"

"We're here to look after you, Cassia." Zar sounded troubled by the idea of my aloneness.

"Are you?"

"Of course we are. Your wish is our—"

"Uh-huh. I'm going to start being more specific about my wishes. How about 'no fighting' for one?"

Hand on his door, Kage looked around, then whistled. Nothing happened.

The first rays of sun stroked treetops with a fiery golden glow that helped to lift my spirits once more.

"I didn't mean to fight with you, Cassia." Zar took my hand, dark eyes round and troubled. "Truly, I'm sorry. I only wanted to make sure we were doing our—"

"I'm not talking about arguments with you. I'm talking about you fighting among yourselves. All night."

He opened his mouth, shut it, then bit his lip, apparently bewildered by such an idea. You'd think I'd told him he and the others had been off skiing last night.

"What?" I asked. "Can you not remember stuff you do when you're—?"

A great, dark figure bounded out of the woods at a run. Kage threw open the door beside us and the wolf flew inside like a gazelle.

Zar spun away from me as Jason brushed past his shoulder. "Jason! *Ni*, get in the back, *Vinu stura*."

"Move over." Kage flapped his hand, though he didn't seem to care what Jason did.

Jason stepped to the far seat, giving Zar room to follow. He did not get into the back but panted, once more seeming to smile, untroubled by Zar's words or tone as Zar still snapped at him in Lucannis.

Kage started the engine.

From the passenger seat I said, "I need coffee before we go back."

# ○ Chapter 15 ○

We took twenty minutes in the village bakery where I was able to find my espresso and plug my phone in for that long. Jason waited in the Jeep, inconspicuously curled up in the back. I hoped.

Kage and Zar sat with me at a tiny table against the wall where I'd found a power outlet. They had steamed milk but nothing to eat, which surprised me. After the display with the burgers, I'd been concerned they might pillage the pastry case. No, they only sniffed, then ignored it. Maybe there had to be meat involved for them to care. Or maybe they were so used to their mealtimes they didn't consider breakfast an option. I didn't ask.

Every early morning visitor to come in that bakery stared at us, making me uncomfortable. Probably locals. Only surprised by us. Yet, with the nature of our mission, and nature of what we all were, attracting attention made my skin crawl.

"Couldn't have got her to have a coffee with you?" Kage asked moodily as we settled. "Why'd she put you off to teatime?"

"She was obviously busy now," I said, both hands on my hot paper cup on the table. "At least she was willing to see us today at all."

"You were marvelous to find her, Cassia," Zar said. "Just like that."

"Bit too easy, wasn't it?" Kage gave me a sideways look. "Makes you wonder."

"What's that mean? You don't trust me?"

"I don't trust *her*." His tone was low, conspiratorial. "Can't trust anyone, can we?"

"So you think Ellasandra wanted the extra time to call up her serial killer buddies and have them meet us at her place? And maybe druids sport hunt out of helicopters also?"

Zar rubbed his ear, looking down at his drink.

Kage also pulled a face and changed tactics. "We don't know who could be after us. Watching us *and* them? Put us all together and...?"

"A bunch of prey in one place attracts predators?" I asked. "If someone is keeping an eye on us, I don't see that we can do anything about it. The faster and more efficiently we work the better. Which is why it's a good thing, not a bad one, to find people we're looking for so quickly. We can't get paranoid just because we find an easy clue. As to me being 'marvelous' I wish you'd have found a caster for help last winter, and you might not be in this situation."

"That wasn't our choice," Kage said.

"But you wouldn't have even if you were leader of the whole South Coast Cooperative, would you? Why do you hate humans? I know you have a secret to keep but you must see them every day. I'd have thought you get used to us."

"Diana did ask once," Zar said. "And most of the pack was against her. Isaac was one who really pushed for it. Only a few did, insisting we could get help from humans."

"It was a right balls up," Kage muttered. "After the way that bloke treated them half the pack started thinking—" He turned his head, looking through tall windows to the gray street.

"Thinking what?"

Neither answered. Zar still looked at his lidded cup. Kage drummed his fingers on the table.

"You think ... casters could be doing this?"

"Of course not," Zar said quickly, finally glancing up. "You're helping us, Cassia. It's not as if—"

"But *some* of your people think these murders are the work of casters?"

Kage gave an irritable shrug while Zar again rushed to answer.

"It can't be casters. The scene, the way they cover their trails, if they had magic—"

"Some say it's casters who mean to make themselves look mundane by the way they're working," Kage said. "Makes sod-all sense if you ask me. If they have magic, why wouldn't they use it?"

"The fact is, we don't know," Zar said. "And our silvers have been firm in trying to keep speculation at bay. Everyone thinks it's someone or other, so the pack gets jumpy."

Bunches of cornered wolves ready to fight back and going on suspicions rather than even solid evidence? My own words came back to me, telling Diana I didn't want to be responsible for a bloodbath. Clearly, neither did she.

As to the caster theory, Kage was right. First of all, it made not the slightest sense that, say, Broomantle members would decide to start murdering werewolves. But, if they did, they'd use all the magic they could and make a clean job of it—no need to chuck gasoline and solvents around. Anyway, I couldn't allow myself to jump on the speculation and paranoia bandwagon. As far as I was concerned no one and everyone remained suspects. And that was exactly how it was going to stay unless and until something pointed to real evidence.

"I'm glad you asked me to help," I said. "They're right to keep everyone in check about running off halfcocked." I sipped my hot drink. "On an unrelated note, what do you mean when you say silver?"

"Silver is top," Zar said. "It originates from Moon silver, you know? Or wisdom; silver-muzzled. Calling someone silver is to say they're alpha, the leader. Any sizable pack will have two or three silvers with one chief, or *cataja*, above the rest. Your *cataja* is your proper alpha. She's the one with final authority."

"The queen? Always a she?"

"Not always, but it's typical."

"No Mayo packs." Kage set down his cup and stretched his arms over his head, shoulders popping. "Anyway, who are you taking along to see this busy old worm for tea?"

"Not you, obviously."

Kage looked at me, slowly lowering his arms.

"You just implied you didn't like her. Why would you want to have tea with her? But forget her for now. What about the rest of the day?"

"We'll need to spend another night," Zar said.

I took a drink, the coffee just cooled enough for it. "That too. Maybe we could get a nap before lunch? And I wouldn't mind sightseeing since I've come halfway around the world to visit Cornwall—as it turns out. It would be nice to see more of the coast. What do you think?"

"You're asking?" Kage frowned. "Or are you just going to pinch my keys and give them to someone on the street to drive you around?"

I sighed. "I'm sorry I hurt your feelings yesterday, Kage. Really. I didn't mean to upset you. But has it ever occurred to you to be sorry about terrorizing your passengers, making them sick, endangering their lives, and reckless driving while towing a caravan and potentially endangering others on the road as well?"

He didn't answer. I kept looking at him and eventually he gave a little shrug.

"If I ask Isaac to take me to meet with Ellasandra this evening are you going to try to kill him again tonight?"

"I didn't do that," he grumbled and drank. "Why'd you think he was still up walking around this morning if we'd meant him dead? The Moon-cursed bastard." Under his breath.

I shut my eyes and savored the rich, sharp espresso. Just half now. I could finish the rest cold. I'd had about six minutes of sleep last night, and none of them could have managed more than an hour either.

Rest, lunch, take a few minutes to be a tourist, solve a murder case.

Maybe a campfire tonight? Hot soup? That would be a treat before bed.

And do our best to get through the day without it becoming an endless bickering session.

It wasn't like we'd be trapped together much longer. Even the ones—Isaac and Zar, maybe Jason, maybe even Kage—who I would like to know better.

We soon returned to the Jeep and started back for the nature preserve at Kage's usual brisk pace.

As we set out south, the black wolf stuck his face up between the front seats to lick Kage's ear. Then he took a pass at me.

I leaned away. Those teeth by my nose made me jumpy. I offered him my hand, as if he might want to sniff it like a dog.

Jason licked my palm and I stroked his cheek with the backs of my fingers. Fur around his face was short and soft, still very thick. Past his cheeks and at the base of his ears it started to grow out until it formed almost a mane around his neck and up his shoulders. Here, the guard hairs were long and coarse, yet the undercoat remained soft and wooly as a lamb.

With more light shed on the matter, it was still intimidating to have his face, the long muzzle and intense golden eyes, right in mine. At the same time ... it was pretty cool to have a wolf in the car.

It also seemed to me that Jason was still Jason. I wasn't sure how I felt about this, however, given what they'd done last night. It might be nice to think that their shift into a wolf form caused savagery to rise to the surface. At least it would have made a nice excuse.

"Get your arse over." Zar was shoving him to stay in his own seat.

Kage braked and down shifted. Jason lost his pawhold on the console, slipped, whacked against Kage's left arm, and tumbled into the floor.

"Get in the back, Jay," Kage said. "We don't need your help."

He regained his footing and licked across Kage's neck.

"Shove off!"

Jason climbed over the seats into the back.

## o Chapter 16 o

SOMEONE HAD LEFT bluebells on the step up to the trailer. I saw them as I opened the door to go in. Also that they'd been slightly crushed. I'd stepped on them coming down a couple hours previously. So someone last night. Zar. Though ... maybe Isaac? Thinking of the necklace and the way the white wolf had seemed to catch my eye in the dark.

This reminded me that I'd seen him limping. And what about the rest? Did anyone need medical care? Would they attack Jason because I'd let him come along? Or more fights in general just because they were back together and some still in furred form?

And hadn't they promised to look out for each other as well as me? My brain was too fogged to remember the details but it seemed like Diana had brought up the matter of them being in this together.

Still, I wasn't the caretaker—or teacher or mom—or in any other way the responsible party. My concern was saving them from a far worse nemesis than each other. I didn't go around asking if everyone was all right or proposing we could all be friends. I just went back to bed.

So much warmer now with the sun up, I opened all the windows again, locked the door, and was asleep ten minutes after getting back.

The fight that woke me was a verbal one.

Insults, oaths—plenty of bloodies, moons, and arses.

I reached for my phone. Only late morning. Three hours sleep. It would do. Time to finish my drink.

I did my little bit of washing up and readying for the day. How long would the water last? One more night. I could shower back at Melanie's.

I sent her a text, saying how beautiful Cornwall was, throwing in a couple details to make myself feel less like a total liar and fraud of a sister. I'd taken a picture of the lighthouse yesterday that I sent.

The weather report, which I had to convert from Celsius to Fahrenheit, said hot. After last night, I was aching for it and gladly pulled on my one change of clothes—blue shorts and a sleeveless yellow blouse. I would keep the hoodie with me in case of wind.

"Of course I didn't! He blames me or Jay for everything just for being in the room." That was Andrew. A name I'd been avoiding since we'd met.

Working in a hotel? What did the rest of them do? They couldn't all be involved in mundane jobs or they would know humans better.

"We had to stay around the Jeep anyway," Jason said. He sounded worried, voice hushed as if he didn't want to wake someone. No one else seemed troubled about such details.

"Why'd we have to bring the *kir* thing anyway? We should have our bikes." A snarl from Jed.

"The caravan, moron," Kage said. "How were we supposed to tow that?"

Bikes? Remembering the mobile home park, I wasn't surprised to think bicycling was how young werewolves tended to get around. But Jed had wanted to bike to Cornwall?

I noticed the cup of bluebells I'd put in a dab of water on the table and smiled. Patches of sunlight filtered into the trailer. Three hours of sleep wasn't so bad. Just like one druid rather than none wasn't bad.

Lots to be thankful for today.

"We'd have caught something if someone didn't trip over his own paws like a yearling learning to run," Andrew said.

"Want a better look at my paws, maggot?" Jed.

"Go ahead." Andrew laughed. "Let me grab a book. You're so slow I'll have to pass the time."

Lunch. That was what we needed. A warm turkey club with a pickle spear and a side salad, maybe an iced latte. But I was thinking of my favorite quick lunch spot at home in Portland.

Lunch in Cornwall? A pub. Or Indian food. I didn't even eat fast food at home. Not going to make a habit of it when I could be trying new things in a new place.

I stepped out to dappled sunlight through thick leaves and found all in their upright forms and dressed.

Kage and Jed faced a tree, in which sat Andrew. Jason stood below. Isaac, reading on a tablet, sat on the fallen tree that Kage had hit the night before.

Zar sat by the caravan, leaned back against a tire, chewing a long stalk of grass and reading from a thin paperback in a plain brown binding. He smiled up when I emerged, scrambling to his feet.

"Morning again, Cassia." He tossed away the grass stalk. "We were making plans for lunch."

"Were you?" I returned his smile. "You have such an interesting way of going about it."

"May I?" He offered his hand and I gave him mine, not sure what he meant. He kissed my knuckles. "My apologies for being out of sorts earlier."

This confused me just as much. "You didn't do anything."

"You're too kind." He still held my hand. "I've thought of you in every birdsong and rustle of leaves this morning. Though your voice is more musical than either. The sunrise was a shallow brushstroke compared to the masterpiece of your beauty."

"Uh-huh."

"I wish I were worthy of this journey with you, Cassia. I've never met anyone like you. My fumbling efforts to contribute must seem trivial—"

"Zar?"

"Yes?" Beaming, eyes lighting up like fireworks when I said his name, pressing my hand. I could practically see him wagging his tail.

*What are you on?* I swallowed as I repressed my own words. Instead, I said, "Are you okay?" And withdrew my hand.

"I'm brilliant now that you're here. You've made this the most perfect morning of my life." Sincerity poured off him like sunbeams.

Goddess, he made me feel ancient and cynical and just ... mean. Although I doubted he was more than a couple years younger than myself. He wasn't a wolf. He was a golden retriever. A gorgeous, poetic one with wavy black hair.

"I'm ... glad I could help," I said quietly, easing back.

"Would you allow me to walk you to the village for lunch?"

"We all need lunch, Zar."

"Your desire is my quest." Bowing his head. "Your goal is my passion—"

"What?"

"I'll take you all for a meal."

"That's a kind offer, but it's Kage's responsibility. And you're already helping with my goals by finding Ellasandra. And, in the short-term, I'd be happy with none of you doing the others a serious injury."

While I spoke, I stepped toward those around the tree. The argument died and they looked at us, Kage nearest.

"Lunch?" I offered him a smile.

Kage frowned, perhaps due to his favorite pastime of snapping at his cousin being interrupted. Then he looked about in a businesslike way. "All right, wolves, here's the day: meal, visit the coast, then Cassia will see our druid—"

He seemed about to elaborate but Jed cut him off. "Who made you silver?"

Kage spun to face him. "You want to explain the plan, vulture-face? Go on and tell Moon and wolf what we're doing since you know."

"Not me," Jed snarled. "The witch is silver here. She can speak for herself if there's a 'plan' to know."

A backhand since he didn't bother using my name. Still, I was more appreciative of an acknowledgment to my position from Jed than for the gushing from Zar. I'd had no idea Jed thought I was anything other than a nuisance to be followed around.

"For right this minute, lunch and sightseeing," I said. "But we can't fit everyone into—"

"I'll ride in the back," Jason said. "So will Andrew."

"We can't drive around with seven people in that Jeep."

"We're supposed to protect you," Kage started.

"So you've said—"

"Not asking you to ride in the back. What difference does it make?"

"It's illegal for one," I said. "Even if it was safe and comfortable, which it's not."

"We'll keep low," Jason said. "No one has to see us."

Kage opened his hands, facing me with a *We have the simple solution* gesture. It was weird how he made me feel so demanding and unreasonable all the time.

I stared at him, and the rest, all watching me other than Jed, who scowled at the ground.

"Are you going to argue and bicker all the way out to the beach?" I asked.

"Am I going to drive?" Kage asked.

"No."

He looked into leaves over our heads.

I sighed. "The door's open. Do you all want to wash up? Shave? Be sparing with the water, please. And leave your bags here in the trailer so you have more room."

While Zar was telling me how thoughtful and kind I was, Andrew hopped out of the tree as if he'd been waiting for nothing but this invitation all along.

"What are you reading?" I asked to get Zar to shut up about me as Jason slipped past us into the trailer with thanks.

Zar held up the spiral-bound paperback. "I beg your forgiveness. I don't know humans well, like Isaac or Andrew. I hope to get to know you better, Cassia. And show you how much you mean to me."

"Mean to you?" I looked up as I took the book from him. "Zar ... you're sweet but you just met me."

"The greatest moment of my life—an eclipse time."

I wanted to tell him to stop, but, dammit, he was too cute for that. Instead, face hot, I studied the thin book.

It was a quick guide to social customs and smooth relations with humans, illustrated with simple cartoons and covering such topics as work, sports, mealtimes, offspring, authority figures, and etiquette at gatherings. There was something very odd about the book—aside from it obviously being self-published and probably limited to about ten copies.

I flipped to the front.

"Zar...? This was published in the fifties."

"That's right. Our great-grandfather wrote it. He served in the human army in World War Two. He knew everything about humans. A brilliant wolf, but I never met him."

"I'm sure he was. Did it ever occur to you that the social customs and lives of mundanes may have changed in the past seventy years?"

His smile faltered.

I handed back the book. "Have your people stayed the same for that long?"

"Yes. Well..." With another chuckle. "We have better bikes."

"Better bikes...? So you don't work around humans? What about school? What about ... going to the grocery store?"

"I'm a crafter. My work is home with the pack. We're homeschooled by core, and supermarkets and all that are up to core."

I didn't ask what he meant by core. Every few minutes one of them said something I wanted to understand, wanted to ask about, but I struggled to rein in my own questions and curiosity.

One more night, help them be the ones to gain information, and be on my way. I couldn't let myself keep getting more invested—allow curiosity to run away with me, or dwell on moonlit beach strolls, or gold necklaces, or learning more about their language, customs, or anything else.

I let out a slow breath. "I was homeschooled for a few years by my grandmother also. But that was mostly to study our craft once I went to live with her. Diana seems to want your pack to get along better with humans. I'm surprised you don't go to school and learn to blend in better."

"It wouldn't be safe. Young pups don't understand about keeping our secret. And once we reach Moon's transition and learn to change we can't always control it at first."

"You can't?"

*Stop it. You don't need to get to know them any better.*

But I wasn't used to repressing my own curiosity.

He shook his head. "Hellish difficult. Mastering the change is half our education as yearlings."

"But once you learn you have total control?" I looked away, trying to spot something to busy myself over. Zar was too eager to talk for my own good.

"Oh, yes, perfectly."

"Except?"

He shrugged. "Nothing."

"No, you were going to say more." I met his eyes.

"Well … it's not that we can't control it. It's just not always … comfortable. Especially at our ages… It's supposed to get better with time."

"I'm not following you."

"It's … it's hard to…" He screwed up his face.

"'Compulsion' is the word you're looking for."

I turned quickly to find Andrew at my shoulder, waiting to go into the trailer while Jason and Kage were in there.

"Compulsion?" I asked.

"That's what lady-hair is trying to explain," Andrew said, smiling into my eyes. His smile was nothing like Zar's. Where one was a golden retriever, the other was a fox. "Like your coffee. Like a triple chocolate layer cake on your birthday. Or that perfect pair of shoes that just happen to be on sale. Or having sex. You *can* exercise perfect control." Andrew stood much too close, allowing me to see his hooded amber eyes in rich detail. "But who does? Who ever has?"

I addressed Zar. "So wolves have control over changing once they've matured? But you'd rather change all the time? It would be hard on you not to change regularly? Like celibacy or giving up a substance you're dependent on?"

"I don't have to change," Zar said, eager, ignoring Andrew. "If you'd rather, I'll stay in skin for the rest of the trip. No fighting, no noise—"

"That's not why I'm asking you about this," I said.

"Then why?" Andrew asked.

I glared at him. "Don't you have somewhere else to be?"

"Wolves have asked him that question for years." Kage stepped from the caravan and Andrew took his spot inside, giving me a bow before he retreated.

I wanted to ask Zar about the mindset. Jason had seemed normal, perfectly aware, but surely there was more to their change than skin-deep. I bit my tongue.

"Are you two ready to go? Zar, do you want in the trailer?" I asked. "Let's get going. And Zar? Be careful about what that book tells you, okay? I'm not a fifties housewife."

He nodded, finally looking uncertain as he glanced down at his book.

I traded from flip-flops to walking shoes and exchanged good mornings with Isaac as Kage, then Jason went off for the Jeep, which was now parked a hundred yards away at the real car park since we'd come back that morning and left it. They sang under their breaths while they walked and I remembered stifled howls of the night before.

Why did they live here? Why weren't all werewolves howling down the moon at their leisure in Canada?

More questions. Plus something else: feeling sorry for them. Struggling to let go of both, I faced Isaac and very nearly overflowed with both questions and concern.

He looked fine: hair combed, calm, quiet, offering me his gentle smile.

I had my mouth open to ask if he was all right when I stopped.

Instead, I'd just started to ask if he would accompany me to meet with Ellasandra when Andrew emerged from the trailer—clean shirt, freshly shaved, and with his hair damp. I interrupted myself, having the presence of mind to tell Andrew to empty his pockets.

"Me?" Shocked. "Did you ask everyone else?"

"How stupid do you think I am?"

He laughed. "In a battle of wits, never give the first answer. Just like in a negotiation—never be the first to say a price." He started to stroll away, as if he thought he'd sufficiently distracted me. He was even more handsome at his jauntiest, like he was strutting down a runway with cameras flashing.

"*Andrew.*"

He stopped, glanced at me, then Isaac, who stood silently by my shoulder.

"Go on," I said.

Andrew fished around in his pockets for longer than needed. At last, he produced my mascara brush and a hair scrunchy. His eyebrows jumped at the sight of them, like someone had put them in his hands by prestidigitation.

"Moon strike me," Andrew murmured. "You never know what a modern bloke might be carrying."

"Right. Were you going to keep those in your man purse?" I held out my hand.

Andrew placed the mascara tube in it, making a point of stroking my wrist all the way to my fingertips. The touch was burning, tingling to the soles of my feet with a strange eroticism considering what should have been a normal exchange. Maybe it was the slow way he felt my skin, or the eye contact all the time he touched me.

"And?" I kept myself stiff, glaring back at him.

Andrew didn't give up the hair tie. He pressed it to his nose, inhaling deeply with his eyes closed, then opening them slightly to roll back in his head as he shuddered.

"Oh, Moon," he murmured. "Moon, yes. Oh, Cassia darling, yes…" Another shiver, breathing quickly.

Slowly, only gradually focusing his eyes, he withdrew the scrunchy from his nose and slipped it onto my thumb as I still stood with my hand out. He stroked the back of my hand, lazy and sensual, while his gaze flicked up from our fingers to my eyes.

Burning, breathing a bit too fast, I couldn't force myself to break the contact. On the contrary, I longed to move toward him.

He held my gaze as long as he could while he lowered his head over my hand. At last he lost eye contact to touch his mouth to my fingers, lips around my nails, his hot tongue caressing skin under them where nerve endings were concentrated. I ached to slide my fingers into his mouth—on the verge of it—but bit my cheek and remained rigid. I knew I was flushed. And it wasn't from the embarrassment—other than having an audience for the event.

Andrew kissed my fingertips, then straightened and walked away, joining in the earlier song about a wolf wandering in a willow grove.

Uncomfortably aware of how much my chest was rising and falling, I muttered, "Thanks," to Isaac.

"For what?" He cocked his head. His expression was just as mild as it had been before. I loved how secure he was.

"For backing me up. I don't think he would have taken me seriously enough to give my stuff back if you hadn't been here. Thank you."

Isaac nodded. "Anything."

Just the one word, yet the way he said it, the nature of it, wasn't helping me get my composure back. Having trouble shaking the feelings conjured from Andrew's touch, I faced Isaac.

"I was going to ask, would you accompany me to the meeting with the druid this evening? I don't want to overwhelm her, but one or two of you. You'll be able to fill her in on what's happening on your side and maybe we can start putting a bigger pattern together with her help. You seem to be better with humans than the others."

"Thank you." Another nod. "I will be honored. Any ally would be welcome right now. We're grateful to you for what you're doing, Cassia. You didn't have to be here."

I looked up to his green eyes. I was no shrimp, about five-six, but he was awfully tall. The way he said my name, somehow, was as magical as his unflappable demeanor and that word, *anything*. I wanted to hug him. It had already been a long trip.

I sighed. "I only hope I can help. At least we're on a trail. Let me get my bag and I'll join you at the car."

But Isaac waited and offered his arm to escort me back to a real trail in the woods and on to the car park beside the river. He smiled as he did so, letting me know he knew he was being ironic. He understood our living in a modern age.

I returned the smile and took his arm to walk with him. Again, I very nearly asked if he was okay, about what had happened the night before, was that him, would it happen again?

I said, "Should we be concerned that someone could discover the caravan while we're away and tow it for being illegally parked on government property?"

Isaac shrugged. "It's possible."

That's what I'd thought before. "I'll just ... run back and get my overnight bag."

I grabbed it, locked the caravan, and hurried out again to Isaac.

Now a simple lunch and sightseeing with this pack to look forward to until afternoon tea.

## ○ Chapter 17 ○

"How would you know, corpse-nose?" Andrew laughed. "You're guessing."

"You're going to be the one with the dead nose in a minute," Kage growled.

"He's right this time," Jason said, one hand on Kage's shoulder as we walked, keeping Kage moving forward rather than veering off to punch Andrew. "That is a Subway."

Zar nodded. "Down here to the left."

We were walking up the street in a coastal town known for surfing and a filming location from the movie *The Witches*, among other things. And we were looking for lunch.

I'd already voiced my opinion but, as everyone turned left, spilling from sidewalk to street without concern for traffic as they avoided human tourists, I tried again.

"Why are you looking for fast food? Can we get one decent meal on this trip? I didn't come around the world for Saucy and a Subway sandwich."

"What did you come for?" Jason asked.

No one else seemed interested once they could smell a meal.

"To visit my sister and have a vacation before starting work at the end of August." *And meet Englishmen.* How thick was I that that almost slipped out? They were intense enough when I wasn't encouraging them. And why? What was the interest when they didn't even like humans?

"Is your sister as fetching as you?" Andrew asked.

*My point exactly.*

"She's married," I said.

"And that did something to her appearance?"

I sighed.

They crashed their way into Subway and out of July sun on Newquay's Bank Street, then waited impatiently, arguing since they had to stand in a "queue."

Once the six actually got up there, things went from bad to scary, almost everyone talking at once, snapping at the bewildered youths behind the counter.

"Why do you put one tiny row of meatballs on these things? It's supposed to be a *meatball* sandwich."

"Get off my bloody foot, Zar."

"What's the one called with ham and salami?"

"Moon curse you, Jed, you were the last in. Back off."

"Is there one with fish? Steak and fish?"

"Can you keep the peppers and onions off the steak and cheese? Bloody daft putting onions on a sandwich called 'steak and cheese.' It's not steak and onion and cheese."

"Chicken tikka with the meatball marinara. Can you do that in one? No, wait, what about the beef melt with meatball in one?"

"I told you to fucking move, vulture-face!"

The only one who actually seemed to be trying to place a real order by the time Kage grabbed Jed's shirt and shoved him against the glass barrier above the sandwich bar was Isaac. He didn't appear troubled by what was going on around him. The employees he was addressing, however, did. Hands reached for phones. Other patrons were clearing out.

"Enough!" I shouted as Jed twisted and Kage caught his fist coming at his face. "Kage, let him go! All of you get out! Now! Give me your wallet. Go!"

It took a minute, and I thought Kage or Jed might take a swing at me next, but, again, they did as I said.

My heart was hammering by the time the place was empty. The two young women and man behind the counter all stared at me, wide-eyed. But no one seemed to have actually called the cops.

"I'm really sorry," I said, clutching Kage's wallet. Deep breaths. "It's been a ... horrible weekend. Sorry. I'll just order for everyone and take it to go."

Was Subway always to go? I couldn't remember the last time I'd been in one.

They nodded, glancing past me to the glass and sidewalk beyond, where Jason and Zar were breaking up a fight. What had made me think coming out in public with all six could possibly be a good idea? Or even a tolerable one?

"Okay. I would like six foot-longs on the cheese bread with the steak from the steak and cheese, and also the meatball marinara. Provolone cheese on top. No vegetables or condiments. All the same. Can you do that? And a six-inch Spicy Italian and a bottle of water. Thank you."

They set to and, with all three working on the order, it was ready in no time, even with heating the six large sandwiches.

I customized my own, paid with purple twenty pound notes—I love their cash—from Kage's wallet, and carried out four bags.

Everyone had settled down by the time I emerged. Yet they sprang for me exactly like my dad's old hunting dogs when he used to rattle the kibble bin. At least those dogs had been well trained.

"Wait!" I clutched bags to my chest, arms around them.

They stopped.

"What are you going to do? Stand here on the sidewalk and eat? Let's get to that park and the grass. You can all spread out and not have to look at each other."

I led the way to the grassy park overlooking a public beach, which was down long flights of stairs. They shifted impatiently as I stopped to read a plaque commemorating a visit to this spot by The Beatles. Andrew offered to carry the bags.

"Is that supposed to be funny?" I asked. "Or was I right that you think I'm stupid?"

He lifted and dropped one shoulder. "Always worth a try."

People were out on grass or benches, eating ice cream cones, taking pictures, or leaning back in the sun.

There were only a few shady patches from small trees. I needed one. I burned easily with my spring complexion and sunscreen hadn't made the cut into my overnight bag.

I passed out their sandwiches, one by one, and started for the only nearby shade with my own. Zar had already flopped down there. I would have joined him but I had reason to suspect he wouldn't be his usual charming self with lunch in his hands.

I also hated to give up on shade. This was the only near patch with a view by the edge. I was the tourist.

Also the one who took a long time over lunch; enjoying the spot.

"Zar? would you mind if I shared your shade?" I smiled at him.

Zar looked up from unwrapping, then around as if surprised to notice he was in shade. Jed, who'd been last to snatch his sandwich for some reason and was just starting away from me, stalked over. Growling.

Zar growled back but fled, retreating to sit on the low wall along the sidewalk.

"Jed, really…" I started.

He was already walking away, throwing out his hand in a *There it is* gesture to indicate the shade he'd cleared for me. Did he think I'd be grateful?

By Jed's standards, maybe it was a sweet gesture?

I sat in the shade. Sunglasses, royal blue ocean, green grass, sea breeze rippling enough to be pleasant on the blistering day. Not enough to tear my meal out of my hands. And I'd thought to pull my hair back this time.

I took another picture to text Melanie. A bite of sandwich, the photo still just sending, when Andrew flopped down beside me.

I looked around, startled. "Something wrong?"

"Only that we were previously kept apart by distance of summer grass. Now, everything is right." He lay on his side behind me, legs stretched to my left, propped on one elbow to look up at me on my right. So close his abs touched the small of my back.

"No, I mean…" I narrowed my eyes as I tried to look into his, also shielded by sunglasses. "You did *not* already finish eating." The photo delivered and I dropped my phone in my bag.

"Why would you say that?" He leaned in to touch his nose to my bare arm, inhaling.

"Meatball sandwiches must be the hardest kind in the world to eat. No way."

"A skeptic." He smiled. "I like that."

"For a people who don't like anyone by them while they eat, you certainly don't allow others the same personal space."

"No worries." He looked up at me over sunglasses, his cheek touching the curve of my elbow as I chewed. "You're human. You like it. You would offer me a bite if you were in the mood. Or maybe you are in the mood?" Arching an eyebrow.

I swallowed. "So you know humans well from your hotel work?"

"You'd be amazed," he murmured, so soft I could hardly hear in a gust of wind. He kissed the crook of my elbow. A soft, warm touch like this perfect day.

I didn't pull away. I should have. Yet I wouldn't have minded if he kept going all the way down my arm. Wouldn't have minded another chance to slip my fingers in his mouth.

"Will you tell me something?" I asked. "With all that wisdom."

"I'll tell you anything." His voice remained soft, smooth as butter. "I'll tell you all my secrets if you'll tell me yours. I'll tell you what I like if you'll tell me. I might even tell you the truth. Careful, though…"

"Why are you all so interested in me? Don't you have eligible females among your own kind?"

"Not many. But it hardly matters. Have you looked in a mirror lately?"

"Believe it or not, guys who are only interested in me for my looks are a huge turn-off. I don't need one more male seeing me as an object rather than a personality worth knowing. You know nothing about me. And, unless you actually want to and are interested in me as a person, you can back off."

"That's how you think of me." He curled closer, bringing in his knees and pressing his hips against mine, at the same time leaning his head and shoulders back into grass, smiling up at me. "I'm not a person. I'm a pretty face. Such is the, uh ... appalling fate of beautiful people, darling. No need to be hypocrites here. Tell me something about yourself and we'll start to get to know what's behind doors number one and two."

I ate while he talked, trying to think. He eased tighter against me and I felt more than his hipbones through his cargo shorts. What was unsettling me now, though, was that he was right.

Was I thinking of all of them in terms of their good looks? No. I really did feel that I was already getting to know them. Even if I shouldn't.

But not Andrew.

Andrew was indeed a pretty face. Which he knew. That was part of it, wasn't it? He used and flaunted his beauty where the others did not. Maybe Kage some. Where Kage had an *I'm too cool for this* attitude, Andrew was inviting.

"Okay," I said after a long pause and eating. Something about me. "I've been a witch all my life, trained by my mother, then my grandmother after my mom died. But I'd never met a werewolf until your pack. So you have the edge. Tell me something about yourself."

I reached for a paper napkin that I had between my knees to keep it from blowing away. Andrew stopped me, catching my hand in his.

"I love mustard," he said, drawing my fingers to his face. "Most wolves don't." That was his secret? As he lowered his face to lick mustard off my skin, he kept eye contact for a long time, breaking it when he finally turned down too much—as he had outside the trailer.

I shivered at the touch of his tongue.

What about keeping a bit of distance? And, if I wasn't going to bother about that, what about Isaac? What about Zar?

I had no business flirting with any of them. Much less all of them.

Still, I did not withdraw my hand as Andrew sucked the tips of my fingers—his mouth hot and wet and making me feel the same. He rocked his hips against me and I thought of leaning down, imagining the feel of his mouth on mine.

Instead, I gave him the end of my sandwich. I was still hoping for an actual English tea later—maybe a scone.

Andrew did not object to the peppers or other vegetables. He gulped the last quarter of the sandwich and went back to smiling lazily up at me while I drank from my water bottle.

He trailed his fingers down my left leg from my shorts to my knee and back up. He didn't try to slide them below, but along the hem, across my thigh.

I capped the bottle and looked from the aqua view down at him. "Aren't you concerned about this?"

"About what?" Rolling his hips, curling himself tighter around me to kiss my leg. "Imagining your fantasies of my making love to you?"

"About what the others might do to you after this? It's not like we don't have an audience." Which was bothering me, feeling disloyal to Isaac in particular for having accepted the necklace, even if just for the trip.

Andrew laughed. "They can't catch me."

I had to smile at that, remembering seeing him sit in a tree that morning. Even in fur he must be no heavyweight like Kage, Jed, and Isaac.

"All right, gingerbread man," I said. "Up to you."

"Is it?" He pressed himself upward on one hand, moving toward my face.

I pushed him back. "And to me. Don't get carried away."

"One kiss? A trial? You could do a lot worse. Those barbarians know nothing about pleasing females. It's all finding a mate to them. Like I said, I know humans."

I lifted an eyebrow. "Careful, Andrew. If you know women so well you should know that boasting about legions of experience is not necessarily a good move either."

"Did I say legions? More like ... enough practical world knowledge to be an experience you'll never forget." He tried to sit up again, reaching to touch my face, lips parted.

If I didn't have Isaac and Zar, even the others, on my mind—both my own misgivings and genuinely being concerned for Andrew's later safety—I'd have let him. Never mind staying detached.

Of course I was being played. Still ... if the player's good enough sometimes it doesn't matter. At least not on vacation.

He let me shove him to the grass, smiling. "Mind letting me in on a secret?"

"I guess that depends what it is." I took another drink.

"What is it you fancy so much about Isaac? Is it the beard? Because just give me a few days…"

"I don't fancy Isaac." But I blushed, dammit, and instantly regretted defensiveness.

Andrew lifted his eyebrows in delicate mockery. "Surely not."

"All right," I said. "He's decent to me. He's mature and not pushy."

"You don't like pushy?" He cocked his head. "Because I'm seeing just the opposite. Was it the gift?" He looked at the necklace—or at my breasts. Hard to tell with the sunglasses. "And what about the skin virgin, lady hair? Perhaps the poetry? Writing songs for you?"

"Zar? He hasn't been spouting poetry."

"Oh—" Andrew chuckled. "You just give him time."

"Although, now that you mention it, he has also been decent to me. And not pawing me." I added pointedly.

Andrew scoffed. "You're too kind. Think there's anything clever about a chap who jerks off before he starts a conversation with a tantalizing female? Forget Zar. I'm the only one here worth bothering about, our mountain wolf aside. The rest of them… Kage is busy, of course. Jason doesn't care so he doesn't count. Jed is a stranger and a proper bastard. And I mean a proper bastard even by human standards. You'd have to be really thick to fall for him. And we've already discussed his yearling brother. That only leaves Isaac and myself. So that's why I asked about him."

"What do you mean by 'stranger'?"

Speaking of compulsions: curiosity nailing me again.

"A wolf spending most of his time in fur," Andrew said. "Becoming estranged from life in skin with his pack. I hadn't seen Jed in skin for such a long stretch since he was a yearling." He stroked my leg, turning in again to glide his tongue over my knee. "It'll be why Diana sent him. She'd rather see reform than see him go the same way as his father." He kissed my kneecap. "How do you have skin like fresh cream? The magic touch?"

I'd spent a whole afternoon at 88 in the Pearl District before the trip, since I'd thought I would be on the beach. Waxing, face mask, spa, whole deal. Obviously, I wasn't about to tell Andrew that.

"Just my natural healthy glow," I said. "Why is being a stranger so terrible that it requires reform?"

"The first one's free, darling. After that..." Kissing my leg.

"I'm not paying you to answer questions—in any way, shape, or form. I was just asking."

"You'd pay if you had an inkling of the truths I could tell, oh noble Cassiopeia. You'd be begging me to be the teacher, offering anything. 'Please, Andrew, please, you sexy beast, tell me all you know about ... Isaac, and ravish me till sunrise.' But—" He sighed. "You don't have any idea what you're missing so we can't expect you to start begging yet."

"Yet?" I tried for my, *Oh, please,* patronizing stare, but I was fighting a grin. His American accent had been flawless.

"Yet," Andrew repeated firmly. He licked my knee again, then stood. "May I escort you down to the beach?"

I missed the pressure against my hip. I also wished almost painfully that I could ask him for everything he knew about Isaac. All of them. All their secrets. All of his own.

*Slippery slope; don't get too attached; curiosity killed the witch; and all that.*

"Please don't," I said. "But I do want to walk down there since we're here."

He nodded, starting away.

"Andrew!"

He looked around.

"My phone, please." I held out my hand.

One corner of his mouth turned up. He pulled my phone in the blue case from a pocket in the cargo shorts and tossed it to me. As I caught it, he blew me a kiss, then strode away.

No one tried to push him off a cliff or otherwise attack Andrew during our sightseeing. Though he kept a good distance between himself and the others all afternoon. Except for Jason—as chummy with Jason as ever.

When we got ice cream later—which they still ate quickly but not insanely—those two even tried one another's flavors, caramel for Andrew and strawberry for Jason.

Watching them reminded me that Andrew had said something odd about Jason. And Kage. I wished I'd used my allotted question for that.

Best to ask Zar, or Jason himself. Everything was free with them.

After the ice cream, then a few pizzas because the sandwiches had been insufficient, we had to return to camp and drop most of the pack off before making our way to tea.

# ○ Chapter 18 ○

KAGE LET ISAAC DRIVE without him. First, though, I had to point out what a short distance it was, how we couldn't all go barging in on this old woman, asked his permission politely to take the Jeep, and kissed his cheek when he mumbled agreement.

One hurdle out of the way.

I was afraid to take Zar along because of the whole old lady/tea/manners thing. He might know druids and the kindred and his own people. Not this. Andrew seemed a more likely choice. Yet I could not stomach the idea of being alone in the Jeep with Isaac and Andrew for over an hour round-trip. Kage and Jed never even crossed my mind as options.

So it was Isaac, Jason, and myself to tea. While we were in the car going over I forgot to ask Jason what Andrew had meant. Maybe something I should ask in private anyway? Kage busy? And Jason didn't care? Not what either of them had been acting like.

Instead, I talked with them about druids. What I knew of druids and how surprised I was to learn that our hostess was the last in the area. Then Isaac asked about my work, leading me to talking of my own graduation and Portland school districts and my impending career. Usually I'm much more comfortable being the one asking questions.

The trip flew past before I could ask Isaac about his own work.

*And what about not asking questions and keeping this impersonal?*

*Screw that. What's the harm?*

*Are you sure? Someone could get hurt. You're here to offer help, then move on.*

*Move on. Exactly. We'll part ways tomorrow. No one's going to be emotionally damaged just because you get to know each other better or ask what the word* kir *means.*

Maybe not that word. I was pretty sure it was rude.

But I would like to know what they meant about "core" and what their lives were like in the pack, and to learn a little Lucannis. I spoke some college French. How cool would it be to speak some wolf language?

Weighing these arguments crowded my brain while I had to navigate to our destination. By the time we got there, I still didn't have answers.

Ellasandra lived in a whitewashed cottage on a bluff on the way into a village not far from Saint Nectan's Glen. The modest space and winding, narrow drive to reach it were more than made up for by views that took my breath away—even after the day on the Cornish coast.

The sun remained well above the horizon in an endless blue sky without a hint of cloud. The ocean, below cliffs that jutted up from it, was rich royal blue and turquoise shades. If not for the lashing wind, I'd have asked if we could take our tea out back in her garden. But that element was also intense, almost blinding.

Instead, Ellasandra had the door open and I knocked on the frame, calling a hello while Isaac and Jason waited respectfully back from me without having to be told.

"Come in. Is that you from the glen?" Her reedy voice sounded from across the cottage.

"It's us," I called. "Cassia, Isaac, and Jason. Thank you so much for the invitation, Ellasandra."

"Thank you for finding me, dear. Come sit down in the kitchen. I'm sorry I don't have a proper parlor, and my hands are full."

"No worries. Your home is beautiful. This setting…"

The stone floor was dusty to the point of debris blown inside, so I didn't bother to remove my shoes, but walked slowly in to find the kitchen at the back overlooking that view. She had a window open here as well and I was glad I'd thought to zip the hoodie on over my blouse. The cottage was chilly with all that sea air, despite the day.

"Look at that," I said, stepping into the kitchen. "Stunning. Have you lived here long?"

"All my life." Ellasandra looked up from a floured counter where she was kneading out dough to cut for a baking tray.

"No…"

"I have indeed." She smiled at me. There was flour on her nose. "I was born in this very house."

"Are you serious? Your own personal corner of the world?"

Ellasandra laughed. "No one can claim a share of the world any omore than of nature. But I like to think I'm borrowing. Anyway, my father was from London so I'll always be an 'incomer' to proper Cornish folk. An emmet, as they say. Leave it abroad," she added in a raised voice again to reach the others. "That is to say, leave the door open. Our brother the west wind is feeling playful today and I love the company."

I grinned. Another sister of the wind. "Me too. I hope you're not going to a lot of trouble just for us. Can I help?"

"No, no, sit down, dear, and ask your friends in." Gesturing with her chin to the ancient wood table in the corner with two built-in benches and two chairs. On one wall of this corner were more wide windows looking out to sea. "The moment I heard your voice this morning I thought, 'That young lady needs a proper cream tea.' I usually do a bit of baking early in the week anyway, and I bet you've never had tea in a real English cottage over the sea before, have you?"

"I'm glad my accent gave me away. But, really—"

"No trouble. Have a seat and I'll just get these in the oven."

I beamed at Jason as he stepped into the room, wishing I had Melanie there to grab her hand in lieu of a happy dance. She would understand. I squeezed his anyway and gestured to the benches to sit. Isaac took a chair that he could shove out for his long legs. I pushed Jason to slide into the bench with his back to the glass so I could sit and gaze out the window.

Ellasandra greeted them as they came in, asking us all what kind of tea we would take.

The kitchen was also white, old in every bone—low ceiling, windows too small for the view, stone floor, exposed beams that had been whitewashed over, tiny oven and great, deep sink. Even with the eat-in part, the room could not have been more than twelve feet across on the longest side and it seemed we filled the little space like sardines.

With currant and orange scones in the oven, our hostess set out cucumber sandwich quarters and chocolate "biscuits." Tea, jam, and clotted cream followed to the table with little china plates for each.

I could hardly believe it, completely forgetting why we were here. It was such a cliché, yet so perfect, I kept thanking Ellasandra for the lovely spread while she chuckled appreciatively.

Jason was slow to take anything, even after Ellasandra invited us to tuck in, herself pouring boiling water into a china pot for the table.

He watched Isaac, who gave him a glance. Isaac demonstrated eating one of the finger sandwiches in five delicate bites—more than I was taking on mine—then added one of the cookies to his plate, but didn't start on it. Jason imitated him. I doubted they cared much for the sandwiches, though cream cheese probably helped.

Even though I was certain Ellasandra knew exactly what they were, I appreciated the effort they made.

We talked about the glen, the waterfall, and Cornwall in general until Ellasandra settled with us, hot scones in a basket on the table, ready for the jam and clotted cream to melt into them and ooze over fluffy edges. Even though it embarrassed me to do it, I explained I had to take a picture of the table to send to my American sister who'd married an Englishman.

"I was visiting her in Brighton when this whole thing started," I elaborated, and was reminded there was a "thing" that had "started" and I'd better attend to it.

Ellasandra prompted me at this comment.

With a little feedback from Jason and Isaac, I filled her in on what Diana had said.

"The starting point we have," I finished, "are druids. I saw druids at standing stones on a cliff when I scried and Diana said your people had also lost someone recently. I'm glad we found you since it sounds like you may be even more rare than shifters these days."

"True druids are indeed scarce." She nodded her white head gently, holding her tea mug in both veined hands, now clean of flour and dough. "Only a few scattered around the South of England and a full, though small, order up north. I wondered how you'd managed it. You must be a gifted seer."

"I don't know about that. If they had my grandmother helping we'd already have this case solved. She died years ago."

Ellasandra reached over to squeeze my hand at this and, to my amazement, I felt a lump in my throat. "That doesn't mean she's not still helping you, dear."

"I know."

She patted my hand. "For our part, I can tell you it's the same."

We all looked at her.

"How you described yours," she said. "Bled out bodies? Eyes, clothes? It's the same for us. But we've only lost two, one just this month. If they are meaning to go after both, they're only now starting with us. As I said, we are very few. It is perhaps most worrying, most telling, that whoever is doing this is able not only to find your people but mine." She paused and took a slow breath.

It crossed my mind how scary this must be for her and I reached to return the favor of pressing her hand. She held onto mine.

"Now ... what help is that to you?" She looked up, sadly gazing from one of us to the next. "I've been thinking all day, is there a way we could put this information together and follow a path? Is there a way nature and spirit will guide us to answers if we find the right door? Everything you've said encourages me to think my one idea may indeed be a valid one." Another breath. "Though I hesitate to mention it."

She looked from Isaac to Jason and dropped her gaze.

"Please," I said. "If you know something, if you have any ideas at all. The wolves asked me. And my magic brought me druids. This has to be right. You think you may know who it could be?"

She licked her thin lips, eyes sad, and, yes, a little scared. "Have you questioned the wolves in London?"

Isaac frowned.

Jason sat back. "There are no wolves in London."

Ellasandra looked him in the eye. "Are you sure about that?"

## ○ CHAPTER 19 ○

"You think wolves could be doing this?"

Silence in the Jeep—aside from that horrible diesel engine.

"You couldn't have said that?" I looked from Isaac beside me to Jason in the back seat.

Jason seemed deeply interested in the countryside out the window.

"It's not that we think wolves are responsible—" Isaac started.

"But you *do* think it *could* be a possibility?"

Jason muttered something in the back.

"What?" I asked.

"How could there be wolves in London?" Jason asked.

I shook my head. "What is going on? The druids think there are wolves in London and you"—looking to Isaac—"say you don't know about that but, yes, the cooperative had considered that wolves could be the murderers? Now she's speculating urban werewolves may be trying to kill you off, going for druids also because city wolves hate what they represent, you already wondered if it could be an inside job, and no *one bothered to mention this to the one person* you asked for help? Is that right? Because you're making me feel crazy."

"Let's ... just wait until we get back to the others," Isaac said. "Jason and I may not be the best to fill you in on that."

"I don't know anything about it," Jason said quickly. "I've never even heard of wolves in London and I don't know the Beech Pack either. Jed's the one who knows them."

*The Beech Pack opted to forgo...*

"The pack that left your cooperative?"

Silence.

Isaac said, "Diana didn't like anyone sniffing toward our kin. Not with everyone so reactionary lately. She's right. However ... it's true they have isolated themselves from other wolves and..."

"And none of them have snuffed it," Jason said suddenly, now sounding angry. "Diana doesn't want infighting. She says we're all wolves, all in this together. But it's rubbish. We can't help infighting. We've been forced to live crammed together. We can't get out and start our own packs because there's nowhere to go. That's why we're at each other's throats. Kage and Jed are just one example. Our silvers are afraid to face the idea that the Beech Pack could be killing off the rest of us because they won't admit that the lives of wolves as our forebears knew them are over. But the Beech Pack knows it. Could be they've decided to put an end to the unnatural way we're living, destroy the South Coast packs as quietly as they can."

"That's the kind of reasoning Diana's been trying to stop," Isaac started but Jason was still talking.

"Wolves in London, though ... Moon, they could be ... who knows what they could be like? If there were wolves in London they may be even madder than the Beech wolves—mad as a bag of cats. Capable of anything. Got to be more than coincidence that wolves and druids have died and both sides suspect it's wolves, doesn't it? We thought the Beeches, they think there are urban wolves, but either way… And remember how she was when she saw Kage and Zar? Scared. Her pulse went right up when she saw them. She'd never have met with us at all if it weren't for you, believing that you were trying to help us find the killers, not that we were the wolves doing the killing."

I watched him while he talked, first to me, then looking at window glass again, voice harsh, speaking fast as he rambled.

"How do you know that?" I asked. "That she was scared?"

"Watching you lot, wasn't I? And she was scared now. Just a bit."

Isaac nodded.

"If she was so afraid and so sure wolves murdered two of her people, why did she invite us home at all?"

"She trusted you. Like I said." Jason glanced at me. "Maybe druids have their own sorts of sixth senses about these things. She believed you were who you said you were. If we'd showed up to ask them questions alone, like that one Elijah says hasn't been around lately, they'd have legged it. Could be the Aspens will never see their druid pal again. Now we know why."

"Did you notice, though, they don't have solid evidence either?" I said. "She says there are urban wolves and they hate everything that their more natural kin and her people stand for. But they don't know who killed those two druids any more than we know who killed the seven wolves. Just because both sides of the victims happen to think this could be wolves doesn't mean it's *not* a coincidence either. We can't run back to your pack and tell your silvers, 'Why, yes, turns out, all the paranoia was right, your own people are murdering you.' This is the kind of information that leads into an investigation. Not the kind that leads to convictions."

Jason pulled a face, back to looking out the window. "What?"

He didn't say anything.

I looked to Isaac. "Does that not make sense to you?"

"It does make sense, Cassia." Isaac watched the road as he drove. "It's a lot to think about. None of us want to believe that wolves are killing wolves. How to prove it or disprove it, and the consequences either way, it's only ... a bit overwhelming. If packs are murdering each other, we could have a civil war on our hands. If they're not, then we still don't have any answers. One way or another…"

"Overwhelming." I let out a breath, also looking ahead. After a long silence, I added, "I'm sorry. For what's happening to you. That wasn't ... what I'd been hoping to learn."

"You've no account to be sorry for anything, Cassia. You made contact with the druids and gained information and a lead to follow. Just for finding Ellasandra we're in your debt."

Jason was probably right that she'd only trusted us at all because of me. Maybe right also that she had some sixth sense born of her connection to the natural world. It made me want to know druids better. But what I really needed to know better right now were wolves. And so did they.

I watched the road in evening sunlight.

So much different, somehow. Thinking what they had was an inside job. And *were* there wolves in London? If that was true, Jason must be right. Those wolves could be anything. Dangerous was the first adjective that came to mind.

Then there was the Beech Pack. Apparently top suspects all along. But justifiably? Or only fear and mistrust of a group of outsiders?

And why was I upset about these new realizations, about what Jason had said, and them not bothering to tell me what they'd already believed?

Wasn't I done? I could scry and see if I could spot a werewolf in London, but what good would that even do? Surely they were best at finding their own kind.

Another reason to suspect wolf killers, though: it takes a wolf.

I thought about my breathing and didn't say anything else on the way back.

I'd meant to stop for snack food and a can of soup. There was a pot in the trailer. A mere dot of a fire would be enough to heat it. Now, after the cream tea with Ellasandra, I was more than satisfied. At least when it came to food. For everything else ... I felt painfully unsatisfied.

## o <u>Chapter 20</u> o

BACK AT CAMP, Andrew scouted to make sure no one spotted them, and Kage and Jason tidied up from the crushed brush tracks for Isaac to pull the Jeep through the wood up to the caravan. They wanted to reconnect it so we could haul it out in the morning.

While Kage and Andrew were asking us about the druids, I was already looking around for Jed. It was the first time I'd wanted to talk to him. And the first time I couldn't find him.

"Where's Jed? And Zar?"

Kage shrugged.

"Could you elaborate?"

"What's wrong?" Kage crossed his arms.

"I'm sorry, Kage. I'm … happy to see you. I'm looking for Jed to ask a question."

"That you can't ask us?"

"Where is Jed?" I almost shouted.

Kage hunched his shoulders and frowned. "He and Zar changed to go over to the river."

"In broad daylight?"

"Keep your skin on. It's evening. They're around. So what'd you find out?"

"I found out you already had a prime suspect and didn't bother to mention it."

He tipped his head to one side. Andrew, though, also watching, didn't look like this was much of a shocker.

"The Beech Pack?" I snapped at Kage.

"Oh ... right. We're all supposed to act like there's nothing wrong with those carrion-eating tossers and they're not mad or anything."

"Is it true that Jed knows the most about them?"

"Should be." Kage shrugged. "Involved with them not too long ago."

"He was? He knows the pack?"

"He must. Ran with them for seasons, didn't he?"

"I wouldn't know." I glared at Kage. "That's why I'm asking you."

"If I understand correctly, Jed thought he'd picked out a mate from the Beeches," Andrew said. "It didn't end well. No idea why or what happened, though." He glanced at Kage, who shook his head.

"If you're wanting information out of Jed, you'll need more than putting his skin back on," Kage said. "Maybe strong drink and an electric goad."

"He won't talk about what happened because a female hurt his feelings?" I asked.

"Well—" Andrew chuckled. "If you talk to him like that he'll fess up, no problem."

I pushed a hand into my hair and stood there a moment. "You're right. That was uncalled for. I'm just frustrated that I was asked to help but no one bothered to give me half the information in this case. And there's more." I dropped my hand. "The druids believe there are wolves in London."

Andrew frowned at the leaves over his head.

"How?" Kage asked. "There can't be wolves in London. They'd go mad."

"That's what Jason said. But I think it's worth exploring since you already had a hunch this was wolves killing wolves. Maybe rebel packs like the Beeches. Maybe urban wolves who really are not right in the head. Could you let me know when Jed gets back? And ask him to change so he can talk to us."

"Sure, because he'll do whatever we ask," Kage said.

"Then just let me know. I'll speak to him." I retired to my trailer while Kage asked the others what else the druids had said.

Isaac filled them in on the two matching victims.

I'd only been inside a few minutes—bathroom, wash hands, wipe neck and face with a cold washcloth, still water left—when someone tapped at the door.

There were only two members of this company I could imagine tapping and one of them was currently running about the woods with claws and a tail.

"Hi, Jason." I opened the door.

"Are you all right?"

"All right?"

"Yeah…" He looked uncomfortable, dropping his gaze. "I didn't mean to be short with you."

"You didn't do anything wrong, Jason. I'm just tired. And now … I don't know…"

"That was the other thing. You … this isn't your fight. I know you're trying to help, to figure this out for us. But you did what you said you would."

"Funny how it doesn't feel like I've done anything. Only brought up more questions and brought you back to something you already knew."

"Sort of knew. The elders won't believe that wolves would turn on wolves. They're living in denial. They're living in a different century." He still didn't look at me.

"Do you want to sit down?" I remembered as I indicated the little table and bench that I had a question for him as well. This may not be the time.

Jason hesitated but I stepped back.

"Come on. No one has even a shred of evidence about this Beech Pack, do they? This really is only suspicion?"

He followed me to sit on the table bench. I sat on the edge of the bed, leaned forward and sipping from my water bottle.

"None of them have died as far as we know—not like they stay in touch other than a rare exchange with Diana."

"That's not evidence either. You think Jed knows them well?"

He nodded. "Digging a den, according to some. Convert and everything. All for some Beech female."

"Convert?"

Jason shrugged. "They don't think like us. The Beeches follow their own Moon."

"Religious differences are hardly a reason to suspect murder."

"It's not that. They're different, the way they live, and they hate us. That's what was so weird about Jed running with them. Usually, they won't let outside wolves around their territory. I don't think there are any other wolves in our packs who know anything about them the way Jed does. And I've never heard him talk about them."

"Surely for this—matter of life and death? If he knows something…"

Jason didn't answer. After a minute, he said, "Anyway, Cassia, I respect what you're doing. You didn't have to help us at all. But … you don't need to keep trying to solve this. You know that, right? We'll take you home tomorrow and we can tell Diana what we found out. Perhaps we'll…"

"Look for wolves in London?"

Shaking his head. "I just can't believe it could be true."

"Thank you, Jason. I know I'm not bound by a blood oath or signed into a contract. I only … if I can help you, I want to. I'll try to scry for London wolves and talk to Jed and … we'll go from there, okay?"

He looked at the tabletop. Watching him, I thought of hair and fur color—matching versus not. Jason's hair was as jet black as his fur had been. All around dark, lean, sinewy, brooding. It was hard to explain other than the hair, but, somehow, he did look a bit like the canine he'd been that morning. One striking difference was his eyes. Jason's eyes were even darker than Zar's, looking black in indoor light. Really a deep umber. In fur, however, they'd been bright gold—pure wolf eyes.

I thought again of all the questions I had for them about who and what they were, how it worked. This time, though, watching those eyes, how miserable he looked, I refrained from asking for entirely different reasons than before.

"Jason?" I said quietly after a pause. "What about you?"

He glanced up. "What about me?"

"Seems to me you're the one who's not all right. What's wrong?"

He looked out the open window, toward the camp clearing and site of last night's carnage and this morning's piles of fur. Kage, Isaac, and Andrew stood out there talking about the druid meeting and the Beeches.

When he didn't answer, I said, "Why are you here? Why did you come along?"

He rubbed the back of his neck, dragging his gaze from the window to my eyes. He always looked into my eyes when he did look at me. No wandering downward.

"I told you, I wanted to come with Kage."

"For real? That's the only reason you're here? Are you another close relation?"

His brows creased. He looked confused. "No ... we're involved."

"In what?"

He stared at me.

I stared back.

"In a relationship."

I still waited for the punchline.

Then I blinked. "You're *what?*"

*Jason doesn't care so he doesn't count.*

"You're gay?" I asked—bewildered, not as much by him, but by Kage.

"Sure," Jason said with a lift of one shoulder. "That's what humans say. Wolves still use gay like ... bright or cheerful." He smiled weakly.

"Why didn't you tell me?"

"Tell you?"

"I'm sorry, it's not like you owed me anything. I just wish I'd known. I—it's—" I took a step and slipped in across the table from him. "The world feels so much more normal thinking there are a mere five guys harassing me or showing off as opposed to six."

Jason laughed. "Glad to help ... if that does. I didn't know you cared. I wasn't trying to keep anything from you. Andrew says worms can be weird about that sort of thing. Wolves aren't fussed."

"It's never an issue for you—with your family or anyone—that you're gay?"

"Why would my family care who I sleep with? It's my life."

"I think that's a lovely point, but yes, he's right that humans can be ... weird. Would you mind telling me about something else, though? Kage? Because I didn't think I was that stupid with reading signs from a guy and I really thought he was interested in me."

"He is."

"Uh-huh." Once again, waiting for the punchline. "Could you fill me in a little? You're in a relationship with Kage?"

"Yeah."

"And he's into me?"

Jason nodded.

"And is this ... what? A normal part of your relationship? Him going after someone else? A female someone else? And you're okay with that? Maybe this is none of my business either but I'm feeling kind of involved here."

Jason rubbed the back of his neck again. "Not really. Females, yeah, sometimes. Kage doesn't go in for distinctions like that. Which is fine. I don't care. Only I guess I thought we were ... more ... settled."

"You thought you were in a committed relationship and that's not what he's thinking?"

Jason bit his lip. "We're committed. It's not a lost kill for him to like someone else. Moon knows we've had ups and downs. That's fine. He just gets distracted with something new like a pup spotting his own tail.

Once he's had a good chase and nip at that, he comes back. He knows I'll be around."

*Wow. That sounds like such an unhealthy relationship I don't even know how to answer you.*

"Okay," I said after way too long a pause. "Well, I'm sorry you're having a hard time with him. I don't know Kage well but I certainly understand that he can be difficult to deal with. And, I must say, I admire the way you're treating me. You've been nothing but civil to me and if I were involved with a guy who started chasing after another woman, the first thing I'd do would *not* be to apologize for existing and ask if she had enough drinking water."

Jason gave me a funny look. "It's not your fault Kage is attracted to you. I don't mind you being here. It's just uncertainty about where he and I stand that starts to feel like a problem."

"Maybe those are usual sentiments in a situation like this for wolves—if this is a 'usual' situation—but, believe me, for humans, that's radical thinking. We have murders in the human world for this kind of love triangle."

"Why?" Jason's eyes widened. "And who?"

"In a comparable dynamic? You, the first wife, would probably be the killer and I, the adulterous lover, would be the victim."

Now Jason chuckled. "Worms are mad. No offense."

"Maybe we are. But we worms weren't trying to tear each other apart last night. Don't forget that."

"Sorry. We'll keep it down tonight."

"Is that before or after skinning Andrew?"

"Andrew?"

"We drew attention today in the park."

"Oh." Jason didn't look much interested. "He can outrun Jed and Kage. He can outrun any of us by miles. He'll be okay. Cassia?" He looked around from the window again. "Do you mind if I change? Are you needing me to talk about what's going on tonight? I just ... I think I need a break."

"You're not going to go drown yourself in the river, are you?"

Another weak smile. "Maybe just a swim."

"Sure, Jason. I don't care if you change. Isaac and I know what was said. All I want tonight is information out of Jed. We can decide on the ride tomorrow what next steps you all need to take. If we can hear each other. Maybe keep the windows up some."

Speaking of road trips, that was why they were all more agreeable to Jason than to each other. They didn't see Jason as a threat in this competition they had going.

So five wanted Cassia? But one wanted Kage.

What did the seventh want?

I thought of Isaac and the necklace, Zar and the hidden coves, Andrew's tongue on my fingers. Then of getting away from this situation, Jason's reminding me of that reality, and of my sister and Brighton and those men she planned for me to meet.

To think, I'd imagined four men in one trip was ... wild.

Jason stood, still looking miserable, and I hugged him on impulse. He returned it, though touching me gently even as I felt the solid muscle of his abs and chest.

"I'm sorry about Kage. If there's anything I can do, or you want to talk, just..."

"Thanks." He gave a nod as he stepped away. When he pushed open the door, he stiffened and added, "Someone here who you're wanting to see."

## ○ CHAPTER 21 ○

NOT ONLY WOULD Jed not talk, he wouldn't even change into a two-footed form so he *could* talk.

After Isaac made a simple request, then Kage threatened him, I asked them to back off and leave him alone.

The sun was taking a last look over the land before twilight. Shadows of trees and ourselves ran on endlessly to the brush or dip to be cut off. These intense purple streaks and vivid golden light were nearly blinding, yet beautiful.

Zar retreated to change, presumably going to wherever he'd left his clothes. Kage grumbled and stalked away. Jason was gone. Isaac also left us. I approached Jed, who sat under the same tree Andrew had occupied that morning.

He was ... huge. His paws were not the size of my full hands with splayed fingers, but way bigger than simply my palm. His coat was not quite black like Jason's. It was chocolate, touched in white around his toes and a spot on his chest, then tipped in true black around his head, ruff, and back. Maybe it was the light, but it seemed he had golden hints in his undercoat as well, a mottling of shades to make what looked like a black wolf layered in an oil painting. His eyes were paler in fur than in skin. Soft brown and gold.

He was beautiful. As striking as the white wolf, though in very different ways.

Walking up to him made me so uneasy I felt my heartbeat quicken and my knees almost lock. But I'd gotten used to Jason in the Jeep and I knew I could get used to Jed if I gave myself a moment.

He sat stiffly, already put out because Kage had been ordering him to change so we could talk—as if Kage were silver. He glared as I approached, sitting upright, but with his head low and forward, hunched. I remembered Kage calling him vulture-face. He had the posture of one as he sat watching me.

Goddess, he was big. Noticeably larger than Jason in fur. He could have held my skull in his jaws.

I stopped several feet from him.

"Jed? You're very handsome in fur." I said it on impulse because it was honestly something I was thinking. Yet, the moment I did, I realized it would sound patronizing. Like I'd say it to butter him up and in a minute he'd be eating out of my hand.

Jed laid back his ears at my words, eyes narrowing more.

"I'm sorry," I said quickly. "But I mean it. You are. I'd had no idea you spent so much time this way. Do you change every night?" I stopped myself mentioning that Andrew had been telling me about him.

Jed's eyes softened, as well as his stiff posture, at least a bit. He studied me as I took a few more steps and sank to my bare knees on the ground. I was close enough that, if I stretched, I could have reached out to touch his fur.

"We talked with the druid. She doesn't know who's killing wolves. Only that it seems to be the same people who have murdered two druids. And she suspects ... other wolves."

His gold-flecked eyes flickered. His ears had eased forward.

"They say ... you're the only one who really knows the Beech Pack."

At mention of the Beeches, he lifted his lips from below his nose all the way back to his molars in a soundless gape that was much more alarming in your face than when you see something like it on a screen.

"Jed, please, if you know about them, if you think there's *any* chance they could be behind these killings—"

He started to growl. Expression the same, about a hundred white fangs staring me down, only adding a low growl in the back of his throat.

"Don't you want to know what's going on? To save your own people? If this pack could be dangerous, we need to know. If you have reason to think it's not them and we need to keep looking, we should know that also."

The growl moved forward, lifting in pitch, starting into a snarl as it neared his teeth.

"What are you going to do? Never tell anyone what you know? I'm sorry if you were hurt, if you had a bad experience with that pack, but that's something that could be important. Please, Jed."

The noise reached his mouth. His lifted lips quivered. His tongue shot between his teeth and back in a truly diabolical snarl while his head lowered more and his eyes rolled white to look up at me. He might have been a creature straight from the gates of hell.

I considered my breathing as my heart raced. I did not suppose Jed would really rip my face off. Yet ... might he? No, he just wanted to be left alone and he thought he could intimidate me.

"Jed," I said very calmly. "If this is painful for you maybe you could share your most basic observations about them? Just your thoughts on whether or not they could be involved. You can just talk to me. You don't have to involve everyone else."

His eyes flickered again. The volume lowered a bit.

"I know something about breakups," I said quietly. "With someone you thought was the one, right? That's what makes them the worst. If it's just any old guy, you move on. Any old female and you go sniff out another. But sometimes it's not. Sometimes you find that special fit. That other spirit who gets you, who walks through your dreams, touches your soul, holds your heart in the palm of her hand."

His lips still quivered, but the volume had definitely subsided.

I heard voices and steps of the others behind me. Rucksacks zipping, doors opening and slamming. The last vestiges of sunlight were only in treetops now.

"That's why they hurt the most," I continued. "That's why we don't get over them. We can move on and have new relationships. But we never really forget them. Not that sort.

"You don't have to tell me anything about her. Now or ever. I'm trying to help your people, though, Jed. And what would help, right now, is a little feedback about this rebel pack and hearing your take on them. I don't know if they're killers or not. You probably don't either. I'm not saying one way or another they're good or bad, right or wrong. I just want to know more. Do you think you can help? Just talk with me?

"Want to come inside and sit down? But change and put something on first? I'd really appreciate it if you'd be willing."

His gaze drifted to the trailer some distance behind me, his growl gone.

Then his eyes widened. Noise returned with a fresh snarl.

In the same moment, I heard the footsteps, and Zar's voice. "Bloody hell, Jed!" He'd seen Jed showing me his teeth and was jogging over.

"Stop it, Zar—leave him alone!"

Jed sprang to his feet, mouth open, tongue flicking out, ears back.

"Sod off!" Zar shouted at Jed. "What's wrong with you? She's the one we're protecting."

"No, Zar, it was just a misunderstanding. We're fine. Leave him—"

All happening in a blink of Zar dashing in and Jed leaping up and me still on the ground, only able to protest.

Zar threw out his arm in a sweeping point, *Get out of here.*

I threw out my own to catch him.

Instead of fleeing, Jed sprang to bite his brother. And he got me instead.

## ○ <u>Chapter 22</u> ○

THERE WAS A WHACKING impact that made me feel I'd been hit with a bat, the force throwing me onto my back, and a sharp pain bursting from my arm. Even in the first second I thought how ironic that I'd been nervous about them and they'd only hurt me because of the others.

In an instant, Jed leapt clear and dashed into the woods. Zar and I were shouting, me at him, him after Jed.

Isaac, Andrew, and Kage ran over.

"Leave it!" I yelled at Zar as he was trying to look at my arm. "What the hell is wrong with you? Jed was fine!"

"Why are you mad at me? He's the one who just bit you!"

"He didn't bite me! He bit *you*. My arm just happened to be there! Get your hands off me."

Zar retreated while I scrambled to my feet, taking Isaac's hand instead as everyone was trying to figure out what happened.

It was too dark for a good look at my arm but there was no gushing blood.

After more shouting—Kage wanting to track Jed, but Andrew getting in on dressing Zar down when he'd figured out what happened, which made me feel better in a perverse way—and Isaac taking me back to the trailer, we assessed the damage.

"It's nothing." I washed my arm in the sink while Isaac held the lantern. "It's not even bleeding."

One slight puncture wound where a tooth had struck the skin hard enough to crack through. But the whole bite had been a ram. Jed must have realized what he was hitting as he made contact and jumped back. He certainly hadn't tried to bite down. A punch with teeth. Agonizing right now, and there would be bruising on the inside of my forearm—not great for my beach look—but that was it.

I told Isaac this and he left the lantern to get something from the Jeep. Then Kage was at the door, asking gruffly if I was all right. I heard claws on the metal step and looked around to Jason poking his head in.

"It was an accident," I assured them. "Jed snapped at Zar and I reached up at the wrong time. That's it. Please leave Jed alone."

Isaac brought a tube of arnica ointment, which was a relief as I realized I had scant first aid material in my overnight kit.

Zar came to apologize but I told them all to clear out—the show was over. Only Isaac remained rubbing in the arnica with a fingertip, going over the bruised skin with a gossamer touch from his large, powerful hands.

I sighed and rubbed my temples. "He was going to talk to me. Now that's that. And I thought Zar was supposed to be the brains of the operation. At least in some things."

"He was worried for your safety," Isaac said quietly. "Jed is dangerous."

"We were fine. He wouldn't hurt me."

"He just did."

"It wasn't his fault. What? You think I'm a soft touch and a bleeding heart? 'Oh that poor brute, he didn't mean to hurt anyone'? He *wasn't* going to hurt anyone. We were fine."

Isaac nodded, saying nothing.

"You're not going to make a thing about this, are you? You and Kage? I'm telling you, he didn't mean to hurt me and if you go after him, he's just going to be more upset. So am I. Leave him alone and I'll try to talk to him again tomorrow."

He capped the tube and left it on the table.

"Isaac? Will you promise you won't give him a hard time about this?"

Isaac stepped back. He made the trailer seem even smaller. "No," he said quietly. "I won't. But I'll tell the others what you said. Moon bless." He left.

*Goddess.*

Afraid to stay in, I went to sit on the metal step a minute later. I rested the lantern on the ground out before me instead of a campfire, pretending it was one, wishing I had another cup of tea and scone from Ellasandra.

I only saw Zar and Andrew talking beside the Jeep by the time I emerged.

Jason trotted up to me from the gloom. He sat against me with his chin on my knees, ears sagging to the sides as I absently stroked his head.

"If I go in to bed, will they go tearing after Jed?" I asked him in a whisper.

Zar and Andrew came over. Zar sat cross-legged beyond the lantern and Andrew hung back beside the trailer to my right.

"I'm sorry, Cassia—"

"Forget it, Zar. Did Jed take off?"

"Right there." Andrew jerked his head.

I had to squint, making out only the glint of the dark wolf's eyes just where he'd been before, sitting below the tree, now with night settled around him.

"We have a long day tomorrow." I addressed the group at large. "Maybe you all wouldn't mind actually sleeping tonight?"

"Steady on," Andrew said. But he grinned.

"Sound like a wild idea?" I asked.

Jason nudged my negligent hand and I rubbed him behind the ears, which he leaned into.

Two pale shapes paced into reach of the lantern's glow from the wood out beyond the Jeep. Both large, one much paler than the other. I didn't look that way, only seeing them from the corner of my eye. Jed remained where he was, watching me. If they would clear out of Subway maybe they would respect me on this as well.

"Tomorrow," I said, "let's get an early start. If we're not gone by sunrise someone might see us sneaking out." I suppressed a yawn.

Zar nodded without looking at me, shoulders hunched. He was making me feel like I should be the one apologizing.

Jason turned to sit up on his haunches with his forepaws crossed on my knees. I rubbed his chest with the back of my hand. He didn't seem so intimidating anymore. His fur was remarkable with its deep thickness. I longed to bury both hands in it. And, as fresh night chill settled over the wood, I remembered freezing last night and wished I really could.

"In the morning, or once we're back with your people—at some point that feels right—I'll scry for you. With a new clear intention, I may be able to see if, and where, there could be London wolves. Or if wolves are really who we're after at all. Right now I'm too tired." I sighed as Jason licked my bruised arm. Not on the bruise, though, where the ointment was, but above the tender area. That had to be clear thinking.

Just like their sense of smell was sharper and they were able to growl like wild animals in their upright skin forms, they had holdover from that form into their fur as well. Enough to keep Isaac and Kage from trying to kill Jed the moment I went inside?

"Okay." It took me a minute to stand as Jason kept nudging into my hand and I relented in stroking his face. "Good night. And please don't hurt each other." I grabbed the lantern, using my left arm rather than the painful right.

Zar scrambled to his feet with me, still looking anxious. "Moon bless, Cassia. I hope you're all right."

"I'll be fine with a good night's sleep." *Not that it's possible here.*

Jason wagged his tail after me while I slipped inside and shut the door in his face—so ready for bed maybe I really would sleep. But I'd hardly latched it when the fight started.

## ○ C̲h̲a̲p̲t̲e̲r̲ ̲2̲3̲ ○

It wasn't Isaac or Kage.

Jed had Jason by the neck when I threw the door open. Jason yelped and snarled back, kicking with his hind legs, struggling to get his face around and bite into Jed's while Jed crushed him into the trailer tire and dirt with superior weight.

As I jumped from the trailer, dropping the lantern and gathering the magic, Kage bounded in at Jed, making a noise like a lion, fur on end and teeth flashing.

I was so angry with Jed it went beyond his jumping on Jason the moment my back was turned—just because I'd given Jason attention. The anger was also how I'd defended him. Of course he hadn't meant to bite me. But, either in spite of, or because of this, one way or another, I'd expected him to feel bad about it. This was no remorse. This was—as Andrew had warned me—a proper bastard.

All this anger channeled into the energy as I rushed out. Kage—large as Jed, looking like a classically marked timber wolf—was midair going for Jed when I hit Jed first.

The magic was a ball of tightly coiled electricity; fury, my own pain, injustice, vengeance, and fear for Jason. It exploded from my hands like a shotgun blast.

Almost silent, yet causing a ripple in the air like a sonic boom. And almost invisible, yet leaving a flash of light and color that seemed more like a blink gone wrong than a real image. And entirely energy: a feel beyond any sight, sound, or smell.

It thundered into Jed's face and sent him flying across the clearing, along with Kage. I didn't see Andrew, but Zar ducked and the white wolf crouched as Jed plowed through the dirt, ripping brush, smashing into a tree trunk and finally stopping with an agonized final yelp in his howl of terror as he'd gone flying. Kage, not hit as hard, bashed into a tree and staggered.

Jed struggled to get his paws under him, gasping and whimpering.

Jason cowered at my feet, flat in the dirt.

Zar stepped back, staring from Jed to me, eyes like plates in the weak light. Andrew had run up from the right, his shirt in his hands. He didn't come in close, staring at us. Isaac's eyes, the white wolf, reflected the toppled lantern's glow as he backed away. So did Kage's. He pressed himself into underbrush, tail between his legs.

Jed shook himself and staggered, almost falling.

Jason trembled violently, panting.

Except for much ragged breathing, the campsite fell silent.

All six watched me, most moving away, but slowly, inching, in fact. All eyes wide, bodies tense as tripwires.

Afraid.

It was the first time it struck me that they had this particular wolfish trait beyond the surface. Deep down, they were afraid of humans. Avoidance and dislike did not come from inherent hate, but inherent fear. For all their mockery, it only took a look around to know humans were the world's top predator.

And magic. Not being magic users themselves, never having associated with casters, they had no idea what I might be capable of.

I stood straight beyond the doorway in the eerie white glow, light to my back, and faced them while their eyes gleamed in the dark wood.

"The fighting on this trip is over." My own voice surprised me, very firm and calm.

No one moved.

I looked down. "Are you okay?"

Wobbly, Jason pushed himself to a standing position. He tried a faltering step, then leaned into my leg, holding up his left forepaw.

I bent to feel his arm, my own still aching. Hot, sticky blood smeared my fingers.

Angry all over again, I turned back for the door. "Come on."

Jason held his left forepaw clear of the ground as he hopped after me and up into the trailer.

I locked the door, set the lantern on the low counter by the sink, then ran water into the washcloth to wipe over his wounds.

I sat on the edge of the table bench while he sat on his tail on the floor with his left paw out to me, watching me with big, soulful eyes.

"You're not going to bite me if I hurt you, are you?" I asked.

Jason licked my hand.

I found a gash on his forearm and cuts around his face, including a slash above his left eye and a bleeding left ear. I dabbed these off and held the cloth in place against his arm until bleeding stopped. It all appeared superficial. Not exactly a broken arm.

As I rinsed the cloth the water stopped.

Still bottles of water for in the morning and I could use the toilet once more, but...

"Getting out of here not a moment too soon," I told him as I returned.

Jason nosed my wrist.

I hadn't realized how much I'd been petting him—how he'd been soliciting it—until that fight had erupted the moment I'd turned my back. With Jed, of course, having watched the whole time, waiting for his chance to commit a murder while that was supposed to be what we were preventing.

"Did you want Jed to pummel you?" I asked, holding the washcloth over his eye.

Jason pinned back his ears.

"What then? I wasn't thinking about distributing attention, but I bet you were. Is it Kage?"

His ears eased forward.

"You want to make Kage jealous? I don't think Kage sees you as a threat when it comes to me. You could stay in here all night and he'd probably not be terribly bothered. Do you want him to be jealous of me? Not you?" I sat back, removing the washcloth from his face.

He cocked his head.

"You know that's a horrible idea, right? Deliberately trying to provoke jealousy in anyone is first of all not a good sign of a healthy relationship and, second, not a healthy thing to do around here in particular."

Jason rested his chin on my knee.

I held the cloth against the oozing cut over his eye, glad he wasn't too scared of me now to do this.

I didn't say anything about the magic or humans.

Soon shivering, I remembered last night: wretched cold, lack of sleep.

"You'll live. But do you want to stay in here to guarantee you'll make it through the night?" My teeth chattered.

I shut the window looking out to the noise zone and the tiny one over the bed. This left one for ventilation but the place hadn't aired out much. I couldn't bring myself to close them all.

Jason lay on the floor with his back to me, chin on his paws, while I changed and quickly brushed my teeth. Since I'd gone when we'd gotten back, I could wait to pee again until morning. I hoped.

I started out with socks on this time and pulled up the wool blanket and my hoodie as an extra cover.

"Okay." When I lay down, I slid over on the bed as far as I could without crowding the wall. The space was tight, seeming more so in the dark.

The great creature leapt with surprising lightness onto the platform, pinning the duvet against me. I resettled as he tried to turn in a circle, hunched against the ceiling that I'd hit my head on. He gave it up after one awkward turn and flopped alongside me to lick his forearm.

I stroked his unhurt right ear, on my side to face him, already warming when I pressed in close and buried my hands and face against his ruff. He smelled like pine and earth and wild places, though we weren't in a pine forest.

He heaved a sigh and stretched out his neck, resting his head against the edge of the pillow. I remembered how disconcerting it had been this morning even to look into his eyes or see him close up. It seemed like a long time ago.

How strange this vacation was. Alice tumbling down the rabbit hole. Already in Wonderland? Or was this only the fall?

Cream tea. I'd had a real English cream tea. And I must be the only human woman in the world right now in bed with a gay werewolf.

My right arm throbbed.

I hung onto Jason's fur, inhaled, and noticed how quiet camp was. Like a grave.

I hadn't even had a chance to talk with Zar about London wolves or Beech Packs, or any thoughts from him on the idea that wolves could be doing this to wolves. He was the one who might have the most general insights. He should know if there had ever been other cases like this. But I still wasn't feeling kindly disposed toward Zar.

As to talking with Jed tomorrow, now I wasn't feeling kindly toward him either. I should have known better—even if Jason had meant to be a fool. I shouldn't have sat there stroking him like a mindless human with her pet dog.

Such thoughts trailed past as I lay there, already drifting off.

I should have been glad to think of my freedom tomorrow. I should have looked forward to seeing the back of them: returning to Melanie and getting on with my vacation. Should have. Instead, I dreaded having to say goodbye.

# ○ <u>Chapter 24</u> ○

Tall spires of black buildings, snapping teeth and running paws, a field bathed in blood, flash of fangs, blistering smoke. A wave washed away the standing stones, turning to blood, filling eyes, mouth, lungs. A jagged howl ripped through the night.

Something touched my nose and I jumped awake, gasping. My arms were clasped around a hot bearskin rug. I was covered in sweat, yet trembling. Fur and warm breath pressed my face.

Jason panted in the dark, hot and nervous.

I pushed myself into a sitting position, careful about the ceiling. I peeled off the sweaty socks and rolled up my pajama bottoms, then fanned the tank top from my midriff.

The black outline of Jason lay there on the edge of the bed like the Sphinx, head up, eyes closed, still panting.

I pried the window open beside me, welcoming the breeze and cool night. Not nearly so cold as last night.

"Sorry," I whispered, wrapping my arms around my knees. I dropped my head against them.

He touched my arm with his muzzle, whiskers tickling my skin.

"Vivid dreams are a blessing of the seer. That's what my grandmother used to say. 'Blessed with the sight, do not expect limits to your gift and you will find none.' So much of my education with her was about sight. And so much of all my education was about … not using it." I paused, swallowing, and sat back.

Once I felt cooled enough, I settled into the duvet with the wool blanket and my hoodie pushed aside.

Jason's head remained over me in the dark.

"It's so quiet tonight," I whispered. "I didn't mean to scare you with magic. I don't use magic in my normal life. It was all 'gift' and 'blessing' and 'connection to Goddess' from Nana on the one hand, while the other hand bore the constant refrain, 'Hide it, hide it, hide it.' If we're so blessed … why are we hiding? If we're so divine … why are we ashamed? Because that's what it feels like. Like hiding a crime—a heritage that could destroy you.

"I was ready to stop before this—commit to living mundane. Looking forward to it, in fact. I would hold a place in my heart for those memories, that time with my mother and grandmother, learning with two great witches, but set it aside. Grow out of magic, if you like. And, when I have my own children, pray to Goddess they have no natural talent whatsoever and I never bring up the subject with them. A normal, mundane family in the normal world."

I sighed and shut my eyes in the dark, still speaking in a whisper. "No one had ever asked me to do anything with my magic before this. I mean, a couple of lectures, being part of support groups. But … this… I thought I wanted to help because I felt horrible about what was happening to you. If anyone came to me, any group to help people or animals… What are we here for if we can't do something for each other and our planet? If we can't leave something a bit better than how we found it when we came into this lifetime?"

I looked to the starlit window just above us. "But I might have been wrong. I may only be out here now for selfish reasons. Because no one had ever asked me to really be a witch before. At most, a magic teacher. Not a witch. Never in my life."

Jason rested his chin on my chest and I stroked his head behind the cuts.

"Your pack was brave to reach out. Even if some didn't agree to do it—and the methods used by the two who came to recruit me were asinine. I'm only sorry … I haven't been much help." I rubbed the soft tip of his slightly rounded ear between thumb and forefinger. "If you can find wolves in London, whether they're killers or not, maybe they'll be able to help you more."

Jason moved his head off my chest to stretch his neck on the pillow, his nose in my hair. I rolled on my side to face him, arm across his back, but I was afraid to sleep again, and I lay there a long time, thinking of eyeless, bled out, staked bodies covered in gasoline.

Werewolves and human druids. Both part of the magical community, yet totally different. Both living lives removed from humans to some extent, closer to nature, keeping to their own.

Who would want both dead? City-dwelling wolves who hated the old ways?

Or humans.

Casters? Why?

Mundane humans who had found out? Who knew, somehow, how to find wolves? Top predator humans. Humans who had already caused the extinction of hundreds of species. Confused humans who might have superstitions playing in to make them stake hearts and carve out eyes—make sure their job was done.

I found that idea more terrifying than the thought that there were werewolves living in London.

At last, exhaustion won.

I woke in gloom to cold and songbirds encouraging the morning. And an apparent man beside me in bed.

Jason had changed into his skin in the night. This was unsettling, bringing on a disquieting *What did I do last night?* feeling as if I'd been on a bender.

Indeed, my head ached, my arm felt like a horse had kicked it, and I was stiff and achy all over—hungry, tired, mouth sticky. Dehydration I suspected was some of that. Ironic since I really had to pee.

The trailer remained so dark, Jason was mere profile and soft details like a sketch with very little pressure used on the pencils. All the same, that profile was beautiful, elegant. Not as solidly built as Kage, not as elfin and unbelievable as Andrew, but in between the two.

Gray outside the windows foretold we had an hour before sunrise. Even so, time to get moving.

Jason lay on his back, looking at the ceiling, listening to birdsongs. Maybe more? How well could they hear? I detected the river only faintly in the background, birds close, as if in the trailer with us. Nothing more.

I turned my face into the pillow to yawn. "You okay? I don't see any blood." Looking at him again and rubbing my eyes.

"Cassia?" He also turned his head, bringing our noses close as he looked at me. "What do the standing stones mean?"

I shivered, thinking of my first vision scrying for them and the stone circles in my dreams. Until the dreams, I'd almost forgotten the stones through this treasure hunt.

"What?"

"Why did you keep talking about standing stones?" Jason whispered.

"I don't know what you mean. I didn't mention stones." Or ... had I? No ... I did recall going rather maudlin last night, waking from nightmares. But not a word about stones.

Jason looked at the ceiling again, brows creased. "You did. You kept saying, 'We'll just find the standing stones.' Or similar. Off and on all night."

"Was that before or after me waking up all sweaty and giving you a witch sob story about needing to give up magic?"

He looked at me again and his expression cleared to a soft smile. "I don't remember any 'sob story.'"

"I dreamed about the stones. I'll look. I should scry again this morning. I was so distracted by the time we found her, I didn't think to ask Ellasandra about stone circles."

"You can ask Zar. Maybe it's still important. But I can tell you that you're wrong about one thing. You've been a big help. We're going to keep tracking the murderer and we have something to go on now with your help."

"I can do better." I turned my face into the pillow again. "Sorry about last night. Keeping you up and ... I don't know why I started oversharing."

"You didn't. You just don't have anyone to talk to. I like to listen, so it works out."

"I have Melanie. And friends at home. I didn't need to go all therapy on you."

"Does your sister know you're a witch?" He waited, then, "Because that's not really the same…"

Living lies. No true friends. Or any other kinds of relationships. I'd never even had a lover who'd known what I was. Not that I'd had loads of those. But I'd cared enough in a couple cases that each lie I'd let drop carried a little bereavement.

"Could you hand me my water bottle?" I asked. "And what about you? You're okay?"

I looked at him as he leaned to grab the water. In dim light, I saw only pink marks above his eye and on his arm. Healed wounds that looked like they wouldn't even leave scars.

"I had to change to get then to close up."

"Your shape-changing heals wounds?"

"Sure, we reform, don't we? Broken bones are a problem. And serious wounds make shifting impossible, or deadly."

"I didn't know." I drank, rinsing my mouth out, wishing I could spit, and offered him the bottle. "Is that why you all act so invincible?"

Jason smiled. "Wolves can be killed like any other mortal. Only we'll take more damage on our way down —and can potentially heal so rapidly that daft legends like silver bullets get started. If you're proper torn up, though, and try to shift, throwing your insides around, you'll end up losing some. We're still only mortal. Or we wouldn't be here having this conversation."

"But the way they've been killed? If it's not necessary to take those steps to kill a werewolf…" I shook my head. "Maybe I should ask Zar more about legends and myths. Who would think they needed to stake a werewolf and a druid like vampires?"

"Someone … ignorant." He looked away.

I took a slow breath. "I also thought of mundanes doing this but ... let's hold off on that. There are other possibilities to explore. Even the idea that mundanes could find your packs ... hard to imagine."

And if they could? If they knew how to track and kill and protect themselves against werewolves?

"It's best to focus on what we do know," I said. "Not go off in random directions."

"That's how Diana talks about the Beeches." Jason sighed and dragged a hand over his face. "But one's got to be right. It's either shifters or humans. It's not unicorns."

"What about undead? Those stakes..."

"There are no vampires around us."

"There are 'no wolves in London' either. Let's take this piece by piece."

"Touché." He dropped his hand over the side of the bed and grinned at me.

"Get up so I can. We need to wake everyone and get out of here."

"They're awake." Jason rolled to sit up, hunched to avoid the ceiling. He was naked, of course. With the wool blanket slipping off him, he stretched his arms.

"They are?"

"Uh-huh." He yawned and rubbed his hair back and forth. The muscles of his back and arms were so deft, so ideal, he looked like a Roman statue enhanced.

He was on another yawn when someone knocked at the flimsy door. "Morning, princess." Kage's voice came clearly through the window. "We're trying to uncurl early but didn't want to disrupt your beauty sleep."

Jason walked to the door. I didn't care much about watching him, already mad.

"You male chauvinist pig, Kage." I scrambled from bed in my tank and pajama bottoms to follow, slipping into flip-flops. "All you have to do is say morning and you're ready to go."

But Jason waved a hand at me, unlocking the door for Kage. "He's not talking to you."

I hesitated, standing against the table.

"Missed you last night," Kage said, stepping up as Jason opened the door.

"You did?" Jason sounded suspicious.

Kage was dressed in his old jeans and scuffed boots, nothing else. He kissed Jason on the mouth as he moved into the threshold.

"Fancy you smelling like a lady—taking after your brother." Kage encircled his bare waist with one arm, stepping sideways.

Jason had started to answer when Kage yanked him off balance and Jason staggered out the door. In a flash, Kage had the door shut: *wham* and the whole trailer shook.

"Kage!" I shouted.

But one punch from outside was all Kage allowed. He opened the door, grabbed Jason's arm, and pulled him back in with his nose streaming crimson.

Zar was muttering out there and I caught a glimpse of Jed—who must have been the one waiting to punch Jason—in the doorway.

"What did I tell you? " I yelled at Kage while he slammed the door. "No more fights!"

"That wasn't a fight." Kage laughed. "Jason knows how it is. Get these things over with and move on— since he wasn't able to enjoy our night out." Kage turned his head to lick blood off Jason's upper lip while Jason was still blinking and dazed.

"Did he break it?" I went for the washcloth in the sink.

"It's all right." Jason breathed through his mouth.

"Kage, what the hell is wrong with you? What kind of thing—?" I'd forgotten I had to wet the cloth from the water bottle.

"You don't want us fighting later," Kage said. "And don't want us to settle differences quickly. What do you want?"

"No bloodshed! I don't feel like that's too much to ask!"

Which Kage was still licking from Jason's lips as it trickled unchecked from his nose. It was a bizarre sight even by standards of this trip, unsettling to watch.

"I don't want him to get hurt," Kage said. "But we need a moment to clear up hard feelings or we'll not get anything done today. You can't show him all this favoritism and not think anyone else is going to notice."

"Show him favoritism!? He was *hurt!* He has been kind to me and I was kind in return. Maybe you should all try it if you're jealous. And stop that! You're not going to help by drinking his blood. It needs pressure."

I shoved the washcloth at Kage and he lifted that to Jason's face instead.

Jason had his breath back and was grinning. Also a disconcerting sight. He flinched at the touch of the washcloth, then pressed his hand over Kage's to hold the pressure.

"Saved your clothes," Kage murmured in his ear, his lips also bloody. "Jed would have ripped them up. I had to get all our stuff into the Jeep and keep him out. No fighting, of course." Giving me a quick smile: *See what good wolves we are?* Noticing what I was wearing for the first time, his gaze lingered on my breasts.

"Thank you." Jason kissed his wrist, all he could reach with the white and red mottled washcloth there, and chuckled, apparently at the pleasant image.

"Does this not bother you, Jason?" I asked. "What he did?"

"He had to do something," Jason said happily. "I couldn't have just walked out there after being in here all night. He was trying to help, like he said—clear the air quickly."

"Right. Helping. Well, he's a hero, isn't he?"

"Come on, Cassia." Jason's voice was muffled, but took on a wheedling note all the same. "He didn't mean any harm."

"You just keep telling yourself that. And *you*—" At Kage. "Get out of here and take care of him. I'll be ready to go in fifteen minutes."

I locked the door the moment they were out.

Soon after, I was dressed, packed, still angry, and wishing they were just a bit *more* afraid of witches. My arm ached, a purple patch on pale skin, but seemed to be all right. My head still hurt, my back was sore, and I really needed my coffee.

I stepped out with my backpack on and the same outfit from yesterday.

A bit of color caught my eye and I looked around to see more bluebells, along with little white and pink wildflowers I could not identify, on my step. They'd been crushed with the coming and going on that step this morning but I picked them up to poke into the mesh side pouch of my bag.

Andrew rushed to the trailer and I stopped stiffly to face him. Zar hurried to follow. Kage and Jason, dressed, were reconnecting the trailer, which I'd thought they sorted out yesterday. Isaac was cleaning up more tire tracks. Jed leaned against that same tree, arms crossed, scowling as he watched us.

Not Kage or Jason bringing flowers in the night. Of the rest ... my money was still on Zar, yet I wondered.

"Cassia, I have a confession to make," Andrew said seriously as he stepped up. "I've got to tell you the truth. No more dodging."

"Okay..." I watched him suspiciously.

Zar reached his side, bumping into him.

Andrew took a deep breath, stealing himself. "Moon knows I should have told you sooner. I'm gay."

I stared at him.

"Both of us," Zar said.

"Always." Andrew threw his left arm around Zar's shoulders.

"Yes." Zar nodded somberly. "Years and years. You know ... poets and ... I write songs."

"He loves it when I braid his hair," Andrew said.

More nodding, both clearly struggling to come up with details that would sound convincing.

"And Andrew..."

"I have on female underpants right now," Andrew said.

I still only stared at them.

Andrew kissed Zar, his mouth open. Zar grabbed his head in both hands, returning it. They broke apart, panting, to beam at me like Cheshire Cats.

Silence.

Isaac, Jason, Kage, and even Jed watched with interest.

Finally, I said, "Nice try," and walked on to get in the passenger seat.

A scuffle behind me, one shoving the other.

"Get your paws off me," Zar muttered.

"Moon curse your hide, Jay," Andrew hissed.

Jason chuckled appreciatively, as he had about his injury, while he helped with the trailer.

I still hadn't scried. I couldn't get my head in it. Stop for a break first, coffee on the way out of the county. Then take a quiet moment in the trailer and look with the magic. Maybe look for standing stones.

This, with the sun up and leaving Cornwall behind, I did.

Which turned out to be a smart move. After that, we weren't heading back to Brighton at all.

# ○ Chapter 25 ○

I SAW IMAGES OF stone circles, great church towers, ancient city skylines, more stones, blood trickling down them into pools, a horizon of fire and black smoke that filled my lungs and nose until I was coughing in the trailer and had to stop.

I escaped into fresh air of the car park and a surprised bunch of wolves who hadn't expected me to emerge so quickly.

That wasn't scrying. It was the dreams, visions, twisting images. Either my own mindset or something about what I was seeking blocked me.

Magic users could create blocks, of course. But there were other things. Hangovers like spirits bound to old houses, for example. It could be a devilishly tricky thing to scry a haunted house. At best, confusing as you got mixed signals. What was flesh? What was spirit?

So, while disconcerted, I wasn't totally thrown. It would just need more work and a proper thoughtful spell and ritual on my part. What really bothered me was the crossover. I'd never received dream images from scrying before. Or the other way around. This was something I didn't know. Something I needed to ask Nana about. But that time had passed.

The stones. Jason had said I talked about them in my sleep, even though I'd never been a sleep-talker that I'd known of. Had I been a bit awake? Yet I didn't remember wakings besides the one that had me spilling my guts to him for reasons unknown.

I remained upset with him for acting like Kage had just been playful by nearly getting Jason's nose broken. But I was also glad to see that Jason appeared to be in much better spirits today than he'd been in since I'd known him. Maybe in werewolf relationships cleaning up a bloody wound with your tongue was a good way to strengthen bonds and show affection.

I still wanted to talk to Jed about the Beeches. And I wanted to talk to Zar about stone circles. But Jed had chosen today to ride in the trailer instead of the Jeep and Zar was the only member of the company willing to join him and leave room for the rest. That meant I hadn't spoken to either all morning—since Zar's dog and pony act with Andrew.

I addressed him in the car park while the six of them lounged about the curb or sat in the Jeep with the doors open. At least I had coffee, doing much to bolster my spirits.

"Zar, do you know if there are stone circles around here?"

"Sure there are." He proceeded to tell me about Hurlers and Duloe stone circles, and Avebury, circles in Wales and circles on the coast, cairns and standing stones with ancient ties to all kinds of peoples. Not only druids, but all magical sorts could be found to have connections with such structures if you went back far enough or believed the folklore.

This was interesting. More connection. But it didn't actually help.

I tried to listen to him, sipping my bitter coffee while my mind wandered.

Jed, squeezing a thick woolen ball that looked like a dog toy in his hands, stepped into the trailer, ready to go. He'd avoided me all morning. This only made me want to talk to him more, even to say I wasn't upset about last night—Jason aside. It had been an accident. It wasn't his fault. I had no idea if this was bothering him, though, or he was only making a special effort to avoid me because he didn't want to hear the name Beech Pack again.

Kage sat in the back seat of his Jeep, looking bored and irritable. Jason leaned against the side of the vehicle, one foot on the tire behind him, chewing a stalk of grass. He'd brought it with him. We were now surrounded by paved lots and brick walls. I'd noticed they all chewed grass now and then. If one plucked some it seemed to make the rest want a sample.

Isaac stood watching me, though I wasn't doing anything. Andrew sat against the trailer's bumper, also chewing on something. He had a plastic drinking straw balanced across his nose. He wore glasses today that I'd never seen. Not his sunglasses, but sleek prescription ones.

"And there are more up north. They're all over the British Isles. I can get more information for you. Atarah would help. What is it you're looking for?"

"That's the question, isn't it?" I shut my eyes. "There may be something about standing stones that's important after all. Maybe if I could just see one of them ... that energy."

"Moon! What the hell?"

I looked around.

Zar wiped a paper spit wad out of his long hair. "*Verus busipa,* Andrew!"

Andrew was already back to balancing the straw on his nose.

"Stonehenge."

I looked to my right.

Isaac gazed calmly at me, having spoken only one word in his soft voice, yet taking in this crowd all the same.

"Oh," Zar said, sounding confused, still pawing his hair. "Sure. There's Stonehenge. A bit obvious, though. It's not like it's accessible to perform rituals or anything. You can't even walk up to Stonehenge these days."

"How close can you get?" I asked.

"It's only roped off," Isaac said. "Close. You just have to stay on the path a bit back from it. You can still go right around."

"You've been?"

He nodded.

"How long from here?"

"Hour and a half, perhaps?"

"Let's go," I said.

Isaac climbed back in the driver's seat.

"What?" Zar asked. "To Stonehenge? It's a tourist trap now."

"I can live with that—*Andrew.*"

He had lifted the straw to his lips while Zar was turned to face me. At my word of warning, Andrew twirled the plastic in his fingers and Zar whipped around to glare at him.

We set out, heading north and east rather than due east. Isaac knew where he was going.

He asked about my arm but didn't seem surprised by the bruise as some of them had—as if it should have healed by now.

Behind my seat, Andrew went through a marked deck of cards with Jason for tricks he played on hotel guests. Jason helped him refine a new one that involved smelling which card they'd touched. These card games distracted them so he could lift their wallets, which he did in order to return them—"found" by himself—to their rooms later and collect tips from the grateful guests. Jason shared his little stash of fresh woodland grass with Andrew and Kage.

Like having the kids in the back playing road games and eating cookies.

"Grass?" Jason offered me some.

"When you say that to humans it sounds like you're talking about marijuana," I said.

"Sorry, just the standard kind."

"I didn't mean I wanted ... never mind." I sighed and accepted a blade of grass from him. "Thank you, Jason. That was thoughtful." I offered it to Isaac.

He shook his head, watching the motorway, smiling a bit. I wondered if he was thinking we had the kids in the back as well.

"How much do you get from those people in tips?" I asked, looking around to them.

"A fiver, a ten. Never know," Andrew said. "One chap gave me fifty quid and an old lady left me a hundred when she checked out."

"Aren't there cameras in the hotel?"

"I'm just borrowing, darling. I give everything back. I don't want their old bones."

I had to think about that, nibbling grass, which didn't really go with coffee flavor. "That is a disconcerting expression."

"Old dry bones no one wants anymore," Andrew said. "You know. You might say you didn't want that old rubbish or useless junk."

They made so many references to carcasses in some form it grew morbid.

I changed the subject. "Why do you have on glasses? Have you been wearing contacts?"

Andrew made a face. "Wolves aren't supposed to have bad eyes."

Jason smiled. "Sore subject. No natives of the Sable Pack are long-sighted. Andrew joined us from the Aspens. Wolves don't have all the health problems humans do. Good eyes, good teeth, as a rule, heart disease, diabetes, most STDs, and many other things are unknown in wolves. But what's the use in boasting when you're nearly gone anyway?"

I assumed he must mean farsighted when he said long-sighted.

"That's the spirit." I faced forward again, looking to Isaac. "So where are you from? Besides just north?"

"A long story."

"I think we have time."

Isaac smiled, glanced at me and ahead again. "Briefly, my forebears were from Iceland. More recently from Scotland."

"You don't sound Scottish…?"

"No, the Mountain Pack is now scattered from the Highlands to Northumberland and Cumbria. I've lived much of my life in England. I wouldn't mind going back to Scotland. It's more beautiful than this country. And much better suited to wolves."

"Then why join the Sables?"

A long silence from Isaac.

Andrew and Jason were back to discussing new ways Andrew could hoodwink human tourists. Kage remained quiet, gazing out the window behind Isaac's seat, chewing grass. What was he so moody about? I understood Jed, but I hadn't done anything to Kage. Except sleep with Jason. Was that it? Then again, Kage's silence might have nothing to do with me.

"Situations in my life changed," Isaac said at last. "I came to the South of England for my work."

"What do you do?"

"I'm an architect."

I almost jumped in my seat. "You're what? You went to school with humans?"

"In Edinburgh. I've only been out of school, working professionally, for about five years. It's not particularly common among my kind." He glanced in the rearview mirror at the con artists. "But there are some wolves who pursue higher education and career paths that keep their lives fully entwined with humans."

"You work in Brighton? I'd love to see something you've designed."

He glanced at me, the slight smile back. "Why?"

"Why...?"

*Because how freaking cool would it be to be all, "Oh, yeah, a werewolf designed my house. We worked closely together. What'd you do last summer?"*

"Because it's fascinating that you're doing that. I would just enjoy seeing your work. How are you able to take off like this? Shouldn't you be working now?"

"The murders of my friends and adopted family are more important to me than my job. I'll make arrangements for as long as I need to, as long as I can be of service to my pack."

I looked at him for a moment, somehow still neat and tidy after two days sleeping in the dirt. The impossible emerald eyes, light hair. The only one of them close to as light a complexion as myself. The outsider in so many ways.

I thought about how much he wasn't saying. And the white wolf limping that first night when the whole pack had apparently gone for him. I longed to ask him to dinner. Wished he was asking me: that we could stroll the Brighton boardwalk and sit with an English Channel view to eat fresh fish. He knew how to eat politely with humans. The only one of the six who I'd accept such an invitation from if it was offered.

"You don't belong with them," I said without meaning to.

A glance at me, smiling more, and away. "I wouldn't go that far."

"Speaking of them, will you tell me something? If they were human, I'd have expected tattoos on Kage and Jed at the very least, maybe piercings, smoking, a case of beer along for the camping trip ... I don't know. They're not into that?"

"I've never known a wolf who believed in body mutilation."

"Body mutilation?" I had to laugh, thinking of my own pierced ears. "A couple rings or a little ink. Not surgical procedures or amputations."

"A piercing is an amputation. Removing skin for reasons of fashion or vanity? As to substances, that can be a problem in our communities. I suppose it can in any humanoid society, outskirts or otherwise, but it's not common either. Many substances, inhaling smoke for example, or long-term effects of alcohol, are another form of mutilation. When we do see a member of our families starting with such a problem we have to respond. Zar and Jed's father was one such case. I only met him toward the end. He was ... too far gone."

"I'm sorry, I don't mean to be obtuse... Their father became what? An alcoholic?"

"Yes."

"And the family had to step in?"

"Which does not always work."

"And it didn't in this case?"

"No."

"Do they have to keep him home because he's a danger?"

"He's dead."

I felt tight pressure across my chest that seemed alarmingly like fear. "The pack killed him because he was an alcoholic? Is that what you're saying?"

"No, the pack killed him because he wouldn't stop being one. You can see a paper trail about him in the human news. A savage black dog loose around Brighton: many people convinced it was a wolf that someone had kept as a pet. The sightings, the sheep torn to pieces, the little girl sent to hospital who needed twenty stitches in her face and almost lost her eye.

"The pack should have acted sooner and that girl would have no scars on her face and perfect sight today. But the family fought back, tried to keep him in, said they could handle him. Gabriel—that was their third brother—used to help, being responsible for watching him. As you suggested, trying to keep him safe. But Gabriel vanished and the two younger brothers and their mum couldn't stop the drinking or the wolf behind it. The night he attacked that little girl—right in a human's back garden with the parents running out in time to save her life—Zacharias rallied the pack and, yes ... we killed him. Almost Jed as well. Jed wouldn't back down, fighting the whole pack trying to save his father's life. Zar kept their mother away.

"It might have helped if Gabriel were still around. We don't know what happened to him..." Slowly shaking his head. "It was a long time ago, yet, in hindsight, some of us wonder about long past disappearances. The odd wolf leaving the pack, never to be heard from again? A lone wolf is vulnerable. If Gabriel wasn't killed when he left, he most likely has been since. I never even met him. And the death of his father was years ago as well, right after I first came to this area."

The whole time, Isaac spoke softly and calmly as ever. I leaned into the console to make sure I could hear him over the diesel.

When he stopped, I didn't know what to say. More than a tightness in my chest then, but my throat, my whole body. I wanted someone there who I could apologize to; to embrace.

Isaac glanced at me and, after a time, he was the one to say, "I'm sorry, Cassia."

And I still didn't know what to say.

## ○ CHAPTER 26 ○

STONEHENGE WAS NOT what I'd expected, even after warnings from Zar about barriers and tourism. For one thing, I'd imagined it remote—not surrounded by motorways. For another, I hadn't realized how controlled the visiting of it was. Kage, Jason, and Jed didn't bother to come with us, but Isaac, Zar, and Andrew accompanied me to view the stone circle.

I'd never visited any others and the size and scale of it threw me—it just didn't look that big in photos.

"Early worms out for birds," Andrew said cheerfully after we'd paid and walked up the footpath.

"Please don't steal anything," I said absently, gazing at the stones yet seeing blood, smoke, and cliffs over saltwater.

This was not one of the stone circles I'd been seeing, either in nightmares or scrying. It was too massive and close, too distinct with some of the top stones still in place after thousands of years.

Still, I felt the sense even more deeply that this was right. That I should be here. While Zar read the signs and Andrew was scoping out the small crowd, Isaac followed me around the stones like a polite guard dog. I told him I was fine and if he wanted to do me a favor he could watch Andrew instead. I wasn't going to leave here with him carrying stolen property.

Which was why I was alone, standing back to gaze at the stone circle from the less crowded north side, when a man approached me.

"Good morning. Are you Cassia, by chance?"

Goddess, I don't know why, but my instant reaction was terror. Isaac should have stayed with me. All of them. That's what they were here for, right? Not that they'd done much protecting. But this was it. When someone got word of what we were doing—someone sinister—and we should all be sticking together.

Yet ... the guy didn't look all that sinister.

Very young, sandy-haired, glasses that made me think of just discovering Andrew had them. A slight figure, even boney, everything about him, from the preppy sweater around his shoulders to his looking as athletic as a drinking straw, screamed academia. He may be a mage, but otherwise he didn't exactly look alarming.

As I took a step back, then caught my own fear and nodded, it struck me that he was the one who looked nervous.

"I didn't mean to startle you. I saw you on the trail and I thought that might be you coming up. I'm here practically every day." With a tentative smile. "And you were on my mind this morning so it was one of those natural divines."

I nodded, willing my pulse to settle. "Are you a scry?"

"I wish." An embarrassed sort of laugh. "I'm a druid. Ellasandra told me about your visit. She's my great aunt. It's a tight community."

"I see..." Yet I felt more suspicious, not less. Wasn't this a tidy coincidence?

"I've been studying the stones for years. I often come out in the morning or evening and just watch the way the sun moves across the circle. But this morning I came to meditate on you and offer blessings. You see, I've been hoping to track clues in this case myself. That's why Ellasandra rang to tell me about you last night. When I saw you with those three just now, I thought it might really be you."

He paused, taking a breath. "I'm Rowan. And 'druid in training' may be more apt. If I may…?"

I let him take my hand, also with a deep breath, watching his anxious eyes, blue as the horizon and so sad I wanted to ask if someone else had died.

"You're our hope," he said quietly, making me shiver, remembering another's words a few days before. "Natural paths always lead us to what is right for us. Natural divine guided my step and yours today." He pressed my hand in both of his.

"Do you live here? Have you been able to follow up any clues?" Still uneasy, I watched him closely.

"I do, not far, but university studies and personal studies devour my time. I wish I had something to offer. Police have investigated the two members we've lost as well, but nothing from them either—not a lead nor suspect. All I can tell you is we don't know why we're being targeted and we need help as badly as your friends here. If shifter conflicts are beginning again, if we only knew where and why, perhaps we could at least get out of the way."

He shook his head, looking up from our hands to my face. "We only want to preserve natural divine. I know it's a lot to ask, but I wondered if you would be willing to keep in touch? If I discover anything new, I'll let you know."

"I don't understand. What shifter conflicts?"

He glanced away across the stones to the others. Zar and Isaac were walking toward us on the grass.

"All we have to go on are these shifter deaths, with druids somehow caught in the middle. If we only understood what was happening and how we could stay away…"

"So you also think shifters are top suspects? Why?"

"Who else would even be physically capable of this?" He shook his head sadly, still holding my hand, warm and gentle. "Ellasandra said they've lost seven. We hadn't known it was that bad. We may be judging them unfairly. But I've long heard rumors of disenfranchised packs, solitary shifters who abandon packs all together, and those of London and other urban places who shun their own kind. Then there's history to consider. Of course, we don't know for sure. We have shadows and blank pages on our hands."

He looked past me to the others, releasing my hand, but gave me another sad smile. "If there's anything we can do, if you need any aid from the druids, we will do all we can. If we're in this together we can strengthen all our chances."

I turned to Isaac and Zar. Like Ellasandra, he knew what they were. He appeared intimidated by the idea. I couldn't blame him. Isaac in particular looked like he could snap this scholarly youth over his knee.

Rowan introduced himself to them and they shook his hand, neither saying more than their names as I told them how he knew about us.

"It's an honor t-to meet. I'm s-so sorry for what's been happening to your kind." Rowan gulped.

"Could you give us a minute?" I touched the young man's shoulder and walked off with him closer to the barrier and stones, hoping to soothe his nerves now that my own had settled.

Isaac and Zar waited, only watching us.

"You're right," I told Rowan. "If you keep in touch, it might help you both. If you learn anything more, or you experience more losses... And they could tell you if they find out more. How can we send messages?"

"Oh..." He looked even more flushed and uncomfortable. "You mean with magic? Druids aren't really casters. I was hoping ... I could give you my mobile number?"

I almost laughed. "Well, I don't know why *that* didn't jump to my mind. You use such things?"

"Of course." He smiled then. "If we could just text it might be easier than ... performing rituals to send missives on the breeze."

"Wouldn't it, though? Thank you for bringing me back to reality. You have to use international dialing for my phone. And I don't know how long I will even be involved in this, but I'll pass your number along to others working on it."

He nodded and gave me his number to put into my phone with the country code.

I took both a literal and emotional deep breath as I typed.

For some reason, this felt like getting somewhere far more than the sight of the stones. Finally druids and wolves able to reach each other by modern means if they wanted to share new evidence or theories.

"If there's any way I can be of service to you, you'll let me know?" Rowan repeated. "And I hope you'll be careful while you're helping them—helping all of us."

"You too if you're meaning to investigate this for your people. Thank you for coming forward."

"Thank you for listening. I was afraid I'd scare you off. It probably sounded mad that I knew your name. I didn't mean to startle you."

I shook my head. "I'm glad you did."

He thanked me again, I promised to be in touch, and he walked on around the stones, watching shadows and sun, which he'd probably seen in this spot hundreds of times and still fascinated him.

"Quite the collector, aren't you?"

I looked around to see Andrew almost at my shoulder. "Collector?"

"Of males." His eyes were hooded behind the glasses, smirking at me.

"Collecting something implies deliberate action. This is not my fault."

"Interesting word choice." He arched an eyebrow. "Don't judge me because I'm sexy, eh? Ready to go?"

"Don't you care what he wanted?"

"I'm not deaf, darling. Name's Rowan. Thinks we're a bunch of barbarians meaning to kill each other off. Bet he never got a woman's number that fast in his life."

"Where were you?" I looked around. There was nowhere to hide. He might have been behind other sightseers, but he could not have been close without me seeing him.

Andrew stepped forward to pull jingling car keys from my ear. "Ready? Wolves are getting hungry."

Isaac and Zar walked up to us.

"Where did you get those?" I asked.

"I just showed you. You ask so many strange questions."

"Give them back to Isaac. Unless you're wanting to drive now?"

"Please." He curled his lip. "I don't drive four-wheels. Most of us don't. Kage is just a freak who likes to compensate for other deficiencies with extra wheels. And Isaac knows how to be a good little worm." He threw the keys at Isaac. "Now, lunch?" Walking away.

"None of you drive?" I looked around at Zar as we also started to walk. So there had only been two options for driver all along?

"We ride bikes," Zar said.

And hardly any phones between them. All fitting.

I sighed. "Zar, is it true there's a history of shifters killing each other?"

"That was a long time ago. And they didn't use tactics like this."

"Even so, no one could have mentioned that? The more I learn from outside sources the more I feel like you already knew what was happening but you're hoping I'll come up with an answer to point the finger somewhere else."

"Cassia?" Zar kept pace with me. "Last night—" He was looking at my bruised arm.

"Forget it."

"It was my fault. It shouldn't have happened. I only wanted to protect you."

"I know that. You all act on impulse. Sometimes you need to slow down and think, see what's going on first. But my arm is fine. It's just bruised. It'll be better in a couple days.

He looked pained, more distressed. As if I'd said it would be a couple of months.

How much more did they know about this that they hadn't mentioned? And what was I going to do about it? Was I still involved? Was it time to bow out?

"Cassia—"

"Don't. It's fine. Give me another minute with the stones." I stopped at a good vantage.

Zar showed every intention of remaining with me.

Isaac, however, gave him a look and Zar followed him to wait at some distance on the trail. Was their hearing really that good?

After more time gazing at the circle, I said, in a soft, normal voice, as if speaking to someone personally close, "Isaac, can you hear what I'm saying?" I glanced at him, thirty or forty yards away.

Isaac nodded.

Maybe he only did because I looked to him?

"What's the square root of four?" I asked, a bit softer.

Isaac held up two fingers.

*Damn...*

"Go on," I said again to the stones. "Let me sit here a minute. See if I can see anything else. Then we'll get out of here and find lunch. And please make sure Andrew doesn't have anything he 'nicked.'"

I sat on grass in the sun, watching those great standing stones, and didn't push, just waited and let my vision run clear.

I didn't see stone circles. Then I knew: I already had that answer. Rowan was the answer.

*Natural paths always lead us to what is right for us. Natural divine guided my step and yours today.*

For him, natural divine. For me, magic and dreams. At the end of the day, weren't they the same thing?

Rowan had been the reason for visions of standing stones last night and this morning.

And this treasure hunt? The next step?

We would just have to keep tumbling down the rabbit hole.

## ○ Chapter 27 ○

We arrived back at the mobile home park early in the evening, Kage driving, as I'd offered for the last leg. He could save face this way, driving his own car back home with his family watching—and he certainly seemed less tetchy after Isaac gave back his keys.

In long shadows a group of children were playing what looked like capture the flag on old bicycles and tricycles up and down the pitted drive to their homes. They left their game to ride around the Jeep, yelling at us, asking questions, as soon as we pulled up beyond the orchard.

"Did you find bad guys?"

"What did you eat?"

"Did the American witch use magic?"

"Did you bring food?"

It took a while for Kage to be able to stop outside their homes. Then he and the others were mobbed piling out the doors. The kids avoided me, keeping clear of the passenger door, casting me curious or downright scared glances, but yammering at the others.

This was a weird experience because I love kids. I'd been a locally sought-after babysitter in my day. The job I was starting at the end of August was upper elementary school level and I couldn't wait. Kids who were old enough to really question and work on complex concepts, but preteen, still eager to have those projects as long as you knew how to get their interest.

According to this lot, you'd have thought I had the plague.

There were six or seven of them, filthy hands and knees, mostly barefoot, dusty, beaming and bouncy. Males and females had short hair and no difference in their dress—mostly cut-offs and T-shirts, though some were shirtless.

"Jason, did you see me take that jump? Elam said I couldn't make it!"

"Andrew, what did the worms give you today? Did you bring me anything?"

"Did you meet the druids?"

"Are druids shifters?"

"What'd you bring to eat?"

"Pick me up!"

Kage picked up a little girl and tossed her to his shoulders as easily as a dish rag.

"Did you eat chicken?" she shrieked. "You smell like chicken!"

"Chicken!" they all screamed, most leaping about.

"Zar!" A couple ran for the caravan as Zar, then Jed, stepped out.

"Do you have chicken?" Scrambling to get a look inside.

"Do me! Me next!"

Andrew had just pulled a pound coin from the ear of a little boy and he repeated the performance for another.

"Chicken! Chicken!"

The littlest, three or four years, was tugging Isaac's slacks and he squatted down for the kid to whisper in his ear.

Zar and Jed were having to display their open hands and open mouths. "We don't have chicken."

"Why don't you show me your jump, Adam?" Jason said. "Did Hannah fix your ramp?"

"Yes! Elam said I couldn't but I did!" Adam grabbed his bike and raced off for a battered plywood jump.

"Where's our cataja, Helah?" Kage asked the girl clinging to his hair.

"With Abraham. He's sick."

"Sick? How's he sick?"

"Mum says he's sick. There was a kitty in the barn. She thought she'd move in and own the place."

"Oh, yeah? What'd you do?"

"Me and Noah said *raaarrr* and chased her up the oak tree. Noah climbed up but she scratched him and he fell. She won't come back. She was soooo scared. Fur like this—" Helah held out her arms wide and, in so doing, fell off Kage's shoulder.

He caught her and put her back. "Good work, Helah. Last thing we need around here's a cat infestation."

"She was a bad cat! I told her. Noah told her. We were a good pack."

"You are a good pack. That's great teamwork."

"Kage? Did you find druids?"

"Yes. And you know what? They had no chicken."

The girl gasped. "Why?"

"I don't know. They're just a bunch of apes."

"Rebecca brought a worm home today."

"That red-headed bloke who smells like motor oil? The one Jason introduced her to?"

"Yes. And she said, 'Don't tell Kage.'" Beaming.

"You're a good pup, Helah."

"Upside down!" Helah screamed.

Kage held her upside down by her ankles and stepped away from the rest to swing her around while she howled with laughter, hands out over her head as if riding a roller coaster.

This distracted chicken seekers as they all wanted rides and Zar spun one as well.

Isaac was walking away for one of the single-wides, holding the tiny hand of the tricycle rider who'd whispered to him. I followed, passing the plywood jump and Jason telling Adam he could do better than that if they moved the jump over to the downhill part of the drive.

I couldn't keep from looking back. Andrew was going through his rucksack from the Jeep to see if he had anything more to hand out. Jed was letting another one search the trailer—presumably for chicken.

Isaac paused on steps to a blue door with chipped paint and a bashed in knob. It stood ajar.

"Are you all right, Cassia?"

"What?" I looked around. "I was just … distracted. You all are popular."

Isaac smiled in that soft way he had that was reassuring and knowing and sexy at the same time. "Pups are life. The whole pack is involved. There's no such thing as an orphan in a wolf pack. Each birth is Moon's blessing and births are not common these years. Reuben? Will you go in to your mum? I'll be right there."

The "pup" pushed on through the wobbly door.

Isaac turned back to me. "I must speak with Susanna. Would you consent to remaining with us until we can gain an audience with our silvers and discuss what has happened? Then I'll take you back to your sister's home, if that's all right?"

"Of course it is. I was assuming I would be seeing Diana, at least. It sounds like she's busy though? Someone sick? Abraham?"

His expression became grave and he glanced to the path down to the next home. "That'll be his mate—a domestic violence situation. Moon knows he won't leave her but he has support if he does. She's already taken off half his ear."

"Oh…" I didn't know how to answer that. "Go on and I'll see you in a bit. Whenever Diana is free is fine. I'll gather up my things."

"Thank you." He gave me a nod and walked on inside.

I returned to the Jeep—the crowd had dispersed—and started going through my bag, making sure everything was back in one place, but also checking that I had it all, especially my phone. Yes, phone, but…

"Andrew!"

He zipped past on one of the kids' bikes with three of them after him, yelling and whooping.

"Andrew! Where's my hairbrush?"

"Your what?"

"My hairbrush!"

"Where'd you leave it?"

"Give it back. That's the only one I brought for the trip."

Down the drive he skidded the bike to make a turn and crash. Those pups were fast. They plowed into him, throwing all four and bike into the long grass verge along the broken fence.

"Elam wins, Elam wins, Elam wins!" A boy of about eight chanted.

"Dry up, Elam!"

"Elam wins!"

"Elam's a git!"

"Was that the best you can do?" Andrew extricated himself while they shouted and jumped around him. "You couldn't catch a bee with a broken wing. Don't you think you could do better? You lot run to the barn and back and show me what you can do when you actually try."

They fought each other to scramble through and over the fence and took off across the field toward the broken down stone barn.

Andrew walked back to me, slightly breathless. His right side from shoe to shoulder was covered in dust and grit and bits of snapped weeds. His right elbow dripped blood. He didn't seem to notice.

"What's the trouble, darling?"

"I want my hairbrush. I can't just go out and replace it at a Boots here. Will you please give it back?"

"What's it worth to you?"

"Don't start that."

"Start what?"

"It's my property. Give it back."

"Cassia?"

I turned to Zar coming up behind me.

"Kage is going to find Diana. If you'll bear with us for a few minutes, we'll get the elders together for a quick meeting. Then I can take you home."

"Thank you, Zar. I don't mind. Whenever you can gather everyone. It's not like I have much to tell them. And that's okay, Isaac already offered to run me home after we see Diana."

Zar stood there a second. Without dramatically changing his expression he still somehow looked like I'd thrown a drink in his face.

"Right," he said after a beat. "Of course." He looked at the purple and black bruise on my arm. His eyes wandered to blood running off Andrew's skinned elbow. Back to my arm. He nodded and walked away.

I opened my mouth to call after, already forming the sound of his name, but stopped. What did I have in mind to say?

"Andrew, I reached the fence first!" All three were back, gasping, climbing the rail fence across the drive from us.

"A big improvement," Andrew called without looking around. "Think you can do it again, or was that enough for one day?"

They took off once more.

Andrew studied me with narrowed eyes. His glasses were lying on the hood of the Jeep—which he must have left before going for the bike ride.

"Smooth," he said quietly. "Especially for someone who doesn't fancy Isaac."

"It doesn't matter how I do or do not feel about Isaac. He asked, I said yes. What was I supposed to do? Tell Zar yes also and then tell Isaac I found a better offer? Isaac was first in line."

"Actually ... I was."

"What?"

"The hotel? I met you before any of them. I was the one who tipped them off to the scrying teacher. I got some of the pack there Sunday morning to scope you out and decide we had to invite you to the meeting. I was first in line."

"You didn't offer. Anyway, I thought you and Zar don't drive?"

"Bikes."

I looked around at the ones scattered on the drive, weeds, against steps and plywood porches.

"Anyway," Andrew went on, "I suppose it doesn't make a difference to you. You did what they asked. You're done with us."

I just stood there, that tight feeling in my chest again that was a mix of things more than what I had a quick name for. Pain, I thought as Andrew turned away. Uncertainty, regret, longing for something out of reach, fear, desire, unanswered questions and confusion, immovable walls, impossible paths. These together made the pain.

"Andrew—"

"Your brush is in Jed's bag." Andrew kept walking toward the fence as the gasping pups stumbled up to it from the other side. "I thought he'd want a memento of you since he went through all the trouble to gather you wildflowers in his delicate little chompers."

Mind reeling, I hurried again to the back of the Jeep. No, Jed had been in the caravan. If his bag was still in there—

But I didn't need to look for it. I spotted him far down the row of mobile homes, walking with his black bag slung over his shoulder. No sooner had I caught sight of him than he turned a corner and vanished.

"Jed?" I called and almost tripped over a pile of wooden blocks. Watching where I was going, I wasn't sure if I was at the right turn. I ran to the next. There he was, walking between two homes, heading for the next row.

"Jed!"

He looked around and stopped.

I slowed to a walk and also paused several feet from him in dust and gravel. "Jed? You have my hairbrush. Would you mind?"

"I don't." He narrowed his eyes—thinking I was playing a trick on him.

"I know you didn't mean to. Andrew stole it and put it in your bag."

He frowned but didn't seem to think this was implausible because he slung the bag off his shoulder. He sniffed it.

"Thank you. I'm sorry to chase after—to bother you." I flushed more than I was already, breathing too fast after having run down here.

Jed didn't even look up. He unzipped the mostly empty bag and produced my pink hairbrush from beside that dense wool ball of his. He stared at it like he'd never seen such a device: rubber handle, long wheat-colored hairs wrapped in the teeth.

For some reason, I nearly told him to keep it.

Jed held it out at arm's length, not stepping toward me, nor looking at me.

"Thanks." I walked forward to take it. "Did you—?"

But I was using my right arm to reach and his gaze flicked to the bruise there. The moment my fingers touched the brush he let go. I didn't have a hold yet and it dropped with a clatter to the dirt by his dusty black boots. Jed walked away, taking long strides.

I grabbed it. "Jed? It wasn't your fault. Zar didn't need to be over there. Anyway, I'm fine. It's no big deal."

He only walked faster, leaving me behind with the scuffed up brush in the dust.

## ○ Chapter 28 ○

Diana and her seconds, the other two silvers, Atarah and Zacharias, listened while I told what had happened with the druids and all I had seen. Jed and Andrew were absent.

We were gathered outside on a porch of a mobile home in lawn chairs or sitting on the boards.

Kage muttered about someone needing to do something about the Beeches.

Jason asked if they really thought there were wolves in London—no one knew.

Zar said of course there was precedent for shifters killing shifters but this was unlike any such event before. General agreement to this.

Isaac had the good sense and simple logic—which seemed to be an alarmingly absent attribute among wolves—to mention that if modern disenfranchised shifters decided to murder their kin, under cover, the only sensible way to do it was one that had never been tried before.

Diana agreed that someone must go to London and search for urban wolves. At which Zar, Isaac, Kage, and Jason volunteered with various levels of enthusiasm. There was an argument about taking bikes, but Isaac pointed out they would be on foot the whole time they were in the city so it would only be reasonable to take the train. They would go first thing in the morning.

Diana thanked me. They kept doing this even though I'd done so little. One clue which yielded one idea? A lead that might not even exist and another that the wolves had already known about?

We had at least made contact with other victims, knew there were others looking, and I had Rowan's number to give Diana. Without me, it seemed they wouldn't have been able to find druids at all. Other than that...? What?

I told Diana I would scry again, look at London, keep looking and let them know if I came up with more. I had Isaac's and Zar's phone numbers—sketchy as Zar's was.

The sun was setting when the meeting drifted apart. My stomach growled. Once again, they had offered no food as part of their gathering.

I felt desperate for a shower and a clear corner of thinking space and a bowl of macaroni and cheese—always my comfort food—yet also for more questions and answers with these people I was leaving.

Questions I wasn't asking. Answers I would never receive.

Isaac was still talking with Diana and gray-bearded Zacharias.

I walked to one of the alleys to wait, watching a couple of kids from before running for home at the sound of a howl, still racing each other.

I wished I'd seen Rebecca again. She was dating a human? Was that common?

I wanted to tell Jason I hoped things worked out with him and Kage—even though really I hoped Jason moved on: he could do better. And to thank Kage for putting up with me and letting Isaac drive. I wanted to have an actual conversation with Jed. And to see Andrew again—to give him something of mine legitimately to keep, maybe a lipstick. I wanted to say I was sorry to Zar, though preferably not have to elaborate.

But they'd gone. No one was even coming to say goodbye.

Once more, only treetops glowed golden. Twilight was settling on the park. Evening birds called. Darting swallows fast as hummingbirds flitted past.

Judging by the smells of grilling meat a late evening meal was being served in some homes. Perhaps later they would go out in their fur in the field to do whatever it was they did. Maybe they hunted field mice and played games when it wasn't just a bunch of young males trapped together who didn't get along. Maybe they buried bones. Maybe they had toys like that ball of Jed's. Did they play fetch?

Suddenly, I wanted to know everything about them. I wanted to wait here and see what happened next, watch them in their fur, dare to be among them. I longed to be a part of this family. Which was insane, first because I'd only just met them, and second because I could never be like them. Lycanthropy was not transmissible like vampirism.

Thinking of which ... what about the stakes in their chests? What about there being vampires in London as well? Shouldn't someone at least ask the vampires? Whether they had anything to do with this or not ... might they know?

Those stakes... And the eyes...

How had we spent these days looking for answers and still had only more questions? How could I walk away from them now?

But they weren't my life.

Melanie and Henry, Portland and my waiting job—I could not possibly have done any better there.

Plus, walking away from this: away from being a witch. That was my life. That was my future. Not worshiping the moon and eating like a shop vac.

"Cassia?"

I turned from watching the broken barn across the field as it faded in twilight, to Zar almost beside me.

I hadn't heard him walk up. No ... I could never be like them. Even if ... but it didn't matter...

"I wanted to say thank you," he said softly, his usual smile for me absent. "I don't know where we go from here, but you helped and what you did ... you're so brave. I've never met a human like you."

"Brave? For being willing to camp? I'm not the homecoming queen I may appear to be. It wasn't a big deal."

"Homecoming...?"

I shook my head, sure he was thinking of the Queen of England. "It's nothing. I'm not delicate. That's all."

"No ... but I didn't mean about the caravan. I meant brave for helping. You were kidnapped by wolves and asked to go off with them as a personal favor. Which you agreed to do for no reason than to help us. I'm not sure you realize how unusual ... how unique you are."

"I'm not afraid of you, Zar. I'm a witch, remember? And ... if I am, a little bit, I happen to know you're a bit afraid of me too. Doesn't that make us even?"

He smiled and dropped his gaze. "Sounds fair. Being around you has been one of the best..." He looked up.

It was strange, but I hadn't noticed him coming closer either. His smile faded with my own as I looked into his face from very close range. Why were they all so handsome? Those good genes? How could they stay healthy with such a limited number? Was it possible for them to reproduce with humans? Any way to expand that pool before it was too late?

Zar's voice became a breath. "It's said ... Moon sighed and dew formed on the grass. Moon wept and frost formed on the grass. But Moon laughed and those drops born of sorrow fell to earth to grow the grass strong for spring." He paused, gaze intent. "I think of that every time I look into your moonstone eyes."

He kissed me. Not a moment too soon or I'd have had to kiss him first.

I didn't worry about the others knowing. Nothing to lose now. Instead of worry, I felt a more intense desire for more in that kiss than any first kiss I'd ever known. I lifted my hands to his face, pulling him in since he was gentle, his lips closed. It seemed he was expecting me to push him away.

His fingers caressed my jaw, down my neck, stroking my throat. I wished he was kissing me there, touching more, pushing more.

I thought again of them going out with humans. Had Zar, at some point along the way, been warned about using a soft touch with human females? Or more of him being afraid of me, tentative? Or was this simply how he was; normal for him? My own vague ideas of voracious werewolves nothing but bigotry?

He stepped in until I could feel his body against mine. Right hand slipping to my back while his left stroked through my hair. The touch was like a dance partner—intimate without demand.

I turned my face to break the kiss and showed him, my fingers connecting at the base of his skull, kissing short stubble on his jaw. He responded in kind and I tipped my head back, eyes closed. His lips caressed my chin, my jawline, down my neck, his teeth on my throat. His own desire showed itself as he held on tighter, kissing to my collarbone. The sensation was stunning: again, like nothing I'd felt from a first touch. Maybe I just hadn't wanted those guys to touch me as much as I wanted Zar to.

I felt his strength even as he did not exercise it—tightness of his muscles, power like a coiled spring. Still I wanted more and more, to see him, feel him, to know his body. And for him to know mine.

I met his lips again. This time they were parted, Zar pulling me to him. His tongue stroked my lips and I opened my mouth for him. I found the hem of his shirt pressed between us and slid my hands under to feel the firm heat of his abs. Zar gasped in my mouth as if I'd reached lower.

When he stepped away, I thought it was because of that touch. But he looked around, chest rising and falling with short breaths.

"Come on." I tugged his hand and he followed.

I was sure he'd heard the last members of the meeting breaking up to walk this way, and I didn't want to be standing here gasping with Zar in the gloom when they wandered past.

Pulse rushing, I imagined more as we walked down the drive to the Jeep where I assumed Isaac would know to collect me to return to town—even if he was bringing his own car and not Kage's.

I loved how responsive Zar had been. Gentle but catching on quickly to my moves, becoming less gentle.

The idea of the next kiss, letting him feel my breasts, down to my shorts, was cut off as I had to shake myself. This hadn't been a first kiss. It had been a kiss goodbye.

We said nothing while we walked, both getting our breath back, still holding hands.

At the Jeep I pulled on my backpack that I'd left in the seat.

The moon was rising, western light down to indigo and violet. Electric lights cast a gentle glow across the drive.

An engine started.

A dozen things I wanted to ask him. None about a murder case. I was sure he would love to teach me their language as much as I would love learning.

I only looked at him.

Zar reached again to my hand, bending, bringing it to his lips. He kissed my knuckles all the way across, letting his lips linger for a long time. For once, he said nothing.

A single headlight pulled onto the drive from one of the alleys and a motorcycle roared toward us.

Zar stepped away, again looking into my eyes.

The motorcycle rolled up and stopped. Isaac killed the engine and climbed off to pull a helmet from the back.

"Are you ready to go home, Cassia?"

I blinked. "You all ride ... motorcycles? I—out of context—I thought—oh. Thank you." I took the helmet. I looked at Zar, who was backing up.

"Moon bless," he murmured and walked away.

# ○ <u>Chapter 29</u> ○

I'D NEVER RIDDEN on a motorcycle. I wrapped my arms around Isaac, held on with my knees, and loved it so much that by the time we were five minutes out of the trailer park I knew I needed to learn to drive one at home. And get one.

The most wonderful, free feeling. Not like being trapped in a smelly Jeep swaying and rocketing around corners at speeds beyond it. The motorcycle curved and leaned in smooth control. It must have had great shocks because the ride overall felt wonderfully silky. Just ... flying. Eating up the road like a rocket, lights and stars and navy horizon streaking past.

If it felt this good hanging on behind, what was it like to be the driver? No wonder these things inspired gangs. Which made me speculate on how many biker gangs were actually werewolves. Maybe that was the norm and even the casters didn't know.

Then again, perhaps being a passenger was better. I had nothing to worry about but embracing Isaac, which, given the guy I'd just left behind, I should not have been enjoying.

Even so, I felt euphoric, hands around Isaac, making no pretense about holding on only for security—wrapped around him.

Thinking of Zar, I was ashamed, as if at a betrayal. Yet I reminded myself, again, this was it. Goodbye. So what difference did it make? I would feel plenty bad about both of them—all of them, the whole situation—later tonight. For now, I held on and only wished the helmet were off to feel coastal summer wind in my hair.

The journey took an impossibly short time. Isaac was speeding, but even so, it flickered past and I was having to give directions to the door.

I'd told Melanie I'd be in tonight. Now I prayed to Goddess she would not spot me or come running out or anything like it.

Isaac did not let me hop off on my own or leave the motorcycle idling. Again, he shut the engine off after pulling onto the sidewalk, through a gap in parallel-parked cars.

I climbed off, reluctant to leave him, startled by the chill in the night once I was no longer leaned into his back.

Isaac left my helmet on the bike—he wasn't wearing one—and walked me up concrete steps to the illuminated red front door.

"Thank you. That was … freedom. A perfect finale to the trip."

"You are most welcome, of course." He stopped one step down while I stood on the landing. He was still taller than me, yet this greatly helped to level the playing field.

"And thanks for all your driving and … responsibleness. I'm grateful to you."

"My pleasure." Looking into my eyes. Right down to his smile he wasn't like them. That smile was so much more about his eyes than his mouth. This was no Cheshire Cat but a real Prince Charming. There was something so courtly about Isaac it crossed my mind he hardly seemed to belong to this century. Perhaps no wolves did.

I stood on the edge of the landing, too close, hand on the rail, my backpack still on yet not feeling it. I wondered if my hair looked crushed and horrible after the helmet. It hadn't been on long, though.

"If you need anything," Isaac said, "please get in touch."

I nodded, mouth dry. "I have your number. Maybe you can let me know what happens? And if I see anything more—scrying, clues, locations in London—I'll call."

"Thank you, Cassia."

The way he said my name was exactly like his smile. Slow, relaxed, incredibly sexy without him doing anything. Just standing there. Gazing into my eyes. Not with a focused or lustful or amused expression. Instead, his eyes were selfless. In his gaze I saw myself as the only person in the world—while he lived to look into my eyes, to do whatever I wished. Calm, respectful, awaiting his next chance to carry me over mud puddles.

That may sound off the deep end for a mere expression. But, looking back into his eyes by the light above the door, that's what I saw.

I moved in no more than a hint, an inch or two.

Isaac took it and met me.

His lips were soft, while the short beard felt rough but not unpleasant. Only a kiss. Count of three while I felt a response all the way to the soles of my feet. Then he broke it, his face still close.

I moved for the next one. Kissing him, repeating the contact and break.

Again, we stood, looking into each other's eyes.

More firsts. I'd never had so little—two very modest kisses—yet wanted so much—him in my bed.

"I'll ... be in touch," I said at last. "I'll be here another ten days or so... If..."

"If there is anything I can do for you in that time, I pray you will also let me know. Anything you need or desire, I am at your command."

I swallowed.

"May I?"

I gave him my hand to kiss.

"Good night, Cassia. Moon bless."

The way he said my name again, Goddess.

"Good night," I said. "And good luck in London."

I was inside, my back leaned into the door, flushed, breaths short, listening to the engine roar away, before I remembered I still had his gold necklace around my neck.

## ○ C͟H͟A͟P͟T͟E͟R͟ ͟3͟0͟ ○

MELANIE WANTED TO stay up and talk, hear everything about my days away. She told me she hoped I could meet this guy named Geoffrey tomorrow—the British spelling of which she explained. Calling a man Jeff when it was spelled Geoff only made my head spin more.

The wonderful thing about my big sister, though, is that she's been my best friend all my life. Instead of spending the night talking my ear off, she got me a fresh towel for the shower and, by the time I was out, she had a cup of macaroni and cheese from a box and a mug of peppermint tea with a few chocolate chips melting in the bottom ready for my very late dinner and dessert.

I told her about Cornwall and the wind and views and sea cliffs.

She told me if I didn't hurry up and start relaxing for this trip I'd never get around to it.

While we sat up in the kitchen, I did laundry—which always seems to be situated in kitchens in this country. I've never seen an actual laundry room in England.

Then she sent me to bed.

*I love you, Mel.*

I did not, however, sleep.

I was much too busy, first imagining having slipped in here with Isaac, unseen, to this room and this bed. Then changing my mind and seeing how it would have been to stay there: Zar taking me back to his home.

Did he have one? He must share. At the very least, they must all have a family member or roommate or still be living with parents. Father and brother gone, I guessed Zar and Jed still lived with their mom or other family.

What about Isaac? Did he even live there? He must have means to live in Brighton if he wished, but maybe that wasn't the nature of the pack?

And who was Susanna to him? Was I jealous?

Rich thinking for someone lying here dwelling on two guys at once.

Oh, please. Who was I kidding? I was thinking of six guys. Even Jason. He and Kage had vanished after the meeting. No goodbye. Hopefully things would be okay between them now without me in the middle. Until the next pretty face, male or female, to come along and distract Kage while Jason hopefully twiddled his thumbs? Why was he so loyal to Kage? Someone needed to slap him.

Maybe loyalty was another trait they shared—if not Kage. Jed fighting his whole pack to try to save his father's life? Himself almost killed. And what had happened to him with the Beech Pack that he'd never talked to anyone about?

Why hadn't Andrew come back to the meeting? Only because he'd been a stowaway and shouldn't have been there? Or because of me?

I relived the kiss with Zar, switching him out for Andrew. Andrew would have had his tongue in my mouth as soon as he touched me. Until this very moment, I'd have said that was a jackass thing to do on a first kiss. *Give us a minute, buster.*

But I didn't feel that way thinking of Andrew. I wished I had Andrew here as much as Zar or Isaac. Which got me thinking about Kage. Kage would be obnoxious also.

And what about Jed? I'd put the wildflowers from this morning in a glass of water beside my bed. They were badly wilted from their journey, poking from my bag all day, but I hoped they'd perk up.

I'd known he wouldn't bite me deliberately. Scary to see those gaping jaws in my face, yes. But, somehow, I'd never really thought he could bite me last night. Had it only been last night?

My arm still ached, incredibly tender at the slightest touch around the bruise. Yet I wished it hurt more. I wished my arm gushed blood or I had cramps or food poisoning or at least a splinter. Anything to distract from this realization that I had tears in my eyes and I didn't even want to fall asleep.

I just wanted to go back.

Well ... I'd have to. Isaac's necklace.

Give it a few days. Cool off with Melanie and the beach. Even if I had to tell her I couldn't start meeting men with her right now.

Then get a cab—I didn't want Melanie up there, no explanations—and return the necklace. Go in the middle of a weekday and hope I could leave it with someone. No way I could hand it personally back to Isaac. Then I might not be able to leave.

I was still supposed to be helping them. Doing what I could from afar. I tried and couldn't draw the magic. I didn't see the faces of any threatening werewolves in London bent on killing off their more traditional fellows. I saw the faces of six werewolves just a short drive away and lifetimes removed from my own.

By the time I did fall asleep, it was for nightmares.

The stones were gone. Followed up, scratched off the list. The magic had called me there to meet Rowan. But if knowing Rowan and Ellasandra were so important, what was next? They were such a tiny clue. Not even as revealing as stakes and amputated eyes. But at least they were solid. The latter two ... as long as I didn't know what they meant, how could they be relevant?

*Make them relevant. Find out.*

Instead of standing stones, I saw the black cityscapes. I saw smoke. And I saw a row of bodies lined up in a field with crosses at their heads. No ... in graves. All dug into graves, crude wooden crosses placed above the head of each. I was seeing through the soil. There was a man walking away. An incredibly pale, sallow-faced man, wiping blood from his lips.

A row of thin wooden stakes were laid out on a wooden table. Carved to points on one end, just right for plunging into a humanoid chest.

I woke again covered in sweat and had to crawl from bed, wanting to tell someone aloud,

*We have to find the vampires.* Druids, stones, shifters, now vampires.

But there was no one to hear. No "we" at all.

I clutched my own head, tears in my eyes.

Just a dream. It hadn't been a real scry. *Just a dream.*

I lay awake again with pain in my chest sharper than my arm.

In the morning, while the sky was only gray, I dressed in indigo jeans and a white cotton blouse. I did my face in a few minutes, brushed my teeth, repacked my overnight bag, and left a note for Melanie on the kitchen counter.

*Mel,*

*I'm so sorry to take off again when I really came here to spend time with you. Something important has come up and there's someone I think I can help. I'm sorry I can't explain more. I'll text you, but I may be gone a couple days again. Thank you for being so patient with me.*

*Love you.*

*Cass*

## o CHAPTER 31 o

I ASKED THE TAXI DRIVER to leave me at the bottom of that last curving, pitted drive up to the trailer park along the rough field. Then I walked in newly risen morning sun, backpack on, still second-guessing every step I took, but striding with purpose all the same.

Would they be up yet? Or would they be *still* up? Some in fur? Or already be gone on an early train?

As I caught sight of the park ahead, a few furry figures dashed into hiding through the alleys. They'd heard or smelled me coming and looked like no more than giant, scruffy dogs from this distance.

So the place was dead quiet, not even birds calling, when I reached Kage's Jeep and stopped, looking down the row of mobile homes. If I didn't happen to see anyone, I didn't know a door to knock on.

I stood uncertainly, only wanting to find Isaac or Zar, or even Kage, when a honey-haired young woman in a threadbare, sky blue bathrobe stepped from around a corner.

"Rebecca?" I smiled, starting forward to meet her. "I may have more information."

"Cassia? I thought that was you." She stepped out, tears dropping from her lashes, and hugged me.

Startled, I returned it. "What's wrong?"

"I'm glad you're back." Her voice shook as she held on, yet her strength was solid and shocking, crushing my lungs. "It's Abraham. They just brought him in. He's dead."

A thrill of horror shot up my spine. At the same time, I knew at once how important this could be—the opportunity it presented.

"I have to see him. Can you show me?" I was breathless, fighting to get the words out.

Rebecca let me go. "Diana was worried about him being upset and roaming too far from the pack last night. She asked for volunteers to track him." She gulped.

"But he's here now?" I looked around. "Can I see him?"

She nodded and took my hand. They were at the top of the park, past a two-story timber building and before a grove of willow trees. Beyond the trees ran a thick hedge and a crop of some kind on the other side, rich with hazy, defused morning sunlight.

Many stood about in their skin, though some in fur as well. Kage and Zar were there. So were Diana and other elders.

A jet black wolf was first to look around at our approach, ears pricking. He ran forward and I knelt to catch his great head in both arms, hugging him while he leaned into my chest.

"I'm sorry, Jason," I whispered in his flattened ear.

His fur was wet, especially around his legs and chest where he'd been through long grass and brush: one of the tracking party. His body felt tense, breaths shallow.

When we continued, the others were all turning to us, the elders parting around the still form laid on a blanket at their feet. Zar started forward, then stopped. No one said a word, yet all eyes followed me as I shrugged off the backpack and walked on to sink to my knees by the naked body, wooden stake still in his chest.

His face was covered in blackened blood, eyes having been carved away. His throat was sliced open nearly to bones, yet there was almost no blood below his neck, only all over his face and hair. The rest of him looked normal aside from the stake protruding from his chest. Around this wound, also, was no blood. Staked after he died. He reeked of gasoline and menthol.

My stomach turned over, bile in my throat, and I was glad I'd had nothing substantial to eat since lunch yesterday. Even that little bit of macaroni threatened to come up, but I clenched my teeth, shut my eyes, and touched the stake lightly with my palm.

I didn't have to work at intention or relaxing my mind into a state of trance. I simply drew the magic and made one request.

*Show me who.*

I saw the driving in of the stake with a mallet while the body dangled upside down from a tree. It was dark, the moon high. A large man in a hood and gloves held him from the back so he did not swing around while another man hammered. They wore jumpsuits and hoods. Abraham's blood soaked the forest floor. Final drips dropping off his hair as it trickled from his neck down the side of his head with the jarring impacts of the stake. His eyes were already gone.

More figures stepped up with gas cans. They splashed this up to his feet, which were looped into a plastic-coated cable from a tree branch. Then down the body, soaking his skin, splattering the ground. They retreated with the cans in use, splashing the area in their wake.

Out of the wood, over a stile, one at the rear threw out fistfuls of cayenne pepper as he, or she, backed away.

Along the grass verge, they climbed into a waiting van and pulled slowly out, still scattering liquid and powder which diminished until they were driving down the main part of the road, blending in with all the other car trails back and forth. They shut doors and windows and drove sedately away in the dark.

*Show me more.*

A wolf pack by moonlight, running like deer in their fur. Then falling, one, two, three, dropping away in sprays of blood as if each had been shot in the throat with a shotgun.

One, two, three, eight, a dozen.

The man from the rows of crude graves, blood on his lips, looked into my eyes. His pupils contracted to slits like a cat's. He smiled to reveal two pointed fangs.

A wolf howled and another crashed into it, teeth to throat.

Church spires ran with blood, roofs crumbled in flames. As the cities crowded into the country, wolves moved onto patches of green that shrank until the green was red with their blood while they fought their way out, leaving only a mound of bodies surrounded by urban progress.

*But not like this. How could wolves kill wolves like this?*

*Find them and ask.* Ellasandra's voice. Squeezing my hand. *Please, Cassia. You found us. Find them and ask. Help us. Please.*

*If shifters hunting shifters, why hunt druids? Champions of nature?*

*If humans hunting shifters and druids, why like this? What do they want?*

The cat-eyed man pressed a finger to his lips to silence me. Then he pointed. There, as far as I could see, were graves with plain crosses at the heads. Miles and miles of them reaching to the horizon.

*They're all gone, you know?* He spoke in my ear. *Can't you see that? It's too late. You're much too late.*

*No!*

I sat back, gasping.

I scrambled to my feet, weak, shaking, but unwilling to remain leaning over that mutilated face.

Zar was there, stepping close. I did not touch him, still seeing the visions.

"Can I speak with you?" I asked Diana quietly, unable to focus my eyes, possibly appearing drunk. "Inside?"

She nodded, extending an arm for me to go ahead. Zar grabbed my backpack.

The black wolf was at my side.

I bent to him, unsteady and holding his face. "Get Isaac, Jed, and Andrew. Ask them to come with us. We can cover more ground that way and stay in groups. I'm not the one in danger. I have to tell Diana what I saw and what we're doing. You all get ready to go and I'll meet you soon."

Jason licked my chin and dashed back to Kage as I walked away with Diana and Zar.

In another hour and a half, Isaac, Kage, Jason, Andrew, Zar, Jed, and myself were boarding the train for London.

## ○ CHAPTER 32 ○

ZAR BROUGHT OLD PAPERS and spiral-bounds much like his manual for getting along with humans from the 1950s. He hoped to find more references than he knew off the top of his head on historical precedents for shifters murdering each other.

We sat at a table in the train, two seats on one side, two on another—Zar and myself across from Andrew and Jason. Isaac, Kage, and Jed sat behind us or drifted around, in Kage's case like he'd never been on a train before, restless and pacing in the aisle.

Zar still tried to talk about what I'd seen.

I felt sick, wanting to talk about anything other than that.

Bloody images of the visions filled my mind with the carved up face of Abraham—the gaping neck and swollen lips and black blood.

Despite the nature of what we'd been doing all along, there on the train heading for London was the first time I'd felt scared over it: about what could happen to my companions if we didn't solve this—even what could happen to me. If they went for druids, they wouldn't mind going for other humans in a pinch. Especially an American witch who they might be able to figure out was on their trail.

A list, a plan, a certainty. I preferred all. Without the latter two, I could at least create the first. An ounce of steady reality. Options to weigh. Paths to truth.

I pulled a slim paper notebook and purple ballpoint from my bag between my feet. I opened it on the table to write so the other three could see.

*Shifters:*
    *Estranged Beech Pack*
    *Urban wolves*
*Undead:*
    *Vampires*
*Mundane humans:*
    *?*
*Casters:*
    *?*

Kage stopped on one of his rounds pacing past our table.

He studied the list, then jabbed a finger at my notebook. "You've seen all those people murder wolves in your magic visions?"

"What?" I looked up at him looming over me. "No. Those are suspects."

"But that's everyone." Jason's brows were drawn, alarmed by my list. "Shifters, undead, humans ... that's the whole bipedal world."

"Yes." I sucked in a breath. "But it seems like much less when you see it as a short list, doesn't it?"

"Um..."

"Don't forget druids," Kage said, still truculent.

"Enough from you about the druids," I said.

Zar rubbed his ear—the way I now knew he did when embarrassed. "Kage, they've lost people also."

"Exactly. What was the first thing they thought when a wolf died? 'Oh, that'll be a wolf murdering another wolf.' Just returning the favor."

"You don't have the kindred on there either," Zar said, getting on board with the speculation.

"Or spirits," Andrew said. "Why stop at the whole world for a suspect when you could look beyond?"

I sighed. "Let's rule out anything that is not capable of holding a stake and appearing in a humanish form. Since I did see that much. We do know for a fact it's not kindred, ghosts, or sheep, for example."

"Just the sort of thing someone says before it turns out to be sheep—"

"Kage!"

"Druids can hold stakes," he mumbled and walked away.

"Does he have something against old women?" I asked Jason.

"He does now. You wouldn't let him go to tea."

"*That's* why he hates druids? Because he didn't get to have tea with us?"

"And you took his Jeep for it." Jason bit his lip as he looked at my notebook.

I rubbed the bridge of my nose, still feeling queasy. These train cars must have bathrooms.

"Okay," I said. "To be fair to everyone, I suppose if there can be estranged wolves there can be estranged druids who could also turn on others. And what about any other suspects? Capable of looking like a human and holding a stake, that is. Anyone else that no one has mentioned who you've already suspected?"

I added *Rogue druids* to my list where Kage could see when he stalked by. Then looked up since no one had answered.

"Well," Zar said, running his thumb down the edge of a book on shifter history. "Nothing that's reliable."

"Neither is the Beech Pack," I said. "Let's try to cover all the bases for this. Who else do your elders suspect?"

Zar moved his lips and didn't answer, apparently working up to it.

Finally, Andrew said, "Your witch pals."

"What?"

"The group putting on the conferences," Andrew said. "After Diana got in touch to ask for help … the mage she saw…" It wasn't like Andrew to hesitate. He looked out the window to green hedges and red brick buildings zipping past along the tracks. "He told her to get stuffed. You can't go around thinking casters are murdering your family just because you meet one who's an arsehole. But he didn't like wolves—made it clear he didn't think we should be here living in civilized areas at all—and the only thing useful he said was that we needed a scry. After that chap, the elders weren't going near casters again."

Jason looked from Andrew to me. "Andrew knew about their history conferences at the hotel. And what they really were. A few wolves were still pushing for human help. Andrew's the one who said he could find a scry from the conference—and someone who wasn't from the South of England. So if that organization really is…"

"If they really have been murdering us, we'd be asking an outsider this time around," Andrew finished. "Someone who wasn't in on the murder plot."

*How many dead now?*

*Of course they keep to themselves.*

I looked at them for a minute, able to think of nothing to say: Jason to Andrew to Zar beside me.

Then I turned the question mark below *Casters* into a B and wrote in *Broomantle*.

## ○ CHAPTER 33 ○

WE WERE MIDWAY through our journey when I had to slip away, leaving Zar busy with his papers on the table, though Andrew and Jason watched me go.

By the time I reached the oval train restroom—an interesting experience with the sliding door and tiny sink like an airplane bathroom, but larger floorspace than one—I didn't feel so sick anymore. Maybe all I needed was to get up and move like Kage. Perhaps that was why he'd been pacing.

I'd feel better with fresh air—if London can be said to have any—and forward momentum.

One lead at a time. And the one now was London. *Shifters. Undead.*

We had to figure out how we were going to find wolves in the city. That was the first thing. In addition, there was the matter of vampires.

Zar had said we'd have to be in the city late to find either. Yet it had still seemed prudent to come over early and spend time in London and make a plan. We could stay the night, no matter the short train trip. Hostel rooms probably.

That's what we should be discussing and figuring out: A to B to C.

*Shifters. Undead.*

They'd brought rucksacks or messenger bags again. I had my backpack. Which made me think of needing to text Melanie, though I had no idea what to say. She'd already sent one asking if I was okay, did I need help?

I wetted paper towels to wipe my neck and arms, catching my breath as I inadvertently touched the bruise.

"Cassia?" Kage knocked at the door.

I was coming out anyway and pressed the panel to open it. The curved door slid wide.

The automated female voice started up with her request not to flush anything that shouldn't be flushed—including "nappies" and "hopes and dreams."

"You all right?" His voice was gruff, like he was trying out the expression but not sure how to use it. "You seemed upset about Abraham."

"So did everyone," I countered, lifting my hand to his chest to stop him. "And if you were actually concerned about me—*Kage*."

He sidestepped in with an agility and quickness I'd noticed even the tallest and broadest wolves possessed. They would make incredible dancers—much less any physical sport.

"Get out—"

"I wanted to see you. When you scarpered last night—"

"You didn't even say goodbye to me last night."

The space was brutally cramped, the air freshener reek making it feel even more claustrophobic. While constant swaying on the tracks created a sensation of instability.

I reached past for the door to get myself out, pressed against him since there was no other way to share the space. Kage locked it.

"You can't count on me for goodbyes," he said. "Chat up your poet friend for that."

His mouth covered mine.

I wanted him to hold me there and kiss me so much it made me furious.

We were supposed to be shocked and grieving. In a smelly little room that was too small for us to share, swinging along on a train track with, potentially, others waiting to use the facilities.

Kage pushed me into the wall at the door panel, his tongue on my lips, powerful fingers on my face. I grabbed his head in both hands in return, pulling him in, breath gone, opening my mouth for him.

We grappled for half a minute, then I found his ear and twisted it so hard his head was wrenched sideways.

He yelped. "*Fuck*, ah—bloody hell!"

"This is not the time and it's *really* not the place to set a romantic mood." I let go. I was shaking—could hardly get my breath, wanting him to touch me so badly, so consumed by it, I was forced to the conclusion that this was one of those crazy repercussions of shock and grief. There was fear and anger and sadness wrapped up in grief, after all. Why not lust?

"What do you want?" He kissed me again. "Flowers and sunset?" His mouth was hot, seeming to mix straight into my bloodstream. "You can have that from your poet." His saliva tasted of something sweet. "With your goodbyes and your hand-holding." A candy or honey flavor that threw me off. But not as much as I was thrown off by his hand on my breast. The other hand was in my hair at the nape of my neck.

I bit his tongue, again pulling him in, feeling his body on mine. Solid force and heat, rocking against me. He kept pushing and I released his tongue to feel him bite my lips.

He cupped my left breast, pushing up with his palm, rubbing my stiff nipple with his thumb. I wanted his hand under my blouse. And my hand under his fly.

He arched his back, having to bend in to hold my throat in his teeth, still pushing, painful. I tipped my head back and fumbled to get the edge of his shirt up and feel his skin. It was weird how little the washboard abs yielded to pressure. Like thinking you were biting into an apple only to discover it was a baseball—too hard to get your teeth through. Speaking of hard, he was still pushing with his hips.

"Kage? You're in a relationship," I panted.

"What?" Tongue to mine and I wanted to swallow him, so eager for him I was already envisioning more.

"Jason," I said. "What about Jason?"

"What about him?"

"For each button you knock off my blouse, I'm going to knock a tooth out of your head."

With lightning speed Kage changed tactics—feeling under my blouse instead of thinking he could rip through.

"Are you in a relationship with him or not?" I asked. "He seems to think you are."

"Sure. Do you want him to be here?"

"Want him to—what?"

"Why are you asking about him?"

"Because you're in a relationship!" I had both hands on his face again, twisting him away so I could look into his eyes.

"So?" He pushed through my hands to kiss me.

"Dammit, Kage! What language are you speaking? Are you sleeping with Jason or not?"

"Of course I am. We live together."

"Live together!" I got a couple fingers into his mouth to push his face away while he bit and licked them.

"Listen. You have to go back to him and honor the fact that you have a relationship. *Or* you have to tell him that you do not have one, because he seems to think you do."

"Then you'd be all right?" Lips on mine, my hand in his hair instead of his mouth. "You don't want me because of him?" He worked his fingers below my bra.

"It's not me. It's him. *You* shouldn't want me because of him, Kage."

"I could call it off with him. If that's what—"

"No! If you break up with him because of me that will do the opposite of earn you points from me!"

"Then what is it you want? He's not really into females, but if you want a three—"

"No!"

"Then what?" Shouting back at me. "Is this lose-lose for me? You don't want me if I'm sleeping with him. It's not acceptable to you for me to stop sleeping with him. And you also don't want both of us at once? So what can I do?"

*Dammit*—this shock and grief and lust thing was getting more complicated.

His questions seemed stupid and obvious. So it didn't make sense that I didn't have answers.

I wished he was pushing even more. I wished he was in my jeans—fingers at least. Then I could feel more justified for my own inability to make sense of this. Much too distracted.

As it was, his hunger and mine were so distracting I wasn't thinking straight. I don't have any better excuse for why I succumbed so much to wanting him in return that I reached to find his erection through his jeans. Kage thrust into my hand, fabric still separating us, while he bit along my neck to the top of my shoulder.

My right arm hurt. His pressure on my breast was painful, sharp. Still, I wanted more.

He needed freedom. I needed him.

But I had enough of a second to think that the craziness caught up.

First get myself under control. Then him.

I held his hips, shoving him away

I owed him a chance. "Kage." I fought to gather my breath and speak firmly. "*Stop.*"

Nothing whatever changed.

I reached lower between his legs. I couldn't get much of a hold with his jeans tight from his erection. For the best, though? Like a pinch on any normal area of skin, I suspected a smaller space may actually be worse.

I fondled him, getting a hold, then closed my fist on what I could reach, twisting savagely upward at the same time—as if ripping a stubborn weed out of the earth.

It would be an exaggeration to say he screamed. But not by much: a string of epic profanity, much in Lucannis, gasping, recoiling. He thought he would simply twist my arm away—big mistake to pull on my hand—then a choked series of, "*Please, please...*"

"So you do have manners? I'm sure your mother would be proud." I let him go.

He was doubled over against the little sink and mirror, puffing like a landed fish.

"All right, tough guy, listen. Again. Your ... odd relationship with Jason is for the two of you to sort out. But when it comes to the relationship between you and me, you only need to know one thing: when I say 'stop', it means you stop on a dime, asshole."

"What's the bloody issue? You wanted this. You were fucking begging!"

I wasn't going to deny that. My head spun and my blood beat as fire for wanting him.

"The issue is I have impulse control. You don't. You're in a relationship. I'm not. I apologize for misleading you—that wasn't fair. But we're just not a good match, Kage. Why don't you finish up alone? Or do you want me to send your boyfriend down here? You need to have a talk with him anyway. If you care about him, act like it. If you don't, tell him. Because he seems to think you do."

I pushed the panel to open the door, leaving him panting behind me.

As the curved door slid wide I prayed—but, no, the corridor was indeed empty. *Thank you, Goddess.*

We were still twenty minutes from London. I spent ten of them walking around before I felt sure no redness was showing, then returned to sit in the same car, a couple of rows down from the others when I spotted an empty aisle seat.

## ○ C̲H̲A̲P̲T̲E̲R̲ ̲3̲4̲ ○

AFTER THE LONG morning—and other circumstances—I wasn't at my best when we arrived in London Victoria. This was unfortunate because my companions were not nearly as street-savvy as they were savvy about taunting each other or locating fast food joints.

While I walked through the crowd in the sprawling rail station, heading for the nearest exit, through the turnstiles and below massive electric timetables overhead, I lost followers.

By the time I reached the archway out by the Italian café and looked around, only Isaac and Jason remained beside me. And Jason walked into me when I stopped because he'd been keeping so close.

Kage was still stuck at the turnstile, arguing with the attendant because his ticket hadn't gone through. Zar stood against a ticket booth, waiting and waiting for the foot traffic to clear before he could move forward. Of course, foot traffic did not clear. You just had to push through. Yet the idea seemed to overwhelm him, his eyes tracking back and forth with the stampede. Jed was being slightly more proactive, slinking along the wall and little shops, all the way down to the Tesco Express before he slipped through and started making his way back in our direction. I didn't see Andrew anywhere.

Jason stared at banner advertisements hanging from the cathedral walls as if they might jump down and attack him.

Isaac's eyes darted to pigeons flying inside, a rolling suitcase clattering past, a paper wrapper blowing through the walkway, a man on his phone, waving his left hand animatedly as he talked.

Everything caught their attention. I saw the crowd and the exit. They saw and smelled and heard and felt the loose strap flapping on a backpack, prepackaged sandwiches in Tesco, click of pigeons' claws on the floor, vibrations of the monolithic station.

I understood as I watched their movements and darting glances, not because I had any special insight into shifters, but because of autistic children I had worked with while in school. Children who may be brilliant, and in many ways rewarding to work around. But who perceived the world in a totally different way than I did. And sometimes, as a result, could not even function in that world.

*Have you questioned the wolves in London?*
*There are no wolves in London.*

Of course there weren't. Unless they were not like other werewolves. So altered, in fact, they may have found some reason for eliminating those who they no longer thought of as their kin.

I waited in the archway until the others reached us. I'm not sure what had happened to Andrew. He just showed up beside me after a minute. With the uncomfortable feeling that I was the only teacher guiding a field trip, I took stock to make sure everyone still had their rucksacks, or messenger bags, then explained the plan that we needed lunch and a park to sit, eat, and decide how we were going to do this.

It should have taken less than ten minutes to walk to Saint James's Park, which I looked up on my phone to keep us from getting lost.

It took about forty-five.

By the time we arrived at the pond, however, everyone seemed more collected. Whatever coping mechanisms they used—zoning out, becoming acclimated, or even their desire to show off for me—must be kicking in to calm stretched nerves.

Andrew did not seem especially troubled. And Isaac was only stiff and watchful. Everyone else, aside from Jed, looked more normal as we found a picnic spot in midday July sun that was growing rapidly hotter, making London—even to my nose—stink. They, however, were sniffing much more, clamoring for the steakhouse they claimed we'd passed, though I'd neither seen nor smelled such a place.

"Do you know how much it would cost for us all to go in a steakhouse?" I demanded of Kage.

"Diana sent more money. They keep a savings for pack emergencies like this—"

"It's not an emergency for you all to get four steaks each in London. How about pizzas?" I found such a place on my phone.

Grudging agreement.

Kage—our treasurer, disturbingly enough—and I walked back to Victoria Street through a maze of winding roads, black cabs, pedestrians, and confusing intersections and turns. Kage jumped when someone hit a sandwich board and it grated on the sidewalk. To avoid having to come into contact with a gaggle of tourists he stepped into the street and a cab driver blew his horn, slamming on the brakes. Kage spun to face the car, growling.

I grabbed his arm and yanked him on. "You live outside of Brighton. I know you've been in cities."

"This isn't Brighton."

Something else about those autistic kids: familiarity. Hang a new painting in a familiar room and you might induce anything from surprise and curiosity to terror or a total breakdown. Kage was probably comfortable in Brighton.

Thinking of those kids, I rephrased how I was speaking to him.

"I know it's overwhelming," I said and took a breath. "I don't know London at all either. I only day-tripped in with my sister and brother-in-law when I was here last year. A couple days of tourist stuff and back and forth to the airport—that's it. It's a lot to deal with when you're not used to it."

He nodded and his head jerked around as a pigeon flew past.

We crossed a last street and had to wait in a queue, giving time to read the menu, then ordering the carry-out pizzas.

A much longer wait after this, sitting at a bar-type table in windows, watching outside. Kage's gaze kept darting to people eating slices.

After a while, I said, "Did you talk to Jason on the train?"

"A few words in passing. Why?" He looked around at me, but his attention was at once caught by a little dog trotting past outside—on a pink rhinestone leash with matching harness.

"For real?" I asked.

He looked at me again. "Oh ... no. There's nothing to talk about."

"Okay."

"And I wish you'd stop doing rubbish like that to me."

It took me a moment to figure out what he was talking about, then remembered his throwing a bag over my head and me kneeing him.

"You stop doing stupid stuff to me and I will. I don't usually try to hurt people I'm around—believe it or not."

"Not as if you were acting like you didn't want—"

"I'm sorry. That was ... momentary poor judgement on my part. Not a deliberate ploy to lead you on."

His tall chair was pushed out: prepared to make a break for it. He crossed his arms on the table and rested his chin on them. His hazel eyes kept darting back and forth with activity in the street and sidewalk through the glass.

I almost told him I was sorry again. Instead, we looked out the window together as if at a movie.

A short time later, we returned to Saint James's Park toting six large meat lover's pizzas with extra sausage and extra bacon, and one Italian salad.

## ○ CHAPTER 35 ○

I KNEW BETTER THAN to think we could sit in a circle and discuss our plans while we ate. Everyone grabbed a box from Kage—Andrew taking two and being kicked in the backs of his knees by Jed, sending him flying. Once pizzas were distributed the pack dispersed to a fifty yard radius to sit down and inhale their meals.

I sat on a bench with my salad, overlooking the pond, and had gotten through five bites when Zar stepped slowly up to my bench.

"Cassia? Would you mind terribly if I ... joined you?" Keeping a little distance. Clearly, Zar thought getting in someone's face while they ate was a dreadful idea, yet he'd watched Andrew get away with this move in Cornwall.

"Not at all. I'm happy for you to."

He smiled and sat inches away, presenting me with his box, which I'd assumed was empty. He lifted the lid and there was a very meaty slice, still warm, smelling of savory sausage, pepperoni, garlic, and basil. Zar smiled from it to me, then my green meal.

"You don't have much," he said. "It's going to be a long day. And probably night. Don't you eat protein?" Hopeful and anxious and eager at the same time.

He had a fair point. I'd wanted the salad because I still felt so unsettled, almost nauseated. But, now, maybe I was feeling sick because I hadn't eaten anything but a cup of macaroni and cheese in twenty-four hours. I hadn't even gotten coffee in the train station because of my stomach. I would find an iced latte for dessert, though. My head hurt and, as he'd said, it would be a long night.

Even so, it wasn't Zar being right that surprised me. He was a smart guy. It was everything else about what he was doing.

"Are you sure?" I asked. "That's yours. I can get something later."

He held the box closer, the slice under my nose. "I'd like for you to have it. And something later too."

"Thank you, Zar." But I didn't need the greasy sausage mound at the tip. I used my salad fork to saw and pull the first inches of the slice off and offer it back to him, taking the rest. "That was considerate of you."

He beamed even more. Again, I had that feeling of him wagging his tail as he swallowed his returned prize.

I'd just started on the slice when Andrew came up behind the bench, dropping his empty box.

"Uh-oh." He flopped in grass at my feet. "You've got a critical case on your hands when a wolf starts showing you what a good provider he is." Andrew idly unlaced my walking shoes. "He'll be digging you a den next."

Zar did not look embarrassed, or even seem to notice Andrew. Still smiling in his adorable way, his focus never left my face. "You eat like a swan—slow and gliding. I wish I were elegant like you, Cassia."

What do you say to a comment like that? *Actually, I was just thinking how graceful you all are?*

I was distracted anyway. "Andrew, that's enough. Don't take my—*Andrew.*"

"You need attention, darling. You've been tense as the Queen's Guard all morning." He removed a sock after the shoe and started massaging my foot, thumbs on the top and fingers kneading the sole.

"This is not the time or place."

"No." He arched an eyebrow, looking up to meet my eyes without shifting the downward angle of his face. Contact lenses in today. "I'd lead you to a feather bed but I looked and…" A sigh. "None around, I'm afraid."

"We need to talk about that—" I started.

"At long last."

"No, about accommodation." I looked at Zar. "Do you have a plan?"

Zar leaned in, starting to turn his head.

"Not a plan about me," I snapped, sitting back before his lips could reach mine. "A plan about our mission in the city?"

"Oh." His smile finally faltered. "I … don't think so."

"Who would know if you do?"

Andrew chuckled.

Zar frowned. "Well, we're looking for wolves. So … that's a plan…?"

"No, that's a goal," I said. "A plan would be a way we could reach that goal."

"But…" Shaking his head slowly. "There's only one way we might find wolves in London. We already know that. So … not much to plan."

I waited. "Are you going to tell me? Because I had no idea you already knew how to go about this."

"We have to track them."

"Track them how?"

"With our noses."

"Noses?" I looked between them. "Your sense of smell is so good you can tell if there's another wolf in London? For real?"

Jason and Isaac walked up to join us, dropping their pizza boxes on top of Andrew's.

"Not like this," Andrew said. "We'll have to change."

"Change?" I asked in horror. "You're kidding. You can't change in London."

After a pause in which Jason and Isaac also settled on the grass, Jason by Andrew and Isaac a bit apart, Andrew asked sarcastically, "Then how, exactly, do you expect us to learn if there are wolves here?"

"You've been thinking you'd come to London and put on your fur so you can scout the area for other wolves? Are you out of your minds?"

"That's why we can only look at night," Zar said.

"Because you're invisible at night? You can't dodge people. You'd be lucky not to be seen in a park at night, much less sniffing up and down every street. Cities this size don't sleep. There won't be a time you could have the place to yourself if that's what you're thinking."

"Not all of us, of course," Isaac said. "Perhaps two? We could split into two groups and cover more ground, each with one tracker. We may be able to do something about our appearance…?"

I thought about that. But what? Paint them to look like huskies? Collars and leashes? Nothing short of throwing a sheet over them was going to make them look less like wolves. There were two, though, that were so dark they might not be noticed in the city at night with a group of people around them…

"Jason and Jed are black, or nearly for Jed," I said slowly. "If we put leashes on them and they stayed close, we might be able to get away with it. Jason's not as big. We'd say he's a cross between a black German shepherd and a black ... bear," I finished lamely.

"The wolf who tries to put a lead on Jed will be lucky to get away with all his fingers," Zar said. "He might not be best..."

"He's right," Isaac said. "Jed's not safe. What about Andrew?"

"If you want a collar on me, darling, you're welcome any time." Andrew told me. He had both my feet exposed, cross-legged and taking turns kneading each.

Kage and Jed walked up, neither sitting.

"What about him?" I asked Isaac.

"He's the smallest," Jason said.

"You could say he's a new breed," Isaac said. "If it came to that. Something out of Russia that's meant to look like a wolf?"

"He has big ears," Jason said. "And a shorter coat. He does look more Alsatian-ish than the rest of us."

"Do you?" I looked down at Andrew.

"At your service." He looked up with a lazy smile. "My ancestors were Australian."

"There are *dingo* shifters?" I asked.

"There used to be. I hope there still are. European mates had advantages. I'm mostly wolf now, but still not like the others. As you've noticed." Lips curving below those hooded eyes.

"Ever seen a North American red wolf?" Zar asked. "That's what he looks like."

"I can't say that I have, but okay. Jason and Andrew then? And you think you can find wolves in this city, with millions of people and animals and sewers and food, by your noses?"

Jason nodded. "If they're here. But..." Shrugging. Which was another point.

"And if we don't find anything?" I asked. "What about the vampires? We need to talk with them."

Silence.

Kage curled his lip. Many expressions darkened.

"What?" I asked.

"Oh, vampires aren't so hard to find," Zar said. "But, like I said, we'll have to wait until night for that also and ... once we do find them..."

"You'll wish we hadn't," Andrew said.

"Will they attack us? Do we have to take stakes and crosses to meet them? Or are those myths? I'm not much help here."

"They won't go for us in a group," Isaac said.

"Not their style, the scheming maggots," Kage said. "They'll wait until your back's turned, won't they? Wait until you're alone?"

Zar was shaking his head. "It can't be vampires. There are no vampires in the countryside. It's the old truce."

"You're barking," Kage snapped. "What's that mean to anyone anymore?"

"What's the old truce?" I asked.

"It's a long story," Zar said.

"If you want to find them, we likely can," Isaac said. "If we stay together, they'll watch themselves. They don't want trouble from the caster community and they won't take on a pack."

"You think everyone is so rational," Andrew said quietly, not looking up from my feet. "If they were, your assessment could actually be right."

"Vampires are not rational?" I asked.

"Off their trolleys," Andrew said. "Mad as hatters, the whole lot."

"Wolves and vampires are old enemies," Zar said. "Nothing about these killings has been their style, though."

"Could be their plan to throw us off," Kage cut in.

"*Also*," Zar plowed on, "there *are none* in Brighton or the whole area. We'd know it."

"A year ago, if someone had told you we'd be losing family to a serial killer, wouldn't you have said then that we'd know with no trouble who that was?" Isaac asked.

Zar didn't answer.

"The truth is, we don't know," Isaac said. "If we knew for a fact there were no wolves in London and no vampires on the coast, we wouldn't be here. That truce was agreed hundreds of years ago."

"But you do have a bad history with vampires?" I asked, glancing around at them. "It seems like you hate them even if you don't normally meet?"

"Like to see you spend two seconds with one and not hate it," Kage muttered.

"I'm going to give it a try. If you all can find one, I'll do the talking. So there's a bit of a plan. That leaves us needing to be here in the city overnight. Maybe for a few? We need a hostel if we can find space on such short notice. Can you all stay in dorm rooms with humans sharing?"

"Of course we can," Zar said. "But we need to stay with you also. We can't leave you alone in a room when we're supposed to be watching out for you. What if our hunters know we're looking for them?"

"Let's figure out if we can even find beds first. Then we'll worry about placement."

Soon, we moved on. It took me a while, having to pull my socks and shoes back on—although my feet really did feel much better, lighter somehow.

Kage stood on the boxes to smash and roll them up for a bin. They didn't fit so he wedged them in, blocking the whole thing. At least it was an effort.

# ○ C̲H̲A̲P̲T̲E̲R̲ ̲3̲6̲ ○

ISAAC AND I CALLED hostels with frustrating results—all booked. We finally found one with space across town by Saint Pancras and King's Cross stations. This meant the Underground—I thought. They refused. We got cheap Oyster Cards and took a double-decker crimson bus instead.

The not especially well-rated Midland Hostel on Midland Road had scattered beds to offer in four different dorm rooms, one of them all female. This started such an argument about me not being off on my own I backed down and we took every bed they had available in the mixed dorms. Two rooms with three beds each and a third with one bed.

They let us leave bags in lockers, then back out into what was beginning to feel like an inferno of mid-afternoon London.

Zar tried to soothe my irritation, telling me they only wanted to protect me.

"It's fine, Zar. It was going to be a dorm anyway. Not like they had anything private left. Two of you can stay with me this way."

"Which two?" Andrew asked at once.

Everyone else looked interested.

"You'll draw straws." I walked back to the bus stop. "Let's find something cold to drink and go to Hyde Park. We could all use some peace."

I wasn't the only one starting out tired. Jed sat with his eyes closed on the bus. Zar looked dazed. Kage kept yawning.

Off the bus, we went in Marks & Spencer at Marble Arch for cold drinks. It quickly turned into a grocery shopping trip.

Kage found a watermelon. Jason, Andrew, and Zar wanted ice cream bars—a box each. Jed picked up a dozen packages of cold cuts and I gently talked him into just two, suggesting that since we'd be up, he could get a late burger. Isaac, staying on track, got us all bottles of water. I ordered an iced latte from the coffee bar and grabbed paper napkins.

I knew better than to stop early in the bustling park. We walked all the way down Carriage Drive, around to the west side of The Long Water, in view of the lake and the Peter Pan statue. Here, we found a quiet stretch to settle in the grass and shade with scattered trees as well as the edge of a patch of woods.

Jed had already polished off his ham. Two boxes of ice cream bars were also gone. Jason was opening a third. All seemed much more relaxed in the park, other than the distraction of masses of gray squirrels that tourists fed and that darted everywhere.

I'd gulped up half my latte as well. Sweat trickled between my shoulder blades into my bra.

Mental note: *London in July—pass.*

I settled in shade, watching Kage as he examined the area, absently balancing the watermelon in one hand by his shoulder. They all had to check out a new place as if looking for snakes and scorpions before they could relax.

"How will you get into that?" I asked, imagining him trying to bite the rind.

Kage tossed the melon lightly up into the air.

*Bash*—on impact with packed earth the watermelon burst into several chunks. Jagged wedges tumbled away in the grass.

He proudly offered me one of these, much to my shock. Another food gift?

"Thank you, Kage."

Andrew and Zar were watching.

Jed took his shirt, boots, and socks off and flopped in the shade a little away from us, lying on his back with his shirt over his eyes. Others also removed their sweaty shirts.

Isaac sat with a chilled water bottle. He kept his clothes on and remained watchful behind sunglasses.

Jason approached Kage and Kage handed over melon slabs. He smiled at me when he did. *See? I can look after you both. What's the big deal?*

So was I the only one who thought this was weird? Yet I knew Jason was depressed about the situation, even if Kage seemed to think he was fine.

Kage gathered remaining melon and sat down to eat.

I avoided looking at him, yet his sharing watermelon with Jason and me … under the circumstances of who and what… It was sweet of him.

I saved the rest of the latte and ate the juicy melon leaning sideways so it didn't drip all over me—first wiping the grass bits and grit off with a napkin.

Zar sat beside me.

I wanted to text Melanie, and our potential informant, Rowan, to let him know we were on the case as well. Then put in earbuds and lie down for a few hours before having to think anymore.

Zar, who had a paper map of London, started telling me how we would search and cover different neighborhoods. He was eating another ice cream bar—essentially like a human would—and I had my melon to enjoy, so I didn't mind him until I was finished. I agreed with everything he said and he warmed more and more to his task of strategizing. Finally, though, I had to explain I needed to send texts and we should all take a break.

He was quick to agree. "Would you like an ice cream?"

Really getting into this food thing now.

"Thank you but melon was plenty for me. And that after the pizza," I added quickly, which cheered him up.

"Want a pillow?" He'd brought his backpack out with him so he could read in the park.

"Oh, I guess so … if it's not hard as books?"

He removed most of the books, then situated the bag for my head. It wasn't half bad.

I started a text to Mel, stopped, started over.

Andrew, who'd been studying the ground on his hands and knees, shuffled over to Jason—who'd finished melon and was just about to unwrap his third ice cream bar.

"Ant trail at Jed's feet." I could just catch Andrew's voice.

Jason's eyes lit up. He handed Andrew the bar and grabbed the last in the box for himself.

Some sort of bond between those two: Andrew giving Jason a milkshake on the drive to Cornwall, sharing the trailer, planning card tricks. Quite buddy-buddy.

Was I still reticent about asking questions, or could I let myself get to know them better? Allow myself to care even more than I already did?

I started a third text to Mel.

Both shirtless, and Jason with his socks and shoes off as well—so lean and toned and beautiful it made a mockery of the snacks they ate—they crept over to Jed, who was apparently asleep. Hard to tell with the shirt on his face.

They ate white chocolate shells off their ice cream bars while Jason observed what must be the line of ants through grass.

I tried again on the text.

Starting out by saying I was fine sounded like there was reason to think I wasn't. But acting like this was nothing out of the ordinary was not right either.

Andrew turned his bar upside down, letting it drip to the grass around Jed's heels, leading the ants.

*I'm sorry I split on you, Mel. I'll be in touch and be back soon!*

I bit my lip and looked at that one.

While Andrew worked, Jason crept up the grass on his knees and cocked his ear at Jed's chest. He must have been satisfied with the deep breathing because he nodded to Andrew.

*Sorry I split on you! You must think I'm crazy. But I'm fine and I'll be in touch. Back soon! XO*

Jason was licking around his bar to make a smooth cylinder of it.

That message would have to do. I sent it. *Goddess help me.* And turned to the matter of adding Rowan's number with the exit code and country code.

Jason put the now rounded ice cream bar down his throat all the way to his fingers on the wooden stick.

Slowly, eyes shut, he withdrew it. He bowed his head over Jed's feet and let a milky white trickle of melted ice cream and his own saliva dribble onto Jed's toes. It ran down the backs of his feet and soles to his heels in the grass.

Jason repeated the performance. Andrew dripped two more trails to lure in marching ants from more directions.

I forced myself to the text for Rowan. This one was easy. Did I have his number right, this was Cassia, we were looking. That was it.

The pranksters leaned over Jed's feet, heads together, watching for progress. They kept their bars from dripping directly onto his skin, perhaps because the cold would have been more likely to startle him awake than skin-hot liquid.

Both grinned. Must be seeing good progress from the swarm. Then they slunk away, finishing their bars and retreating beyond Kage, Zar and myself, then Isaac, to bask in the sun by the bronze statue.

I put in earbuds but didn't play anything on my phone. Only lay with my eyes closed behind sunglasses.

What were we getting into tonight? I needed to ask them more questions not of a personal nature, but of a life and death nature. Shifters attacking shifters in the past? Vampire enemies? Old truces that kept vampires out of the countryside?

But there was something about the moment I couldn't let go. Something starting tonight that we wouldn't be able to turn back from.

Unless we were all torn apart by urban shifters, or our blood sucked out by vampires in a few hours, I would have time to learn more from Zar soon enough. And, if we didn't make it through the night, due to sticking our noses places they didn't belong in the magical underworld, I didn't want to spend my last evening listening to stories or lectures.

I just lay there, listening to laughing children around the water's edge, footsteps on the path, distant voices, birds, squirrels, my own breathing. Close to dozing off.

Then swearing and running. I didn't look up at first.

An impact on the earth not far away made me cave and part my lashes enough to see what was happening.

Andrew ran through grass. Must be why he'd left his shoes on.

Jed was on his hands and knees. It looked like Jason, who'd been lying on his back, now sitting up, had tripped him as he'd started after Andrew. Jed whirled and punched Jason, slamming him into the ground. Kage sprang into my field of vision but Jed didn't stay to fight them both. He took off after Andrew.

Jason sprawled on his back at Kage's feet, clutching his head. And laughing. Kage sat with him.

Zar got up from beside me, dropping his books, and walking out to the trail to watch where they'd gone. Speculating on a way he could assist his brother? Cut Andrew off with two of them? I wasn't sure if Zar would get involved or not. There did not seem to be much of a bond between the two brothers.

More I wanted to know. About their family. About Isaac's. About dingo shifters and how Andrew's ancestors had ended up here.

Isaac and I alone had not moved. He still looked out over The Long Water. I wished he would lie down beside me, just to be there. Or more—wondering again if this was my last evening on Earth.

Six werewolves and a witch? Wasn't that why we were all together? Whatever was out there, I liked to think we could handle it.

Someone jogged up to my spot. He was breathing hard, stepping over me.

I squinted to see Andrew gathering Zar's things; papers and books. He looked around, spotted the backpack under my head, then wisely decided to leave it.

"Jay?" Andrew panted. "Row boat docked just up there. That prat tried to stop me."

Jason, who'd been lying back with his bruised head on Kage's thigh for a pillow, scrambled up to take the papers and trotted off for the boat.

Andrew, bare chest heaving, skin wet with sweat, flopped on grass against me. He lay on his side, propped on an elbow, and kissed my shoulder through thin cotton.

"You didn't save me watermelon?" he asked.

I indicated my earbud.

"Please, darling. You're not listening to anything."

*Dammit, those ears of theirs.*

I pulled out the bud beside him. "Why do you two torment Jed?"

"Don't you remember that bit about a proper bastard?" Murmuring in my ear.

"Did it ever cross your mind that it's the chicken, not the egg?"

"I don't make Jed Jed. If anything, I help bring out his playful spirit."

"Sure ... he looked really playful."

"You don't know Jed. I do. I know them all." His lips brushed my ear. "Information today, they say it's easy to come by. But, if you can't Google it ... oh no. What will we do?"

"I'm surprised you know that term."

"Humans have been my sideline all my life. I know what I'm talking about there too. And I know you're a curious one—keeping an eye on us. You can't stop thinking about my offer of truth telling, can you? Want to know who you're really dealing with here? You need only ask me." He leaned over to kiss my lips and I turned away before he could.

"Andrew, I'm having quiet time, as you noticed."

"So you'll let them have a kiss? Not me? What have I done?"

I looked at him sharply. "How did you know that?"

A slow smile twisted up his lips like the Grinch. "You just told me, darling."

Of course I had. I reached for my phone. "Now, I am listening to something."

As I tried to return the earbud, Andrew's mouth got in the way. "Why does your own desire for me bother you? It's obviously not the wolf thing. I'd ask if I remind you of someone unpleasant from your past but there's no one else like me. So what is it?"

"You're just not my type, I guess."

"As if."

"Some other time and place. I'm dealing with too much attention lately, in case you hadn't noticed."

"Another lie. You love it. Be honest with me and I'll be honest with you."

"Before or after you steal from me?"

"After, naturally."

"What did you take?" I turned my head—a mistake, our faces touching. His lips had hardly brushed mine before I had my face upward again, yet contact left my pulse racing.

"You tell me," he whispered. "Haven't you ever had that feeling before? The shock of waking to discover someone stole your heart?"

I was spared by footsteps: Zar returning and snapping at Andrew. "What are you doing? Where's my stuff?"

"I didn't take your stuff," Andrew said serenely.

"Like hell—"

"By Moon, I didn't, Zar. You can ask anyone."

I put in the earbud, starting Bishop Briggs at random.

The day was sweltering. The grass and shade and latte with melting ice were gifts.

I stopped following the arguments as Andrew was compelled to leave my side.

It didn't seem, in that moment, that we were all about to start risking our lives—placing those lives in each other's hands and paws. It felt like a beautiful day out in Hyde Park with a bunch of sexy British guys. The beach at Brighton couldn't possibly be better.

So I would enjoy the moment, at least for now. Even though it was only a few hours until sunset.

# Dear Moonlight Pack

THANK YOU for being part of *The Witch and the Wolf Pack* family! Ready for the adventure to heat up?

From sweltering tunnels below London to sizzling skin heat below moonlight, killers will be tracked and inhibitions tumbled in *Moonlight Hunters*, Book Two of *The Witch and the Wolf Pack* series.

And why stop there? Come along and run with the Moonlight Pack! You'll find all the links to join in at www.kralexander.com, receive fresh-off-the-press release news and exclusive content when you sign up for the Moonlight Mailing List, and let your own song be heard by sharing a quick review for *Moonlight Desire* on Amazon.com!

Until our next hunt,

Made in the USA
Columbia, SC
12 April 2025